Lucy King spent her adol... glamorous and exciting w... when she really ought to h... ...paying attention to her teachers. As she couldn't live in a dream world for ever, she eventually acquired a degree in languages and an eclectic collection of jobs. After a decade in southwest Spain, Lucy now lives with her young family in Wiltshire, England. When not writing, or trying to think up new and innovative things to do with mince, she spends her time reading, failing to finish cryptic crosswords and dreaming of the golden beaches of Andalusia.

USA TODAY bestselling, RITA®-nominated and critically acclaimed author **Caitlin Crews** has written more than one hundred books and counting. She has a Master's and a PhD in English Literature, thinks everyone should read more category romance, and is always available to discuss her beloved alpha heroes. Just ask! She lives in the Pacific Northwest with her comic book artist husband, she is always planning her next trip, and she will never, ever, read all the books in her 'to-be-read' pile. Thank goodness.

HIS ENEMY'S SURRENDER

LUCY KING

CAITLIN CREWS

MILLS & BOON

First published in Great Britain 2025
by Mills & Boon, an imprint of HarperCollins*Publishers* Ltd,
1 London Bridge Street, London, SE1 9GF

www.harpercollins.co.uk

HarperCollins*Publishers*, Macken House, 39/40 Mayor Street Upper, Dublin 1, D01 C9W8, Ireland

ISBN: 978-0-263-34458-5

04/25

This book contains FSC™ certified paper and other controlled sources to ensure responsible forest management.

For more information visit www.harpercollins.co.uk/green.

Printed and Bound in the UK using 100% Renewable Electricity at CPI Group (UK) Ltd, Croydon, CR0 4YY

EXPECTING THE GREEK'S HEIR

LUCY KING

MILLS & BOON

CHAPTER ONE

THE GLOBAL ECONOMIC FORUM—taking place in a seven-star resort in Switzerland, with the world's most influential movers and shakers from business, the arts, government and science in attendance—had been running for three days.

That afternoon, Alexandros Andino had given a keynote speech to a packed-out auditorium about future trends in climate change investment. Tonight, at this drinks party, the last social event before everyone departed tomorrow afternoon, he was nursing a glass of whisky surrounded by half a dozen people who sought his further insight on the subject.

Up until a moment ago, he'd had plenty. When it came to alternative energies, green initiatives or the rapidly improving rate of return in this sector, there was little he didn't know.

Right now, however, he had none.

He had nothing to say about anything, in fact.

Because he'd just spotted Olympia Stanhope chatting up playboy businessman Sheikh Abdul Karim al-Umani—his most important, most lucrative client—and through the red mist suddenly swirling about his head like a tornado, all he could think was, that was it. His patience was at an end. He'd finally had enough.

When she first burst onto the investment-fund scene as the director of new business for Stanhope's, the exclusive private bank owned by her super-wealthy Anglo-Greek family, he hadn't thought much of it. Who would ever take seriously a notorious wild child with a decade in the gossip columns and a twelve-week spell in rehab under her belt? he'd privately scoffed when he'd learned of her absurd appointment in November last year. She had no experience of financial markets. According to the tabloids that recorded her every move, all she knew about money was how to spend it. No one would pay her a blind bit of notice. She was simply being indulged by her older brother Zander, who ran the Stanhope Kallis banking and shipping empire, and evidently had no problem with nepotism. She'd be replaced within a week.

In retrospect, that arrogant disregard for her talents had turned out to be a mistake. He'd been an idiot to assume that a too-rich, over-indulged party girl was all she was. He'd underestimated the power of her scandalous appeal to the ultra-high-net-worth individuals that his and others' funds served. He'd failed to consider her uncanny ability to sift the wheat from the chaff, to lure the former to her team and subtly discard the latter. Instead of slinking ignominiously from the financial pages back to the gossip columns where she belonged, she was being tipped as someone to watch. A potential key player in the field that she'd entered with zero previous experience and occupied for a mere six months.

Frankly, it beggared belief.

But because the investors she'd won over to date were relatively small fry, and he remained convinced she was a flash in the pan that everyone would soon see through, Alex had contained his irritation. Because he was no more immune to her charms than anyone else—despite the fact that she descended from a woman he hated with a passion, which should have turned him right off, but for some unfathomable and frustrating reason didn't—he'd given her such a wide berth that they'd barely ever spoken.

However, tonight, by audaciously targeting the multi-billionaire Sheikh whose money he managed, she'd overplayed her hand.

This was *his* world, he thought, gritting his teeth as the sound of her low throaty laugh reached his ears and triggered an unwelcome rash of goosebumps prickling every inch of his skin. A world he'd had no choice but to step into in the aftermath of her mother's affair with his father two decades ago, which had led not only to the destruction of his family and the brutal yet necessary severing of all ties with her son Leo—Olympia's eldest brother and his then best friend—but also, thanks to an extremely acrimonious and expensive divorce, the threat of penury.

He'd spent twenty years sweating blood to turn the ashes of the Andino fortune into an empire that managed so many billions of dollars it was too big to ever be wiped out again. Olympia was trying to muscle her way into the industry he dominated on the back of little more than her family name. Her frothy presence in his space and the undeserved interest she generated was an insult to all his hard work. He could not allow it to continue. She needed to be put in her place before she became all anyone talked about, and what was left of his peace of mind vanished.

With his pulse thudding in his ears and a burning sensation tightening his chest, Alex gave a curt nod and a terse smile as he muttered his excuses to those around him. Then, with a set of his jaw and a sharp surge of adrenaline, he set off in her direction.

She stood with her back to him. Her long dark hair shone beneath the soft light of the chandeliers. Her outrageously flashy silver-sequin dress clung to her curves and shimmered like a beacon in a sea of grey, navy and black. Always standing out, he thought grimly as he cut a swathe through the throng, his eyes narrowing at the sight of the Sheikh touching her on the arm. Always the centre of attention. Like mother, like daughter—dangerous, unpredictable and in possession of the potential to unleash devastation.

Steeling himself not to respond to the impact of her proximity, which he knew from the one and only time he'd experienced it was as intense as it was unwelcome, he came to an abrupt stop beside them.

'Good evening, Abdul Karim,' he said, ignoring her completely as he leaned forward to clap the other man on the shoulder in a move designed to demonstrate his authority. 'Good to see you. Forgive me for interrupting, but would you excuse us? Miss Stanhope and I need to have a word.'

'Right this minute?' The Sheikh's eyebrows rose in a way that suggested he was not best pleased at the intrusion, but those choppy waters would have to be soothed another time.

'I'm afraid it can't wait.'

Abdul Karim eyeballed him for a moment. Then, evidently noting the hint of steel in Alex's tone that belied his relaxed stance and easy smile, he inclined his head and took a step back. 'In that case, of course.'

'Mr Andino is mistaken,' Olympia cut in smoothly, addressing the Sheikh with an effortless smile of her own. 'We do not have and never have had anything to discuss. We haven't even met. Not properly, at least. I can't imagine what words he thinks we need to exchange.'

'I beg to differ,' he countered. 'It's a matter of some importance.'

'I have a gap in my schedule tomorrow morning at nine,' she said, flicking him a glance so chilly it could have frozen the Sahara. 'I could fit you in then.'

'Not tomorrow. Now.'

'Now is not convenient.'

'The urgency of the situation dictates otherwise.'

'Perhaps you could elaborate?'

'I will. In private.'

'As fascinating as this dynamic is,' said the Sheikh, clearly bored of the polite but thinly veiled battle for control playing out before him, 'it's getting late, and I should be heading off. I would, however, be interested to hear more of your thoughts about the future of fossil fuels, Alex. Lunch next week, perhaps?'

'I'll set it up.'

'It was delightful to meet you, Miss Stanhope. I do hope we cross paths again.'

'You can count on it.'

'Good evening.'

With a nod and a smile at each of them in turn, Abdul Karim walked off. Vowing that his client and Olympia would never meet again if he had any say in the matter, Alex clamped a hand to her elbow and wheeled her away before she could escape.

'Let me go this minute,' she hissed, instantly losing the dazzling smile as she tried but failed to shake him off. 'What the hell do you think you're doing?'

Steering her towards the exit while ignoring the curious looks darting in their direction, Alex gritted his teeth and focused. Despite having braced his defences to withstand her effect on him, her captivating scent nevertheless ignited his nerve-endings. Awareness sizzled through him. The palm that was in contact with her arm felt as though it was on fire and his pulse raced. All of which was frustrating and unacceptable and meant that he needed to get this over and done with as quickly and efficiently as possible.

'I could ask you the same thing.'

'*I'm* not the one causing a scene. How dare you take advantage of your superior physical strength to maul me about as if I'm some sort of chattel? What's going on? Please remove your hand from my arm at once.'

'In a moment.'

'This is outrageous.'

Ignoring her ire, Alex hustled her out of the ballroom. On spying a fire exit, he marched her across the sumptuously carpeted floor, through the door and into the dimly lit stairwell, which would afford them the privacy this conversation required. The second the door swung closed behind them, he released her and shoved his hands into the pockets of his trousers.

Olympia sprang back and rubbed her elbow, her glare so fierce it could have stripped the paint from the ceiling. 'You made me look like an idiot back there, you patronising, misogynistic jerk,' she fumed quietly, her colour high, her dark eyes sparking with simmering fury. 'It was mortifying and utterly out of order. You've done your very best to avoid me for months, and *now* we suddenly need a word? At a drinks party? When we've been here for three days already and I'm right in the middle of something? What's so urgent?'

Alex's stomach churned. His muscles clenched. Keeping a lid on the heat raging through him, and resisting the urge to lower his gaze to the rapid rise and fall of her chest, was taking every drop of willpower he possessed. 'Stay away from my clients, Olympia.'

Her eyebrows shot up and her jaw dropped. 'I *beg* your pardon?'

'You heard,' he said flatly. 'You've been trespassing on my territory for months now and I've let it slide. The low-hanging fruit you've been picking off to date is of little importance to me. But tonight, by approaching Abdul Karim, you crossed a line. You've overstepped and I won't tolerate it any more. So it stops. All of it. Now.'

For a moment she just stared at him. Then twin spots of colour hit her cheeks. '*Your* territory?' she echoed with a mutinous jut of her chin. 'You *let it slide*? Your arrogance is truly breathtaking.'

So what if it was? As if he'd ever cared about that. 'This is my world, not yours,' he ground out. 'I've been at it for twenty years. I'm the best in the business, the biggest shark in the sea. You are a minnow, splashing around in the shallows. An inexperienced upstart who's waltzed into my industry on her name and nothing else and has ideas way above her station.'

'Yet you evidently see me as a threat,' she shot back, irritatingly uncowed.

'Don't be ridiculous.'

'And you know what? You're right to be concerned about the Sheikh. Because I can be very persuasive when I put my mind to it.'

He could imagine. How many men had she slayed with those dark come-to-bed eyes and the charm that she wielded like a weapon? How many more did she have lined up? Why was he suddenly grinding his teeth?

'The Sheikh is and always will be mine,' he said, unclenching his jaw, scrubbing all thoughts of kissing her from his head and focusing on the point. 'Far more experienced operators than you have tried to lure him away from my company and failed. You're wasting your time.'

'Am I?'

'Your mule-headed naiveté demonstrates how totally out of your depth you are.'

'That's rude.' She took a step towards him and he resisted the urge to retreat. 'But you can think what you like. I may not have been at this for long, and I know I have much to learn, but I have no intention of stopping. In fact, I've barely even begun. There are no lengths to which I won't go to squeeze every drop of success from the opportunity I've been given. I have big plans. *Huge* plans. So I hope you can handle a little healthy competition.'

Refusing to recognise elements of his youthful self in what she said, because identifying with her in any way was the very *last* thing this situation required, Alex inhaled deeply and fought for calm. 'Do not make an enemy of me, Olympia.'

'Or what?'

'You'll regret it if you do.'

'These feel like empty threats,' she said with a dismissive shrug that only intensified the red mist in his head.

'They're anything but. Have you heard of Naxos Capital Assets?'

'No.'

'Lincoln Masters?'

'No.'

'Precisely. Mess with me at your peril. Stay in your lane and out of my business or suffer the consequences. Continue to defy me and I will use any weapon at my disposal to get what I want—your past, your family, every single thing I can find out about you. It will all be fair game.'

'I doubt you'd find anything that isn't already in the public domain.'

'I won't warn you again.'

'And *I* won't be intimidated.' She planted her hands on her hips, the glint of challenge lighting the dark depths of her eyes. 'What exactly is your problem with me, Alex?' she asked as a fire began to burn in the pit of his stomach. 'And don't try and claim that what's going on here isn't personal. We both know it absolutely is. You can't stand me, can you? That much became clear when I tried to introduce myself to you at that awards ceremony back in November. I mean, there I was, holding out my hand for you to shake, and you just looked down your nose at me, then spun on your heel and walked away. It was quite the snub. I don't think I'll ever forget it. Your dislike of me has been apparent ever since. Whenever we find ourselves in each other's vicinity, you avoid me. You glower at me from afar. If looks could kill I'd be dead a thousand times over and I just don't get it. You and I don't know each other. Before tonight we hadn't even spoken. So have I wronged you somehow? Do you take issue with my reputation? I once overheard you commenting that I ought to find a different career to play at, but surely you can't have *that* big a chip on your shoulder. As you pointed out, you're the best in the business and have been for years. If you want the truth, your precious Sheikh was more interested in getting me to agree to dinner than moving his assets to Stanhope's, and believe me I tried. So why do you care what I do? Why do I even show up on your radar? What have I done to make you hate me so much?'

She stopped, her eyebrows raised, her chin up, tension and defiance radiating from her every pore. Alex reeled, buffeted by her accusations and flummoxed by her questions.

So much for assuming that, in response to his proven ruthlessness, she'd accept his vastly superior experience and acquiesce to his demands with a grudging apology. Instead she'd gone on the attack, seizing the upper hand—a development he would never have envisaged—and for the first time in years he found himself on the back foot.

Silence bounced off the walls of the stairwell as their clashing gazes held, but the cacophony in his head was deafening. While the Sheikh's loyalty had never been in any doubt—although they'd be having dinner over his dead body—Olympia obviously hadn't made the link between the past and the present, between her family and his. So where did he go from here? Was he really going to have to explain that he didn't hate *her* exactly, but rather what she represented?

It would mean confessing that she looked so like her mother that every time he laid eyes on her he was seventeen again, trying to block out the arguments, the tears and the callous cruelty, and realising that life had changed irrevocably. He would have to reveal how deeply he resented constantly reliving not only the moment he'd found his father stone cold on the kitchen floor, a mere week after the divorce had been finalised, his hand still clutching his chest, but also his mother's later diagnosis of terminal cancer that he remained convinced had been brought on by everything she'd suffered. And, as if the prospect of exposing those vulnerabilities wasn't unpalatable enough, he'd also have to acknowledge the frenzied lust that she—Olympia— drummed up in him, which he loathed and feared in equal measure.

He too could recall the moment they'd met as if it were yesterday. The instant their gazes collided, he'd felt as if he'd been punched in the gut. Her smile had blinded him. The thunderbolt of desire that had gripped him had been so powerful, so consuming, he'd instantly understood how nations could be obliterated in the pursuit of it. Instinctively, he'd known that if he'd taken her hand in his, he'd have pulled her into his arms. He'd have crushed his mouth to hers, as if they were the last two people on earth and the survival of the human race depended on them doing something about it.

He'd never experienced such a threat to his control. Shocked to the core by the strength of his reaction to her—and horrified at the idea of history repeating itself, albeit a generation removed—he'd had to walk away. He'd had no choice. He would never succumb to such temptation. He could not contemplate the resulting chaos. He would not be that weak.

Ever since, he'd sworn to keep his distance. And he had. Until tonight, this very minute, when they were standing less than two feet apart, eyes locked, the bristling air that filled the space between them thickening and heating to such a degree that, suddenly, he couldn't recall what she'd asked.

His head was pounding and his heart was crashing against his ribs. Her proximity was stealing his wits. Despite who she was, and the threat she posed to his settled, well-ordered life, he wanted to yank her into his arms and propel her back against the deep-red silk-papered wall. To cover her with his body and his hands, until she was melting into him and sighing, clutching at his shoulders and moaning his name. When she touched the tip of her tongue to the corner of her mouth, the need to kiss her surged through him so fiercely, he actually had to hold himself back from leaning forwards and taking what he wanted.

'Ah,' she said, her voice penetrating the swirling fog in his head, with a breathlessness that made him think of twisted sheets and tangled limbs. '*Now* I get it.'

The knowing tone snapped him out of his trance. He stilled. Blinked. Focused on her face, finding her expression had lost the anger and challenge, and, after briefly flirting with astonishment, was now displaying baffling yet unsettling smugness. 'Get what?'

'You want me.'

Shock froze him to the spot. All the blood in his body

drained to his feet. Surely he wasn't that transparent. Surely he hadn't actually *moved*. 'I beg your pardon?'

'You're attracted to me,' she said, running her gaze over him with a shrewd intensity that coated his skin in an ice-cold sweat, even as he burned. 'There's no point denying it. The evidence is indisputable. Your pupils are dilated. The pulse at the base of your neck is pounding. You couldn't take your eyes off my mouth just now. And I'm making an educated guess here, but I suspect that because you think so little of this *"pampered nepo princess"*—your words, as I recall—you don't want to want me. You desire me against your will and *that's* what you hate.'

For a moment, Alex couldn't think of a thing to say. He was utterly speechless. She was so appallingly right about everything, except *why* he didn't want to want her, that denial was his only option. 'Have you completely lost your mind?'

'Quite the opposite. The situation could not be clearer. And you know what I also think? I think this unwelcome desire you have for me is behind the grim, disapproving looks you've been shooting at me these past few months. They haven't just been about my scandalous reputation and the fact that my brother, the CEO, gave me a job for which I admit I have no experience. They've been because of you. You don't know how to handle me.'

His heart was beating so fast he felt as though he were about to pass out. 'That's quite a leap of the imagination.'

'Perhaps,' she agreed with a slight tilt of her head. 'But if I'm right—and I'm pretty sure I am—it would certainly explain what happened in the ballroom earlier.'

'How?' The word was out before he could stop it.

'You were jealous. Of the Sheikh. And I can see how it may have looked. We were standing fairly close together. That room has terrible acoustics. No wonder you were moved to stake your claim. He's a notorious womaniser.'

Beneath Alex's feet the floor shook. Rejection surged through him, blazing a scorching trail that singed the very marrow of his bones. *Stake his claim? What the hell?* Of course he wasn't jealous. Not only was jealousy a destructive, pointless emotion he'd never had any time for, but also it would mean he felt some sort of possessiveness towards Olympia, which was so far out of the question it was in another galaxy.

Although it would explain the white-hot bolt of lightning he'd experienced when he'd first caught sight of her and the Sheikh talking. And the urge he'd had to break the other man's fingers when he'd seen him touch her. The flat denial that had surged through him at the thought of them having dinner too.

But no. All that had just been fury that she had the temerity to invade his space and was daring to try and create a professional rapport with someone she shouldn't. Nothing else. And the only claim he was interested in staking was on the Sheikh.

'This is insane,' he practically growled, the voice in

his head nonetheless urging him to get the hell out now, while he still could, before he was pushed into doing something he'd regret, whatever that might be. 'You are completely deluded. And not nearly as irresistible as you seem to think. Not every man you meet is bewitched by your smile or succumbs to your charms. Some of us manage to remain immune. All *I* want is for you to stay out of my business.'

'So if I touched you, you'd feel nothing?'

Every muscle in his body tensed. 'Right.'

'I don't believe you.'

'I don't care whether you believe me or not.'

'Let's prove it, one way or another.'

Before he could even register her intention, she stepped forward, closing the distance between them, and lifted a hand to his face, its destination evidently his jaw. But instinct kicked in—just in time—and he jerked his head away, catching her wrist in his hand. 'Stop this.'

'Stop this. Stop that,' she echoed, provocation dancing in her darkly amused eyes. 'You're very free with your diktats. Does everyone apart from me do what you say?'

Yes. They did. So how the hell had it come to this? To the two of them locked in a stand-off that she clearly expected him to lose? And how was he going to win it? He'd have to teach her a lesson she would never forget, a lesson that would make her regret ever deciding to take him on.

'Back off, Olympia,' he ground out, giving her one last chance to comply before facing the consequences.

'You first, Alex.'

'You're playing with fire.'

'So burn me.'

CHAPTER TWO

WHAT ON EARTH Olympia thought she was doing at this precise moment in time she had no idea. Twenty minutes ago she'd been trying to keep the Sheikh on the subject of investment and off dinner, while simultaneously wondering how much more of this she was going to have to endure. She was, of course, honoured to be representing Stanhope Bank at the conference this week, and would be eternally grateful that Zander had given her the chance to turn her car crash of a life around, but all this schmoozing was exhausting.

She'd been at it for six months now. Initially, she'd totally understood where her brother had been coming from when he'd told her that she needed to build up trust before she could start managing the funds their uber wealthy clients invested in. After a decade of generating headlines that went along the lines of *Olympia screws up Olympically*, she was well aware that that her scandalous reputation meant she had a lot to prove. Even if she hadn't read the incredulous press reports about her appointment, she would have known that her well-publicised stint in rehab didn't exactly inspire confidence. So she'd been only too happy to show Zander that she could be relied upon in whichever way he deemed fit. And if that meant using her outgoing personality and her notoriety to drum up new business, then that was all right with her.

Such had been her determination to succeed that she'd smashed the target he'd set for her first year in a quarter of the time. Since then, on a roll, she'd doubled the number of investors she'd lured to the bank. She was more than ready to step up and take on the fund management position she'd been after ever since unexpectedly catching the finance bug in rehab. She was champing at the bit to get started.

But frustratingly, Zander still seemed to have doubts about her suitability for the job, about how her reliability and trustworthiness were still publicly perceived, which was why she'd targeted the Sheikh this evening. A richer, higher-profile investor would be impossible to find. Should she manage to lure *him* to Stanhope's, her brother could not fail to recognise her talents and reward them. What more could she do to prove her dedication and persistence?

Of course, she hadn't considered the possibility of Alex bloody Andino showing up and putting a spanner in the works. But then why would she? They'd never crossed swords before, which had always been completely fine with her. She'd had no desire to seek him out any more than he had her. She could still feel the sting of his slight when she'd tried to introduce herself. The stunned disbelief that he had so rudely ignored her outstretched hand and stalked off, leaving her standing

there—red-faced, smarting and feeling like a fool—
had taken weeks to fade.

What was his problem? she'd wondered pretty much
ever since. Everyone liked her. She made sure of it. So
the fact that he very much didn't had stuck to her like
a burr. That he *had* found her resistible—or so she'd
thought—had sorely piqued her vanity.

But that hadn't crushed the desire that had struck
her like a sledgehammer that evening, as she'd briefly
stood before him, her gaze locked to his for that one
charged moment. Which was pretty galling, but unfortunately, attraction didn't care how he felt about her, or
his rudeness. All *that* had been able to focus on was
the darkly masculine perfection of his features. The
deep brown eyes and the straight blade of a nose. The
chiselled jaw and the sensuous mouth that invariably
tightened whenever their gazes collided.

Nor, unfortunately, had it lessened over time. This
evening, when he'd barged into her conversation with
his towering height, powerful physique and shoulders
as broad as the Aegean, she'd almost swooned. She'd
forgotten how incredible he smelled. How weak her
knees went at the spicy, woody notes of his seductive
scent, which tugged at something deep inside her, making her want to get all up close and personal.

But by focusing on her outrage, which had fuelled
through her when she'd realised what he was up to,
she'd kept it together. She'd fought her corner and had
had surprising fun doing so. Because, while he'd clearly
expected her to crumple in the face of his displeasure

and back off as he demanded, in fact, his antipathy had had the opposite effect. In response to the great waves of tension he radiated, and the forbidding stoniness of his expression, the devil in her had stirred. The prospect of locking horns with him had thrilled her. She'd felt more exhilarated, more alive than she had in a year, and very much up for the fight.

And then, having clocked the crackle of electricity that zigzagged between them—and the trouble he had keeping his gaze off her mouth when she'd deliberately touched her tongue to her lips to confirm her suspicions—she'd realised what the past six months' antagonism had *really* been about, and her outrage had drained away. In its place had flooded hot heady desire that begged to be satisfied. The more he'd denied it the more determined she'd been to prove it, to find out how explosive the chemistry that sizzled between them might be, how good they could make each other feel if they unleashed it.

But God, he was a hard nut to crack. Even now, with time and the world at a standstill, her bold challenge hanging between them, he still resisted—even though the hammering of her pulse beneath his fingers had to reveal the effect he had on her.

Excitement was thundering through her. With mere centimetres separating them, he dominated her senses. His eyes blazed and his heat enveloped her. His scent was scrambling her brain, his touch sending tingles down her arm, and all she wanted was his mouth on hers and his hands exploring her body. To experience

the electrifying passion that she'd missed since rein-
ing in the wilder side of her character.

So maybe, because of the recklessness that was turning the blood in her veins to fire, she ought to shake
herself free and step away. The mindfulness tech-
niques she'd learned in rehab to ride out any disruption that might set back her recovery—any disruption
to her composure at all, in fact—were so ingrained she
could recall them at the drop of a hat, and she probably should. Besides, some sixth sense warned her that
prodding this particular beast might not be wise.

But she wanted Alex's surrender more. She wanted
to punish him for what he'd done back there in the ballroom. To finally win this battle of attrition he'd started.
She longed to find out what would happen when his resistance cracked. So she deliberately lowered her gaze
to his mouth and let it linger. She drew in a slow deep
breath, which brought her aching breasts into contact
with the solid wall of his chest, and held it.

For the longest time he didn't move a muscle. He
didn't seem to be breathing either. And it was just beginning to occur to her that sickeningly, *mortifyingly*,
maybe she'd got it all wrong and he didn't want her,
when suddenly he moved. In the blink of an eye she
was up against the wall, the air whooshing from her
lungs. His head descended, blotting out the light, the
stairwell, everything but him, and his mouth slammed
down on hers.

Pinning her there with his big hard body, he took advantage of her parted lips to possess her in a kiss that

was hot and ferocious, no doubt designed to establish his dominance and demonstrate that he was a dangerous man to trifle with. He instantly released her wrist to bury his hand in her hair, angling her head to increase the intensity with which he plundered her mouth, as if he didn't want to just burn her but brand her, as if he were aiming to imprint himself on her memory for ever.

And he was succeeding. She'd never had a kiss like it. Every one of her senses was under siege. Her brain was short-circuiting and her bones were disintegrating. She was losing her mind and her control, so much so that when he lifted his head a moment later and growled, 'I did warn you. I never bluff. I hope you've learned your lesson,' she actually whimpered in protest.

But if his intention had been to put her off with that punishing but thrilling onslaught it had backfired spectacularly. She wanted more. She wanted everything—danger, dominance, every dark desire he possessed. So he might be loosening his grip on her, making to step away, but he and his clever mouth were going nowhere.

Giddy with need, Olympia surged forwards, threw her arms around his neck and pulled his head back down to hers. Kissing him as fiercely as he'd just kissed her, she arched her back so that every quivering inch of her pressed against every shocked, rigid inch of him.

And then, there it was—the moment his control snapped—and it was as dramatic and exciting as she'd imagined.

His arms whipped around her, crushing her in a tight embrace that she couldn't have escaped if she'd wanted to, and her body went up in flames. His fingers were in her hair and his scent was in her head and in her blood, intoxicating her to the point of madness. Within seconds she'd become a pounding mass of lust, reduced to making little moans of pleasure at the back of her throat as he ground his pelvis into hers, his rock-hard erection digging into her right where she wanted him most.

He wrenched his mouth from hers to draw in a ragged breath, then set his lips to her neck. As her head fell back to allow him better access, she trembled and gasped. He trailed hot kisses down the sensitive skin of her chest. As he did so, he tugged down the spaghetti straps of her dress. The soft shimmering fabric fell to her waist, exposing her bare breasts to his scorching gaze, and when his mouth closed over her nipple, her knees buckled.

In response to this delicious torment heat poured through her. The need to have him inside her consumed her. Shaking, mad with desire, she shifted to put a sliver of space between their lower bodies. Her hand found their way to the button of his trousers and his zip, moulding to his straining length in a move that she couldn't begin to claim was accidental.

Alex hissed out a harsh breath and jerked back. He pushed up her dress and, with her help, he yanked her underwear off. She tackled his trousers and shorts, shoving both down while he located his wallet, fished out a condom and rolled it on.

Using the wall for support, he planted his hands on

her thighs and lifted her up, parting her legs, stepping between them as he did so. Panting desperately, clinging tightly to his shoulders, Olympia shifted her hips, and on a rough groan he surged into her liquid heat.

He held still for a moment, a stunning moment she used to familiarise herself with the exquisite feel of him, so big and deep inside her that she actually saw stars, and then, as she locked her legs around his waist, pulling him in even further, he began to move.

Their mouths met in a fiery clash of teeth and tongues. He didn't bother with slow and measured, but struck up a quick intense rhythm that she matched stroke for stroke. With every powerful thrust she lost a little bit more of her mind. The friction of her sensitised breasts against the crisp white cotton of his shirt sent such strong sparks of electricity to her nerve-endings that she thought she was about to combust.

She'd never felt such raw animal passion, such wild abandonment, and she never experienced it in someone else either. There was nothing tender and romantic about what they were doing. It was primal and electric. The fight for completion was instinctive, a mutual goal, a battle which, this time, they would both win. They were volcanically in synch. So much so that when she tore her mouth from his and bit into his jacket-clad shoulder, muffling her cries as she shattered powerfully around him, he buried his head in her neck, thrusting into her one last time, hard and deep, and climaxed so intensely that it detonated another explosion inside her.

For the longest moment, as the blazing pleasure

ebbed and the heat cooled, all she could hear was the thundering of her heart and the raggedness of their breathing. She barely had the strength to open her eyes, let alone speak. But she just about managed when he eventually eased out of her and stepped back to set her on her feet.

'So that was wild,' she said dazedly, as she tugged her dress into place while he dealt with the condom, then pulled up his shorts and trousers and put himself back together. 'I thought it might be good, but I had no idea it would be *that* good. I've never experienced anything like it. You nearly blew the top of my head off. Want to find out what we could do in a bed?'

'No.'

The word shot from him like a bullet from a gun. Olympia stilled. She lifted her gaze to his face. Noting the rigid jaw and blank expression, she felt a tiny shiver of ice-cold apprehension run down her spine, and she frowned. 'What?'

His dark eyes glittered. Tension rolled off him in great buffeting waves. 'This shouldn't have happened,' he growled. 'We will never speak of it again.' And with that, he stalked to the door, yanked it open and vanished.

CHAPTER THREE

Eight weeks later

THESE PAST TWO MONTHS, never speaking of what she and Alex had done together in the hotel stairwell in Switzerland had suited Olympia down to the ground. Not even thinking about it—or him—had suited her even better, because with his parting shot, he'd turned the hottest ten minutes of her life into some of the seediest.

It wasn't that she had a problem with one-night stands. On the contrary, prior to going into rehab, she'd learned to favour ultra-casual flings, which gave her the rush she craved. She was far too screwed up to be trusted with a relationship, and who would ever want to take on her and her issues anyway? No strings meant no disappointment. No possibility of rejection. No danger of swapping one dependency for another and transferring her innate neediness onto a man.

Besides, she wasn't sure she even knew what love meant. She certainly hadn't received any from either of her parents. Before his fatal heart attack when she was nine, her aristocratic British father had been a stern distant figure, only interested in his heir—her eldest brother, Leo. Her scandalous Greek socialite mother had never had time for anyone but herself, and still didn't. And with five older siblings, she'd had to fight for every scrap of attention she'd been given, none of which could have been called unconditional.

It was the way the night had ended that left such a bad taste in the mouth. She'd thought she and Alex had been on the same page. He'd certainly demonstrated an equal degree of feral desperation. She hadn't had sex with anyone since checking into the clinic in Arizona, and she'd been excited by the idea of making up for lost time with him.

But he'd made her feel as though they'd done something shameful, something grubby. She'd been left with the impression that, bafflingly, not only did he deeply regret succumbing to desire, but also he held her to blame for his loss of control. His unexpected and inexplicable anger had winded her. His rejection had stung. Her brittle self-esteem had plummeted, and for the first couple of weeks she'd been back in Athens she'd hated him for all of it.

Nor was she all that keen on herself, if she was being honest. She still couldn't work out what on earth she'd been thinking that night. Acting on impulse had been one of the first problem areas that therapy sessions in rehab had identified. She'd spent weeks learning strategies to control it, and had put considerable effort into working on this particular flaw.

Yet the minute Alex had confronted her in all his

thrillingly dark and handsome glory, she'd forgotten every single one of them. She hadn't questioned for one moment the wisdom of taking what she so badly needed. Had they been caught, the press would have had a field day. She'd have been fired on the spot, her fledgling career over, her improving but still fragile reputation in tatters.

However, none of that had crossed her mind. The second he'd pulled her against him and crushed his mouth to hers she'd been utterly lost. The flicker of triumph she'd experienced at his surrender had been burned to a crisp by the bonfire he'd lit. All she'd been able to focus on was taking what they were doing to its natural conclusion as quickly as possible.

Stupidly, unthinkingly, she'd positioned herself at the top of a slippery slope, at the bottom of which lurked a version of herself she was trying to put behind her. The reckless rebel, who'd taken attention seeking as a child to a whole new boundary-pushing level in adolescence, by first flirting with an eating disorder and shoplifting, then dabbling in drugs and alcohol and casual sex—bad choices all of them. She'd slipped back into old habits as if she'd never spent three months in Arizona working out why she behaved the way she did, then doing her best to create better, less destructive ways to measure her self-worth. She'd thrown caution to the wind and chased the high that would make her feel like a billion dollars without a thought to the consequences.

And now she was paying for it.

Because, as she'd discovered this Friday morning, half an hour ago, here at the clinic where she'd had an appointment to find out what was behind her chronic tiredness and bloating, there was indeed a consequence. The sort that developed over nine months and lasted a lifetime.

She was pregnant.

Not ill, not suffering from ultra-delayed cold turkey, but pregnant.

Olympia's head spun and her stomach churned as she stared at the black and white printout of her uterus, containing the recognisably baby-shaped blob, which she held with clammy fingers that had been trembling for the last twenty minutes. Surely the scanner had to be faulty. The blood tests wrong. Because how could it have happened? She and Alex had had sex just the once and they'd used protection. It didn't make any sense. Had there been a problem with the condom? An application issue? Or had they just been spectacularly unlucky?

More pertinently, what the hell was she going to do about it? She wasn't equipped to have a child. Up until a year or so ago, she'd lived her life entirely on her terms, and those terms had not been great. She'd barely been able to look after herself, let alone anyone else, and even though she'd moved on—she hoped— she was still a little fragile. Still at risk of screwing up if she wasn't careful. And then there was her budding career, her need to prove she had value and purpose outside of supplying the gossip columns with material. What impact would a child have on that?

But despite the inconvenient timing and her many concerns about her ability to cope, she wanted this baby instantly, with a surprising strength that had made her throat tight and her chest ache. She wanted someone to shower with love and affection and to receive it back. To do it right. Her child wouldn't suffer the parental neglect she had, she vowed as she concentrated on breathing in and out, slowly and deeply. Her child wouldn't be left to fend for itself in a sea of older siblings and an absence of guidance.

So there was only one solution. However much she might recoil at the idea of facing him again, she was going to have to tell Alex. He blew so hot and cold that his reaction to the news was anyone's guess, but this was as much his concern as it was hers, and she had no other support. She needed to know whether or not he wanted to be involved and, if he did, what that involvement might look like. Only then could she proceed.

She hadn't seen him since he'd disappeared through the fire door that night, attractively rumpled yet confusingly brutal. Unable to stand the thought of bumping into him, and feeling even worse about herself than she already did, she'd packed her bags and left the conference early the following morning. Thereafter, somehow, she'd managed to avoid him completely.

But that wasn't an option any longer. Nor was sticking her head in the sand and pretending all this would go away in time—it wouldn't. She had to face reality, put the past behind her and focus on the future. There was no point dwelling on the unpleasant manner in which he'd abandoned her. Or bearing a grudge against him for the situation she was in because after all, he was the one who'd taken responsibility for contraception. Regret and blame would help no one, least of all this new life they'd created.

What *would* help was staying cool and in control when she confronted him. Presenting him with the facts plainly and unemotionally and above all maturely. She would not allow lust to throw her off course again, she told herself as she carefully stowed the ultrasound in her handbag and pulled out her phone to try and track him down. Or any emotion for that matter. She would finally deploy the tactics she'd learned to curb her impulsive streak and rise above any unfathomable animosity he might still display towards her.

She had someone else to think about now, someone who needed her to make this work, whatever the sacrifice, and that was all that mattered.

Sitting at his desk in the office suite that occupied the entire penthouse of the twenty-storey Athens building, which housed Andino Asset Management, Alex was in the middle of mentally calculating the money he could potentially make by shorting the yen against the dollar, when one of his three assistants put her head around the door.

'Sorry to disturb,' Elena said with an apologetic grimace, 'but Olympia Stanhope is on her way up. I checked and she doesn't have an appointment. However, according to the receptionist she was very insistent on seeing you. She was threatening to make a scene. I thought it best to contain the situation by complying with her wishes.'

In response to this revelation, Alex barely moved a muscle. His gaze merely flickered from the screen in front of him to Elena, then back again, while his pulse skipped a beat and his brain screeched to a halt. He hardly even breathed.

Up until now he'd done an excellent job of blanking the appalling encounter he'd had with Olympia from his head. Even though it had been the hottest sex of his life, the last thing he wanted to do was revisit such a monumental loss of control with a woman who represented everything he detested, and not just because of her surname.

What the hell had he done? That was the question battering his thoughts as he'd stormed back to his hotel suite, still recovering from the most earthshattering orgasm he'd ever had, while simultaneously feeling sick to his stomach with self-loathing and regret, furious with himself, her, the entire bloody world. He'd allowed himself to be seduced by a self-proclaimed hedonist, a charming, beautiful scandal of a woman who wouldn't know responsibility if it slapped her around the face.

He should never have approached her that night. He should have waited until the morning, when she wouldn't have been wearing an aggravating dress and her thick glossy hair would have been up in its usual neat and tidy arrangement, instead of down in loose alluring waves about her shoulders.

But even as she'd demanded he burn her, he could have salvaged the situation. All he'd had to do was release his grip on her, take a step back and demonstrate supreme control by getting the hell out of there. Yet he hadn't moved. He'd been transfixed by the challenging jut of her chin and the knowing, teasing glint in her eyes. Then she'd deliberately brought her breasts into contact with his chest and all rational thought had vanished.

She needed to be shown that *he* was in control here, he'd thought as he'd raked his gaze over her stunning face, the arch of one fine eyebrow, the hint of a provocative smile on her beautiful mouth. So if she wanted to be burned, he'd burn her. He'd brand her so deeply she'd run a mile whenever their paths crossed, riddled with regret that she'd ever decided to take him on.

But it was he who'd been branded. Because the minute he'd kissed her—in a mindbogglingly stupid attempt to teach her some sort of a lesson—he hadn't stood a chance. The desire he'd had for her was simply too overpowering. And it was his brain that had disintegrated when he'd finally pulled back and she'd thrown herself at him.

His defences reduced to rubble by her extraordinarily effective assault, he'd succumbed to temptation. He'd slept with the enemy. Which meant that not only had he made a mockery of his driving force these past two decades, but also that he was not nearly as strong-willed as he'd always assumed. In fact, he was just as weak as his father, incontrovertible proof that the apple really didn't fall far from the tree.

Who would want to recall any of that? He certainly didn't. Therefore he hadn't, and he was so single-minded that it hadn't even taken much effort. He'd just wiped the entire incident from his head, as if it had never happened, and that had been that.

However, now Olympia was here. Why, he had no idea. But while instinct urged him to instruct Elena to get rid of her, logic told him that he couldn't turn her away. The scenes she made tended to end up on the front pages of newspapers, and his business could do without that sort of scandal.

And really, there was no need for alarm, he assured himself as the shock receded and his brain cranked back into gear. It wasn't as if he'd be blindsided by her effect on him again. He knew what to expect. He would not be hurled off track by memories of how incredible she'd felt in his arms or the soft little sounds she'd made as, together, they found oblivion. He would not look at her and suffer an attack of the past. Whatever she had to say, he'd hear her out, then respond appropriately with icy indifference and rock-solid immunity.

'Show her in,' he said, taking a moment to prepare himself, so that when she stepped into his office a moment later, he was able to bank the immediate response of his body to the sight of her, getting to his feet as if completely unmoved.

Pleasingly, he was so unaffected he barely noticed

the mini earthquake she seemed to be setting off as she crossed the floor, or the rearrangement of the air so that it apparently no longer contained oxygen. He merely slid his hands into the pockets of his trousers and watched her as she came to a stop on the other side of his desk, somehow managing to make blue jeans, white trainers and a biscuit-coloured blazer over a white T-shirt look like haute couture.

'Good afternoon, Olympia,' he said, giving her the smallest of nods and allowing his mouth to curve into a faint but humourless smile. 'You just can't resist invading my territory, can you?'

'It's delightful to see you too, Alex,' she replied with equal cool.

'How have you been?'

'Just fine. You?'

'Couldn't be better. May I offer you something to drink?'

'No, thank you.'

'Please do take a seat.'

She sank elegantly into the chair he'd indicated while he sat back down, refusing to recall how the last time he'd seen her she'd been convulsing around him and biting his shoulder to muffle her cries of pleasure. 'Did you enjoy the last day of the conference?'

'I left early that morning.' She crossed her legs and linked her hands over her knee. 'Things to catch up on. I assume you didn't stay either.'

'I'd been away from the office long enough.'

'Of course.' She gave her head the tiniest of tilts and

smiled. 'I must say, I've been surprised not to bump into you these past few weeks. You haven't been avoiding me, have you?'

'Not at all,' he said easily, thinking that of course he hadn't been avoiding her. He'd simply been so busy with work recently he'd considered it a judicious use of resources to send others in his stead whenever Andino representation was required at an event. 'I've just had a lot on. As have you, I hear. I knew it was too much to hope you'd quit the industry entirely.'

'Sorry to disappoint.'

He arched one sceptically amused eyebrow. 'Are you?'

'Not remotely.'

'I didn't think so. At least you saw sense and backed off my business.'

'I had no choice. Your clients are mystifyingly loyal.'

'There's nothing mystifying about it. Not only do my results consistently outperform everyone else's, but I've also spent years building and curating the relationships I have. Why would anyone jump ship?'

'Yes, well, fortunately for me, others aren't quite so good at what they do.'

While Alex could admit he found this back and forth mildly entertaining, he doubted it was the reason she'd pitched up at his office. He was keen to find out what it was, so he could eject her from his building and move on with his life.

'So to what do I owe this pleasure, Olympia?' he asked, steepling his fingers as he continued to regard her impassively. 'What are you doing here?'

For a moment, she just looked at him blankly, as though she'd forgotten. Then she gave herself a quick shake, took a breath and said, 'I have some news.'

Oh? 'Couldn't you have called?'

'My phone was hacked once and it's the sort of news best delivered face to face anyway.'

A ripple of apprehension shivered down his spine. 'That sounds ominous.'

'It might be. Or it might not be. Depends on your perspective.'

'How cryptic.'

'You must be busy so I'll get to the point.'

Finally.

'I know we were supposed to forget all about what we did together the last time we saw each other and, believe me, I was fully on board with that. In fact, given the way you stalked off and left me there, I would have been perfectly happy never to lay eyes on you ever again. As an exit strategy, yours leaves a lot to be desired. But unfortunately, keeping out of each other's way is no longer possible.'

'Why not?'

'Because that night created a situation.'

'What sort of a situation?'

She pulled her shoulders back and looked him straight in the eye. 'I'm pregnant, Alex,' she said. 'And the baby's yours.'

CHAPTER FOUR

As that bombshell landed Alex stilled. The world skidded to a stop. Every muscle in his body tensed and his head spun. It was a good thing he was sitting down. Had he been standing he might well have keeled over.

But then, cold hard logic kicked in, scything through the shock, and told him no. Absolutely not. That didn't make any sense at all. So what was going on? What was she up to?

Shifting in his chair to get his blood flowing again, he pulled himself together and focused on the facts, which rendered her claim a lie. 'Is this some sort of a joke?'

Olympia's eyebrows shot up. 'A *joke*?' she said on a sharp intake of breath. 'Why on earth would I joke about something like this?'

'I have no idea,' he said with the shrug of one shoulder. 'To punish me for walking off that night in Switzerland? Because the papers need a story? For fun?'

'Are you *serious*?'

'Deadly.'

'I'm not that vindictive,' she said tightly. 'Nothing about any of this is fun or for a story. And it's very much not a joke. I had an ultrasound this morning.' She dug around in her bag for a moment and withdrew a small square of paper, which she thrust at him. 'Here's the photo. According to the doctor, I'm ten weeks along.'

He automatically took it and glanced down at the grainy black and white image below her name, which clearly showed a tiny human being floating in a circle of black. Which proved she was pregnant, but that was all.

'Congratulations,' he said, handing it back as if it were on fire. 'But I'm not the father. I can't be.'

'You can and you are. Unfortunately. Not only do the dates fit, but you're also the only person I've had sex with in over twelve months.'

'Do you honestly expect me to believe that, with your past?'

In response to his cutting tone she flinched minutely, but he refused to allow her reaction anywhere near his conscience. She was a Stanhope and therefore not be trusted. 'It's the truth.'

Ha. 'I used protection.'

'Evidently incorrectly.'

No. That was a preposterous suggestion. He had over twenty years' experience of practising safe sex and not once in that time had he been careless. Not once had there even been the hint of a scare. What Olympia was implying was unthinkable. 'It's impossible.'

'Statistically, it's not. Improbable, yes. Impossible? No.'

'So I'm just supposed to accept what you say?'

'Well, I was hoping you would. But I'm happy to arrange a paternity test if you wish.'

Feeling as though the walls were closing in on him, Alex didn't know what he wished. He couldn't think straight. He was finding it hard to breathe. There were spots in his vision. She was coolly pulverising every one of his objections, but he didn't want to concede she had a point about the statistics. He didn't want to acknowledge the growing feeling that she wasn't lying.

Yet for how much longer could he continue to ignore the evidence? Her ice cool façade was cracking. She looked to be as thrown by this as he was. She was unnaturally still and her face was pale. And what possible ulterior motive could she have for pressing him to acknowledge the paternity of her child? She wouldn't be after his money. She had plenty of her own.

So perhaps the unthinkable *wasn't* all that unthinkable. He'd been so crazed with need that night he'd barely been able to recall his own name. His hands had been shaking. He might well have deployed less haste and more speed. Or maybe the condom had split. He'd climaxed so hard it wasn't beyond the realm of possibility. All of which meant that he *could* be the father of this baby. And, more shockingly, if he was, then it was entirely his fault.

'However, I'm not here to assign blame,' she continued, her steady tone slicing through the storm swirling around his head and the nausea churning up his stomach. 'What's done is done, and thrashing out what went wrong seems pretty pointless. I realise it's a shock—it was to me too—but you *are* the father of my child. I'm here because I thought you should know, and to find out how much you want to be involved.'

'You're keeping it?'

'I am,' she said with a decisive nod. 'The circumstances could not be worse but I am. And what I'd like to know is, what do *you* want?'

Alex stared at her blankly. What sort of an idiotic question was that? He was still having trouble accepting the situation, despite the increasingly obvious truth of it, and he'd never felt so at sea. 'How the hell do I know?' he snapped, pushing back his chair and surging to his feet, overwhelmed by the need to move, to pace, to do something to ease the dawning realisation that, once again, life as he knew it was over. 'I haven't had any time to think about it.'

'I'm happy to wait while you do.'

How long did she have?

He scrubbed his hands over his face as if trying to wake himself from a nightmare, and strode to the window through which there was a spectacular view of the Parthenon, not that he could focus on that right now.

Fatherhood wasn't something he'd ever contemplated before. For one thing, he'd never met anyone who'd remotely tempted him to do so, and for another, the mere thought of marriage and family brought him out in hives. He'd witnessed how fragile relationships could be, the devastation they could cause when they broke down, and he had no wish to either experience the direct pain himself or inflict it on others.

Nor did he have any truck with love. The implosion of his parents' marriage had taught him that the heart was fickle and not to be trusted. That handing responsibility for your own well-being and happiness to someone else to destroy was foolish beyond belief. It was best, he'd decided in the aftermath of that hideously acrimonious divorce, to avoid love and commitment at all costs, which was why he stuck to short-term, sedate, no-strings affairs that came to a mutually agreed end with no fuss and no drama.

What he'd done with Olympia had been anything but sedate, and she was drama personified. And it wasn't over, because with the birth of this baby—which he knew deep down in his bones had to be his—they would be connected for ever. He'd be constantly reminded of the year he'd had to grow up fast. Its grandmother would be Selene Stanhope, the viper that two decades ago had slithered into his family's nest and wrecked three lives. Leo—the best friend he'd brutally cut off out of a sense of self-preservation—would be its uncle. Of all the women he could accidentally get pregnant, Olympia had to be the absolute worst, not least because she drummed up in him the sort of uncontrollable, insatiable lust he despised.

And yet...

He couldn't deny the flicker of primitive excitement leaping about in the pit of his stomach at the notion of another being in this world with half his DNA. He would no longer exist on his own. He would have something else to channel his energies into, not just work.

His bloodline would continue, his life would have evolutionary purpose and, in a way, the family he'd lost would be replaced. Instead of dwelling on the past he'd have a reason to look to the future, which was a confusingly appealing prospect.

The last of his resistance evaporated, and despite the many external complications to this particular pregnancy, an unexpected wave of protectiveness swept through him. Hot on the heels of that was the sharp realisation that there was no way he would allow Olympia to bring up his child on her own. She seemed to be on an even keel these days, if her absence from the gossip columns was anything to go by, but what if she relapsed? What if she wrecked things in some other way?

Furthermore, he was not having his child raised a Stanhope. He couldn't imagine a greater insult to his mother's memory, or a bigger mockery of his achievements. It would be an Andino, brought up on his values—whatever those turned out to be—and that was final.

Olympia had had him on the back foot and dangling from her strings since the moment they'd met, but that stopped now. He was taking control of the situation, nailing it down, so that if and when she screwed up he'd be there to minimise the fallout. To remove her from the picture altogether if it came to that. He would never let his child be subjected to the sort of devastation he'd suffered. Never. Nor could he ever allow a situation in which she waltzed off and cut *him* out of the picture.

So he didn't give a toss if she had a problem with

'the circumstances' as she so euphemistically put it. If he could rise above what her mother had done to his family then so could she. The new life she was carrying transcended his feelings towards the Stanhopes. He would do everything in his power to keep it safe.

Filled with steely resolve and flatly ignoring the voice in his head, which insisted there had to be some other solution because this one could prove a disaster in ways he couldn't even begin to comprehend, he turned to face her and announced, 'You and I will be married.'

In response to Alex's stunning and wholly unexpected solution, the tension that had been gripping Olympia ever since the doctor had revealed she was pregnant drained from her system so fast her head spun. The strength left her limbs, her vision blurred, and it was taking every drop of willpower she possessed to stay upright.

Oh, thank God for that, she thought, letting out a long steady breath as her head gradually cleared and her heart rate slowed. What a result. Some people, she knew, might take umbrage at the obsolete idea of marriage for the sake of a child. Others might baulk at the thought of being tied to someone they didn't know and didn't particularly like for ever.

Not her, though.

All she felt was relief. Blessed, overwhelming relief. Because, despite the continuing friction that existed between them—not to mention his unflattering denial of the situation, which she'd decided to attribute to shock and had therefore risen above—she didn't know what she would have done if Alex had told her she was on her own and turfed her out of his building. She hadn't realised how desperately she'd been relying on his support until she had it. And, quite frankly, that support could not have come in a better form than the one he'd just suggested.

Evidently he was intent on sharing the immense responsibility, which would have been enough on its own, but with this proposal of marriage the future would be secured. In the event she screwed up—entirely possible, despite the progress she'd made with her recovery—her baby would be safe.

Of course, nothing was ever guaranteed, but the set of his jaw and his steely tone indicated a reassuring degree of resolve, of commitment. Formalising their relationship would minimise the possibility of him abandoning them when the going got tough, and it would maximise the chance of making a success of things. So from that point of view, it was a no-brainer.

But it might also have further benefits, she had to admit as she rapidly worked through all the implications of embarking on such a course of action. Ones of considerably less significance, of course, but nevertheless appealing. It could be professionally advantageous. A public demonstration of stability and maturity. Proof that she'd put the past behind her for good and settled down. That, ostensibly, one person at least believed her to be trustworthy and dependable. He would give her gravitas and their union could be presented as a whirlwind romance culminating in a fairy-tale wedding. No one need ever know the true circumstances of the arrangement.

And there was no denying that the physical side of things would be thrilling. The events of today might have turned life for both of them on its head but, despite the shocking impact of this meeting, an undercurrent of attraction still sizzled between them.

When she'd walked in and seen him standing behind his desk, shirt sleeves rolled up, top button undone, watching her intently from behind a pair of black-framed glasses, she'd almost forgotten why she'd come. She'd been hit by the urge to push him down and settle herself on his lap. To set her fingers to his shirt and tackle the rest of the buttons. And he wasn't immune to her either. He hadn't taken his eyes off her once and, for all his stony indifference earlier, that pulse at the base of his neck still throbbed madly. Therefore, assuming he'd got over whatever had spooked him in the stairwell, she saw no reason why they shouldn't indulge that raging chemistry whenever the mood took them.

So what would be the downsides of agreeing to his suggestion? Well, for one thing, there was his surliness, which she was beginning to think was his default setting—at least when it came to her. But she would charm him out of that eventually. As she'd once told him, she could be remarkably persuasive, and she had no doubt that with a little effort she would have him eating out of her hand in no time at all.

Then there was the prospect of binding herself to

him for the next twenty years or so, but it wasn't as if she'd be giving up some childhood dream or anything. Marrying for love, in the manner of her siblings, had never been on the cards for her. She'd done nothing to deserve that sort of happiness, had no idea what love even was, if she was being honest, and as everyone knew, she was a flighty, irresponsible good-time girl. Or at least she had been. Now she wasn't quite sure what she was, but that didn't matter. Career progression and optics aside, all that really mattered was the baby.

After years of doing everything wrong, now was the time to do what was right. And that was providing her child with the best possible life she could, the life she would have given anything to have had. So it was the easiest thing in the world to nod firmly and get to her feet. To straighten her spine, smile brightly and say, 'Great!'

And when he told her 'I'll be in touch' as he walked her to the door, she was so giddily relieved about how well this had all worked out she didn't even wonder how.

CHAPTER FIVE

AT TEN THE following morning, Alex had just emerged from the pool when he heard the roar of an engine somewhere in the vicinity. Irritated beyond belief by the potential intrusion into his privacy, he slung a towel round his neck, then flung open the front door and strode out into the wince-inducing sunshine. A nifty red convertible was zooming up the drive. He didn't recognise the car but he sure as hell recognised its occupant, and the instant he did, the tension he'd worked off by ploughing up and down the pool for an hour returned with a bang.

He had not slept well. Yesterday afternoon, unable to concentrate on anything in the aftermath of Olympia's life-altering news—and utterly drained of the adrenaline that had sustained him throughout their conversation—he'd had his driver bring him home. On arrival, he'd headed straight to his study and cracked open a bottle of *tsipouro*. Then he'd thrown himself into an armchair and had steadily worked his way through it while raking over the cataclysmic events of the day.

What on earth had just happened? was the question he'd asked himself repeatedly as he'd stared out of the window into the twilight, four glasses in. Could he have dreamed the whole thing? It hadn't seemed real. Olympia's ready acceptance of his marriage proposal, all the more remarkable for the absence of defiance, had certainly lent the encounter an air of fantasy.

But no. He hadn't, of course. After years of studiously avoiding any sort of emotional tie, one misstep and he'd suddenly acquired a very real wife-and-child-to-be. What was he going to do with them? How was he going to be able to face the constant reminder of her mother and the damage she'd done? Would he ever get past it? Was there any chance—any chance at all—that this was all some catastrophic misunderstanding?

Unfortunately, the industrial strength alcohol had supplied no answer to these or any of the other questions rocketing around his brain. Nor had it granted him the oblivion he'd sought. All it had done was give him a pounding headache and nightmares that tangled the present with the past, then woke him up, drenched in a cold sweat, his heart thundering so hard it was in danger of cracking a rib.

As a result, he was exhausted and woolly-headed and very much not up to Olympia ambushing him on his doorstep. But it was way too late to pretend he wasn't in, so once again, he'd just have to find out what she wanted and then send her on her way—a plan that today, unlike yesterday, *would* work.

'Good morning, Alex,' she said, briefly raking her gaze over him with a scorching intensity that made him wish he'd pulled on a shirt.

'That's debatable,' he muttered, feeling as if he'd gone up in flames. She got out of the car and, with a slam of the door behind her, marched round to the back. 'What the bloody hell is going on? How did you know where I live?'

'Friends in low places.'

With growing alarm he watched her pop the boot and duck her head, then heave out a small suitcase and plonk it on the cobbles.

'As for what's going on, isn't it obvious? I'm moving in.'

At that, his brows crashed together in a deep frown. His pulse skipped a beat and then began to pound. 'What?'

'I'm moving in.'

'Here?'

'Yes. Of course here. Where else?'

'No,' he said with a sharp shake of his head. 'Absolutely not. This is not what we agreed.'

'I don't remember discussing it at all,' she said dryly. 'Or any of the practicalities of the arrangement, as a matter of fact. And I know you said you'd be in touch, but it occurred to me earlier that we didn't even exchange phone numbers, which was why I couldn't call ahead.' She delved back into the car and extracted a holdall that she dropped next to the suitcase. 'But we do need to hammer out how this thing is going to work. And get to know each other. I live in the city centre. You live out here. A forty-minute drive between us isn't conducive to anything. You must agree cohabitation makes sense.'

Alex's teeth clenched and his head began to throb again. 'I do not have to agree to anything of the sort,' he said, never regretting more that they hadn't exchanged numbers. He did not have the wherewithal to cope with this level of face-to-face assault.

'Well, I guess you could move in with me if you really object to me being here,' she said with a thoughtful tilt of her head. 'My apartment isn't as big as this, naturally, but it would suit equally well.'

At that scenario, a shudder ripped through him. God, no. Willingly enter Stanhope territory? That would be even worse. What if her mother showed up? 'It's out of the question,' he said, weak at the very thought of coming face to face with the selfish narcissistic socialite he held responsible for the detonation of his family. 'All of it.'

'There you go again with the diktats.'

'It's not happening.'

'Why not?' One fine dark eyebrow rose, yesterday's compliance evidently a blip. 'What's the problem? Why would you not see this as an excellent idea, and one that should be implemented right away? I do. I've even taken the next two weeks off work for that very purpose. I admit this situation isn't exactly ideal, but surely we have to make the best of it.'

Not ideal? That had to be the understatement of the century. And as for making the best of things, well, that wasn't happening. At least, not right now. Because for one thing he hadn't yet had the time or the headspace to work it all through. And for another, he couldn't have her in his vicinity until he'd figured out how to get a grip on his response to her once and for all.

Despite his excellent intentions yesterday, he'd still wanted to spread her across his desk and divest her of her clothing. And today, it was bad enough she was standing on his drive in a short yellow sundress, which clung to her curves and revealed far too much sun-kissed skin over long toned limbs for his peace of mind. He didn't dare imagine what might happen if they found themselves in close proximity to a bed. Sure, he could *try* and convince himself that he was particularly susceptible to her allure this morning because he wasn't firing on all cylinders, but the inconvenient truth was that he was *always* susceptible to her allure, and handling it required a plan that he had not yet devised.

Besides, they did not need to get to know each other. This marriage was to be purely practical. There'd be logistics to consider, of course, but a heart-to-heart that would likely strip him of his armour and bare his soul? No, thanks. And as for learning her innermost secrets, that appealed even less than spilling his. Every fibre of his being recoiled in horror at the prospect of forming an emotional connection with anyone, let alone a Stanhope. No one but a fool would willingly put himself in a position that could lead to pain and suffering and destruction so cataclysmic it took years to pick up the pieces.

And anyway, where had all this urgency sprung from? Was he missing something? Had he been too quick to shelve his concerns about her trustworthiness? Could she have an ulterior motive that had nothing to do with money? If so, what could it be? This was all happening too fast, and he now felt a pressing urge to slow it down. 'Perhaps I would like that paternity test, after all.'

'Really?' she said, sounding thoroughly unimpressed as she planted one hand on her hip and gave him a withering look. 'I'm more than happy to arrange one if you insist, but I thought that was settled.'

'You think a lot of things.'

'Why on earth would I be here if I wasn't one hundred per cent sure you are my baby's father? I'm not a masochist.'

She had a point. And deep down he didn't need a paternity test when the evidence was overwhelming. He was just desperate to regain some sort of control over a situation that had none. 'So what's the rush?'

'What's the point in delaying?'

'The baby won't be born for another seven months. Only then will we need to make a decision about the future. You should withdraw your request for leave.'

Her eyes narrowed and her chin came up. 'So are you saying that we won't be married right away?'

Alex pinched the bridge of his nose and fought for calm. Quite honestly, he hadn't a clue what he was saying. He needed some time, dammit. All he *did* know was that, right now, he was getting what he wanted, which was her off his property and out of his head.

'What I mean,' he said, injecting some ice into his

voice, so she could be absolutely clear about who was in charge, 'is that *I* will decide what is happening when. As you intimated yesterday, this situation is most likely my fault and it is therefore up to me to fix it. And when I have come up with a plan, believe me, you will be the first to know.'

'How?'

'Ring my phone.' He gave her his number, watched her dial it and somewhere in the depths of the house he heard the device ring. 'There. No more excuses to show up without invitation. Now go home.'

'And do what?' Olympia reached up to close the boot, her luggage still unfathomably on the ground.

'I don't care.'

'I have a better suggestion. Why don't you work on your plan while I settle in?' she asked, her mollifying tone scraping across his nerve-endings as much as her complete disregard for his instruction to leave. 'Better still, why don't we work on it together? I appreciate your willingness to accept the blame for this but, don't forget, I was there too. This is on both of us. There's no need to be noble.'

'I'm not being noble,' he said through gritted teeth, torn between physically removing her and her luggage from his drive and wishing fervently that he *could* forget. He might have done an excellent job of wiping that night from his brain for the last two months, but seeing her again yesterday had brought it all flooding back, in vividly appalling detail. 'There's nothing noble about any of this.'

'Marrying for the sake of a child is.'

'I simply wish to guarantee my rights.'

'Me too.'

'You already have all the rights.'

'You misunderstand,' she said. 'I want to guarantee *your* rights. I'm under no illusion that I won't mess this baby thing up. I'm hardly the most responsible person on the planet. Not all that long ago I was out every night, partying hard and throwing as much alcohol down my throat as I could. I haven't had a drink in a year, but people do relapse and I'm not so naïve or arrogant as to believe I might not be one of them. This child deserves to have at least one functioning parent, which is why I agreed to the marriage you proposed. I can't risk you disappearing the minute things get a bit tough.'

'There is no danger of that,' he said, thinking it was about the only thing he *was* sure of right now. 'I am fully committed to the baby we've created.'

'Prove it, then. Like I am, by being here, when in all honesty I'd rather be anywhere else. You do realise that I'm not the only one who's going to have to make sacrifices, I hope.'

In response to that very valid observation, what remained of Alex's weakened resistance collapsed. This wasn't about him, he realised with a jolt. This was about their child, and ultimately nothing else mattered. He would never do anything to jeopardise its well-being, so he had to put his misgivings to one side and bury his unfortunate attraction to its mother. He had to do what was best for *it*. And she might think that meant finding out about each other, but he had different ideas.

First of all, while he was certain of his commitment to the situation, he couldn't be certain of hers. She talked about sacrifice and prioritising their child, but from what he'd read she had a history of prioritising herself, and he'd witnessed her recklessness first-hand. What if she changed her mind about his involvement? What if she decided against the marriage and disappeared? He couldn't risk that happening, so forget waiting. Whatever it took, however much it cost, he'd marry her the instant he could arrange it.

Secondly—and concurrently—he would take action to mitigate the vulnerabilities she'd revealed. It was admirable that she recognised her weaknesses, of course, but they were clearly still a cause for concern. So, in addition to preparing the paperwork required for their union, he would have a watertight prenuptial agreement drawn up that would grant him sole custody in the inevitable event she screwed up. His child would never know danger or uncertainty, he vowed. It would never suffer because of the selfish actions of a parent, and if he ever had cause to enforce such a clause he would *relish* the opportunity of denying Selene Stanhope access to her grandchild.

Thirdly, he'd be controlling the narrative from this moment on, so that he could not be sucker-punched again, starting with a phone call to her brother and his former friend to explain the situation before anyone else could, therefore minimising further Stanhope hassle.

And finally, he was rapidly coming to the conclusion that while all this was rumbling away in the background, despite the severe personal discomfort it was going to cause him, he was going to have to move Olympia in. As if her actions in Switzerland weren't proof enough, showing up here unannounced further indicated she was a loose cannon, liable to go off without warning. Who knew what else she might get up to left to her own devices? Very soon they'd be married, and he wouldn't have his reputation tarnished by hers.

And it would be fine, he assured himself, forcing himself to adjust to the idea of allowing the enemy into his lair for the sake of their child. He could keep a lid on the mad desire he had for her. He'd faced tougher challenges. He was sure of it, even if he couldn't think of one at this precise minute. Once he'd given her a quick tour, he'd install her in a guest room as far from his own suite as it was possible to get. With any luck he would hardly notice she was there.

Already feeling more alert with the development of a strategy, and ignoring the myriad doubts still trying to barge their way into his head, Alex strode forward to pick up her bags. He stalked to the front door and turned when he reached it. With a tight smile, he gestured for her to go ahead and said, through teeth that were hardly gritted at all, 'Welcome to my home.'

CHAPTER SIX

WELL, *THAT* VERY nearly hadn't gone according to plan, Olympia thought as she walked past Alex, into the house, nodding distractedly when he dropped her luggage and instructed her to give him a moment before disappearing. Although, to be fair, she hadn't exactly had a plan. The minute she'd come up with brilliant idea of moving in, she'd messaged the firm that handled her family's security. Once she'd had his address, she'd packed her bags and hopped in the car. There hadn't seemed much point in hanging about. There never did.

When she'd swung off the main road and onto the drive, she'd taken one look at the house and decided that there were worse places to hang out for the next couple of weeks while she got to know the father of her child. On the ground floor, four windows extended out from either side of the elegantly pillared porch. On the first, nine windows spread across the entire width of the house. The symmetry was as soothing as the softly swishing trees that lined the drive, and the lush verdant lawns it bisected.

Of course, the pleasing sense of tranquillity had not lasted long. But in light of the conflict that had characterised every one of their encounters to date perhaps she should have anticipated Alex's resistance. It wasn't as if he'd ever made any secret of it, and it had been very much in evidence out there on his drive. At one point, she'd actually thought he'd been about to fling her luggage back into the boot, bundle her into the passenger seat and push her off. But he was the one who'd suggested marriage in little more than the blink of an eye. If she'd given it any thought she'd have assumed he'd got over the problem he had with her.

Evidently he hadn't. Or perhaps he simply didn't appreciate being caught unawares, which, if she was being brutally honest, hadn't had to be the case. She could have easily got his number from the same security firm that had provided his address. It would have certainly smoothed the way. But, although the thought of doing just that had briefly flitted across her mind, in some deep dark corner of her psyche she was aware that interesting things happened when his guard was down. She found riling him thrilling. Had she forewarned him, she most likely wouldn't have been presented with his semi-naked body, which would have been a shame.

When he'd stormed out of his house in nothing but black swim shorts, and a small white towel slung round his neck, she'd practically swallowed her tongue. Such broad shoulders. So many hard defined muscles. She'd taken one look at all that masculine perfection and been hit by an image of him in the pool from which he'd evidently emerged, scything magnificently through the water. She'd recalled how easily he'd lifted her against that wall in Switzerland, and had very nearly swooned all over again. When one mesmerising rogue droplet had trickled down his neck and then his pec, she'd wanted to lick it off and not stop there. And God, she could not *wait* to win him round and get her hands on him.

'This is a spectacular property,' she said, deciding to strike while the iron was hot when he returned to show her around, having disappointingly donned a shirt. 'Have you lived here long?'

'Ten years.'

'And before that?'

'An apartment in the city centre.'

As he took her through the myriad rooms on the ground floor she peppered him with more questions, which were also minimally answered. But her aim was to learn more about him and she was not to be deterred. 'Where did you grow up?' she asked in the second of the three reception rooms, which had French doors onto the terrace.

'Not far from here.'

'Do you have any siblings?'

'No.'

'Parents?'

'They both died a long time ago.'

'So you're all alone in this world.' She ran her fingers over the soft worn leather of a wingback chair, then glanced over to see how he felt about that.

'I won't be in seven months' time.'

'Neither of us will,' she said, frustratingly unable to

discern anything from his inscrutable expression. 'It's going to be quite an adventure.'

'That's one way of describing it.'

'What if we mess up?'

'*I* won't.'

At the inference that she would, Olympia felt a flicker of hurt, which was inexplicable when that was something she herself had implied, so she determinedly shook it off. 'You might,' she said, turning her attention to the books on the shelves, just in case her face reflected the lingering sting. 'It happens.'

'Not to me,' he said with enviable confidence as he strode past her and opened the patio doors. 'Whatever the personal sacrifice, there are no lengths I won't go to for my child. I will do everything in my power to protect him or her. Of that you can be sure. Let's move to the garden. I could do with some air. Mind the step.'

Later, as she unpacked her things in the light and spacious guest room Alex had shown her, before stalking off as if he had the hounds of hell snapping at his feet, Olympia reflected on the aspects of their conversation that had stuck in her mind.

If he followed through with his promise, their child would be lucky indeed. No one had ever looked out for her. She'd had to fight her own battles and she hadn't done a very good job of it. He seemed as determined as she was that that fate would not befall her child. It strengthened her conviction that she'd done the right thing by coming here.

But a desire to defend and protect might not be the

only thing they had in common, she thought as she hung up a dress. Could he be as troubled by loneliness as she was? Was professional success enough or did his chest sometimes ache with emptiness? He had no one, she had everyone, yet she'd never felt as alone as when she was surrounded by people. So perhaps this marriage could be good for them—not just as prospective parents but also as individuals. Perhaps, in time, they could provide each other with companionship. That was something she'd never had before. Had he?

But oh, she had to be careful, she reminded herself as she carried her toiletries into the bathroom and decanted them into the vanity unit. She must not make the mistake of reading more into this than there really was. The marriage proposal, agreeing to cohabit and his solicitousness over the step into the garden weren't for *her* benefit. *She* didn't matter to him. The baby did, as he'd pointed out in no uncertain terms, and it would do her no good at all to forget it.

The sound of her phone ringing jolted her out of these oddly turbulent ruminations and she returned to the bedroom to fish it out of her bag. It was Leo, her eldest brother, calling, no doubt, from Santorini where he built luxury yachts—and lived with his wife, Willow, and their two daughters—and quite honestly, his timing could not be more perfect. She could apprise him of the situation before he found out some other way. She could take the opportunity to spin what had happened as that whirlwind fairy-tale romance she'd decided on yesterday, ostensible proof that she was capable of a mature relationship with someone who wanted her, instead of the rather tawdry truth that was a regrettable one-night stand and faulty contraception. As long as she remembered to keep her feet firmly on the ground, where was the harm?

Dropping into the armchair that sat in front of the large window, overlooking the inviting pool and verdant gardens, Olympia swiped right.

'Hi, Leo,' she said brightly, all in all really rather satisfied with the way the morning was playing out, given the circumstances. 'How are you and Willow and my gorgeous nieces?'

'We're all fine.'

'Great. Good.' She shifted in the chair and braced herself. 'I'm glad you rang,' she said, her heart beating a little faster than usual, even though she totally had this. 'Because I have news.'

'That you're pregnant and getting married?' her brother said dryly. 'I heard.'

She stilled and frowned, the world momentarily tilting on its axis. What on earth? Surely that wasn't possible. It had been less than twenty-four hours and she hadn't told a soul. 'How?'

'I just had a call from Alex. I would offer you my congratulations, but as I understand the situation, it's not that sort of an arrangement. I'm ringing to find out if you're genuinely all right with it. He seemed to think you were, but say the word and I will ruin him.'

Her frown deepened and her blood chilled, the wind whipping from her sails as she absorbed this information. Alex had called her brother? Why would he have done that? How did he even have his number? *She'd* wanted to be the one to tell her family her news, dammit. The needy attention-seeking kid she'd once been, traces of whom still lurked deep inside her, had been looking forward to Leo's reaction. To *her* version of events, which presented her in the best light—not the truth, which didn't.

'What did he tell you?' she asked, trying to keep her voice steady, although confusion, distress and her rising anger at Alex ripping the rug from under her feet made it hard.

'That you'd had a one-night stand, which has resulted in a pregnancy, and you'd both agreed to get married for the sake of the baby. I must admit it came as quite a shock.'

Olympia's throat tightened and her head buzzed. 'Well, you know me,' she said, just about managing to inject some faux levity into her voice. 'Reckless, impulsive, always getting into trouble. Surely you couldn't have been *that* surprised.'

'I didn't mean that,' Leo said with what sounded like a tut. 'Your personal life is none of my business and none of us escaped our upbringing unscathed. As the youngest you must have suffered the worst of it, but you're really turning things around. It's impressive. And don't forget, Zander knocked Mia up after a one-night stand so your predicament isn't exactly unique. What I meant was that I haven't spoken to the guy in twenty years. It was quite the blast from the past.'

Oh. Right. Well, it was good to know that she wasn't being judged for what she'd done, although she was rather taken aback by the notion of Leo thinking her impressive. But, hang on a moment… A blast from the past?

'Do you *know* him?' she asked, her curiosity piqued despite the volatile emotions swirling around inside her.

'Well, I *did*, once upon a time,' Leo replied. 'We used to be friends. Best friends, in fact. But then our mother had an affair with his father and that put an end to that. You probably don't remember the summer I was so angry with Selene that I deliberately dashed her favourite yacht against the rocks. I was sixteen. You must have been about six.'

Olympia racked her brains, a process that was hampered by the impact of this major new piece of information Alex had never thought to mention. 'That does ring a bell,' she managed eventually, dimly recalling the one and only time their father had raised his voice, a remonstration against his eldest son and heir for his unacceptable display of irresponsibility.

'I'm not surprised Alex cut me off,' her brother continued. 'I'd have done the same in his shoes. Still, it took me a while to get over it. Strange how our paths haven't crossed since. I guess they will now. I'm pleased old wounds have healed.'

But had they? she wondered, her head now spinning with questions as the implication of Leo's revelations registered. What if she'd been wrong about Alex's issue with her? What if it had nothing to do with her reputation and nepotism and therefore wanting her against his will and everything to do with her surname? Was he the type to bear a grudge? Could he be out for revenge? Was she simply a pawn in some greater game?

Or was she getting carried away, her imagination going into overdrive? It had been twenty years. Surely it was all water under the bridge. He couldn't be that Machiavellian, could he? There was only one way to find out.

'Well, I appreciate the call,' she said, surging to her feet and stalking across the bedroom to the door, her heart thumping hard. 'And rest assured I'm fine with everything. Please give my love to Willow and the girls. But right now, I really have to go.'

If Alex had known how disturbing giving Olympia a tour of his house was going to be he would never have suggested it. He'd have left her to figure out what was where on her own, because almost immediately the reality of having her in his house had hit home.

First, there'd been questions about his family to head off. He didn't want to dwell on the past. He didn't want to think about the beautiful villa where he'd grown up, which had been built by his great-great-grandfather one hundred and fifty years ago, in his family ever since and then lost in the divorce. He had no doubt that with her determination to get to know him there'd be many more questions to come, and he did not relish the energy he'd have to expend in deflecting them.

Then, there'd been the surge of curiosity he'd experienced at the idea of her feeling as on her own in this world as he did. How was that possible when she had family and friends galore? Surely she was anything but lonely. And why did it warm something cold and hard inside him to know that if she was, then they had something in common beyond the baby they'd created? It made no sense. He wasn't looking for any sort of emotional connection. It was deeply unsettling.

Last but by no means least was the way she'd moved around his space that, up until that moment, had been his sanctuary, his escape from the demands of the city and other people. When she'd run her hands over the furniture, he'd imagined them on his body. She'd examined the books on the shelves and the art on the walls and he'd wondered what she thought of them. After successfully avoiding the Stanhopes for two entire decades, there one had been, pregnant with his child, nosing around his things, and it should have felt like a gross invasion of privacy, a betrayal even, but it hadn't. It had felt somehow right. And that had sent him into such a spin of bewildered appal that he hadn't been able to get the tour over and done with fast enough.

As soon as he'd parked her in a guest room tucked away at the far end of the house's east wing, he'd buried his alarming response to her presence here, which he didn't understand, and turned to the practicalities of the situation, which he did. He'd instructed his legal team to get cracking with the paperwork required for their marriage and the prenup that would protect his child—and him—against any future whim of its mother. He'd then requested that Elena send him a contact number for Leo Stanhope, and when it had come through a mere couple of minutes later he'd called it.

The ensuing conversation had been unexpectedly difficult, he reflected with a frown as he set about making some much needed coffee. He'd embarked upon it with the intention of delivering the news, dealing with any fallout and moving on. He had not anticipated being bombarded with memories of that time. Or, horror of all horrors, *feelings*.

When the affair had come to light all those years ago and his family had begun to implode, he'd been battered by a wide range of emotions. Confusion at what was going on. Guilt over the fact that he'd introduced Selene into his family by way of his friendship with Leo. Resentment that his life had been upended because, regardless of how it had started, his father hadn't been strong or honourable enough to put his marriage and his family above such basic, primitive lust. And then anger, grief and despair as the repercussions continued.

He'd assumed he'd let go of everything apart from the deep burning hatred for the woman he held entirely responsible for it all, who'd casually ended the affair when someone else caught her eye, and still wafted about in this world causing chaos while his parents lay cold in their graves. But the minute he'd heard Leo's voice on the other end of the line, the emotions had flooded back, suddenly bubbling away so dangerously close to the surface that he'd very nearly hung up. He hadn't resorted to such theatrics, of course—he was far too in control of himself for that—and he'd imparted the news as intended, but he'd nevertheless been disconcerted enough to agree to a drink and a catchup.

However, at least it was done. And he could easily get out of any social engagement, he assured himself, noting a shift in the air and glancing up to see Olympia marching into the kitchen, her jaw set and her dark eyes flashing in a way that was becoming only too familiar. He and Leo might have been best friends once, but those days were long gone. He had no interest in rekindling the relationship. He didn't do friends now anyway. He had far too much on his plate with work.

'All settled in?' he asked, ignoring the perverse thrill he felt in response to her evident and intriguing umbrage.

'Yes.'

'Do you have everything you need?'

'The room is very comfortable. Your baby thanks you.'

'It's welcome,' he said and stamped out the part of him that unfathomably wanted her gratitude too. 'So what's wrong?'

She came to a stop at the enormous island that stood in the middle of the room and hopped onto a stool. 'You called my brother and told him I was pregnant and we were getting married.'

Ah. Right. He should have guessed that Leo would be straight on the phone to his sister. He'd always been the loyal, protective sort. Alex had lost count the num-

ber of times the guy had got him out of sticky situations when they'd been friends. He recalled that Leo
had once told him he'd rescued a five-year-old Olympia
out from the bottom of a pool when she'd fainted during
a swimming gala and no one had noticed. Earlier, his
former friend had demanded to know if he—Alex—
had somehow forced his sister into this marriage, which
was so far from the truth it would have been laughable
if any of this was remotely amusing.

'I did,' he said with a short nod as he leaned back
against the worktop, folding his arms across his chest.
'Is that a problem?'

'Yes, it's a problem,' she said tightly. 'It was my news
to share—not yours—and I had a plan.'

'How could your plan have differed to mine?'

'Yours was the truth, mine was not.'

His eyebrows rose. 'You were planning to lie to your
brother about us?'

'You don't have siblings,' she shot back, her colour
high and her shoulders stiff. 'You wouldn't understand
the dynamics.'

'Try me.'

'I'm the youngest. The screwup. The one who's always courting trouble and attracting negative headlines. But I've been trying to change, to put my past
behind me, and I've been doing a very good job of it.
And, all right, so I slipped back into old habits with you
and what we did, and now there's this—' she waved a
hand in the direction of her abdomen '—but when life
gives you lemons you have to make lemonade, right?

I was planning to turn a negative into a positive and dress this up as a fairy-tale romance in which I came out looking good. It was going to be a chance to cement my reputation as a mature adult capable of real responsibility. You just ruined that.'

Ignoring the flare of curiosity triggered by the brief insight into her history, Alex focused instead on the chill that was settling over him. With everything else going on he'd forgotten her capacity for creating drama. Her addiction to the limelight seemed to be embedded in her DNA. Her willingness to manipulate the situation to suit herself made him think of her mother and the destruction she'd caused. If he'd needed a reminder of the importance of keeping Olympia at arm's length, here it was.

'I apologise.'

'It's too late for that,' she said tartly. 'The damage is already done. Would *you* like people knowing you knocked someone up in a hotel stairwell? How would your clients take that, do you think?'

He felt the urge to tell her not to speak of what had happened like that, but because he had no clue why he ignored it. 'They're all about the bottom line and I'm not remotely bothered by what people think of me.'

'Hmm. Well. Aren't you the lucky one?'

'Luck doesn't come into it. I've worked insanely hard for everything I have.'

'And I haven't, I suppose.'

'Have you?'

'I'm *trying*. And anyway, you're hardly one to cast judgement on honesty.'

'What do you mean by that? I'm not the one distorting the truth to further my own ends.'

'My mother and your father. Why didn't you ever mention they had an affair?'

He frowned, his blood icing over in the way it always did when that particular memory was jogged. *She didn't know? How was that even possible?* 'I assumed you knew.'

'I was six at the time, apparently. Why *would* I know?'

'Were there no arguments?'

'None at all. There never were about anything. My parents barely spoke to each other. They were hardly ever in the same room. How they managed to produce the six of us is a mystery. And it's not as if such a thing would have raised any eyebrows. Selene had affairs all the time and still does. Your father was one of so many I couldn't even begin to count them all. Leo mentioned crashing a boat, which I do vaguely recall, but I don't remember if your name came up. He said you cut him off. Why did you do that? What happened wasn't his fault.'

To some extent, Alex recognised the defensiveness in Olympia's tone, evidence of the same protective streak that Leo possessed, but it barely pierced the white noise rushing through his head. All of a sudden his heart was beating fast and hard. His chest was so tight he was struggling to breathe. An event that had been cataclysmic for the Andinos had caused hardly a ripple for the Stanhopes. While his life had been falling apart they'd just carried on as usual, and now she was hammering questions at him as if he were to blame for the fallout.

His vision blurred and a wave of nausea rolled through him. He wasn't ready to talk about it. He never would be. Not with her, not with anyone. He couldn't have her digging around in his psyche. He didn't need her opinion or her censure. He had to de-escalate this before he wound up telling her everything and exposed himself to carnage.

'It happened twenty years ago,' he said, ruthlessly suppressing all the roiling emotion until his pulse had slowed and he could breathe more easily. 'I was seventeen. Little more than a kid. I can hardly recall anything about it either.'

She tilted her head and narrowed her eyes at him. 'Are you sure?'

'Why wouldn't I be?'

'Selene's left a trail of angry spouses in her wake. Why not a clutch of angry children? Maybe you're using me to somehow get back at her. I do look like her, after all.'

'That's ridiculous,' he said, choosing to ignore the fact that the resemblance had occasionally spooked him. 'What's going on here has nothing to do with then, and if I'd wanted to get revenge, which I don't, I'd have done it a long time ago.'

'Right. Lincoln Masters and Naxos Capital Assets.' She looked at him shrewdly for a moment before nodding. 'All right. Fair enough. I did think it was a bit of a stretch. I mean, twenty years would be insanely long to bear a grudge.'

Not in his opinion. Not when it fuelled his drive to

succeed, his abhorrence of drama and his determination to avoid commitment at all costs. 'And let's not forget,' he said, refusing to consider for even a second that she might have a point, '*you* seduced *me.*'

'Does that happen often?'

'Never.'

'No wonder you were so angry and ran away in such a hurry.'

'I did not run away,' he said with a grind of his teeth. 'I simply don't like losing control.' His jaw clenched tighter when a faint smile curved her gorgeous mouth. 'What's so amusing?'

'You must admit there's a certain symmetry to it.' An unsettling glint lit the dark brown depths of her eyes. 'I mean, your father and my mother, then you and me, all this time later.'

'It's not the same thing at all,' he said, a cold sweat breaking out at the thought of being sucked into her orbit, swallowed up and spat out when she was done with him. 'What happened between us was strictly a one-off.'

'Why? I agree that there are a lot of unknowns about this whole arrangement, but you know as well as I do that the sex would be great. I mean, the way things ended notwithstanding, that encounter in Switzerland was scorching. And we still share an uncommonly intense attraction. It was there yesterday and it's here now. So why fight it? Are you a fan of celibacy? I'm not.'

Well, no, of course he wasn't. But lust had got him into this mess in the first place and he was never succumbing to it again. Prioritising their child and avoiding screwing it up through reckless and selfish indulgence was the whole bloody point of this. He would fight the attraction—that unfortunately he couldn't deny—until his dying breath.

So his body, which was all for closing the space between them and spreading her out on the island, could forget it. And Olympia should abandon any designs she might have on him too. Perhaps she assumed she could wrap him around her little finger, as no doubt she had with countless other men, but if she did, she was dead wrong. She might be as dangerously beautiful as Helen of Troy and as doggedly persistent as Genghis Khan, but he wasn't a toy to be played with or a land to be conquered. And she was obviously used to being indulged and getting her own way, but not this time and not by him. He'd built an empire out of nothing. He'd overcome bigger hurdles and faced down tougher opponents than her. He would not be swayed. He would never yield to her allure, no matter how loudly the voice in his head demanded it. He would never be that weak.

'Further complicating an already complicated situation is a terrible idea,' he said in a tone that even he could hear brooked no argument. 'We owe it to our child to stay focused. To give it one hundred per cent. So there will be no sex. Either now or in the future. And that's final.'

CHAPTER SEVEN

OLYMPIA FOUND THE knowledge that the affair between their parents remained in the past reassuring. Not only would it make the future tricky if Alex still had a problem with her mother—who had a tendency to pop up unexpectedly—but also she did not appreciate the thought of being manipulated and used for revenge.

Other elements of their conversation, however, gave her grave cause for concern. What gave him the right to bulldoze her perfectly valid observations about their relationship? she thought, as they monosyllabically munched their way through a lunch of prawns, olives, tomatoes and bread, which his housekeeper had laid out beneath the vine-heavy pergola that covered the terrace. Who'd made him the boss of this? Confidence was one thing, but arrogance and presumption were something else entirely.

She was developing the impression that he actively wanted to make their arrangement as difficult as possible, although for the life of her she couldn't work out why that would be. It didn't seem at all complicated to her. As they'd already established, they had seven months before the baby put in an appearance. There was plenty of time to indulge the attraction before having to switch their attention elsewhere.

So maybe *everything* was a battle for control. Maybe he got a kick out of catching her on the back foot. Or maybe he was simply a masochist. Who knew? One thing she *did* know was that having him eating out of her hand clearly wasn't going to be as easy as she'd assumed, which was not only irritating but also alarming, because she liked being liked. It made her feel good about herself. When people did what she wanted, her self-esteem rocketed.

Conversely, rejection, which she'd always hated, invariably triggered a painful sense of unattractiveness and invalidation. In the past, this had brought about some pretty self-destructive behaviour. One night, after a few too many tequila shots as a result of being ghosted by a guy she'd briefly hooked up with, she'd danced naked in the fountain at Trafalgar Square, which had led to an embarrassing brush with the police, a one thousand pound fine and headlines the next morning that had not been kind.

It was obvious that Alex didn't like her. He clearly found her aggravating and considered her manipulative. He didn't trust her not to mess this parenting business up and he had no respect for the effort she was trying to make with regard to her career. In fact, his opinion of her could not be any lower and that was worrying. Despite his apparent commitment to their baby, her situation felt precarious. What if she did something that made him back out of their marriage of convenience?

What if he decided she was too much to take on—or too little, for that matter—and realised he could provide just as well for their child without having to be involved with her?

She couldn't allow that. She needed his protection, and therefore she had to mitigate the risk of him disappearing and bind him to her and the baby a little more tightly for both their sakes. Perhaps she should seduce him again. Bamboozle him with sex. That might raise her in his estimation. He was adamant that it wasn't happening, yet their chemistry was still off the charts. It would strengthen their connection. The boost to her self-esteem would be just what she needed. So what if she took to floating about the place in nothing but a skimpy pair of bikini bottoms and asking him at intervals to rub sunscreen into her back? She reckoned he would last five minutes tops with her stretching and purring beneath his hands.

And what if she combined that plan with something else? Like, say, a party to celebrate their engagement with family and friends. Wouldn't that double down on achieving the security she was after? Marriage would be harder to get out of once they'd announced it to the world, surely. And quite apart from that, it would have myriad other benefits, benefits that were crashing through her thoughts even now.

'Alex?' she said, so convinced by the rightness of her inspired idea that she couldn't keep it to herself.

'Mmm?'

'I think we should throw an engagement party.'

In response to this bald announcement, which sounded oddly loud after such a long period of silence, Alex's head shot up and his brow furrowed. 'An engagement party?' he echoed, evidently not as enamoured of the idea as she was, if his look of horror was anything to go by.

'Yes,' she said, her brain already beginning to ping with ideas. 'Nothing big. Just a couple of hundred or thereabouts. Food. A DJ. That sort of thing. We could have it here. In the garden. Lights in the pool. In the trees. It would be quite the event.'

'Absolutely not.'

'Why not?'

He sat back and stared at her as if she'd sprouted horns. 'What on earth makes you think an engagement party is necessary? I hope you haven't forgotten already that nothing about our arrangement is real.'

Something twanged in her chest at that, but she ignored it. 'Don't worry,' she said firmly, although she wasn't entirely sure which of them she was trying to convince most. 'I haven't forgotten anything, and I am well aware that nothing about this is real.' Which was fine, of course. Because that had been the plan all along and would continue to be. 'However, there are a number of reasons why it's an excellent idea.'

'Such as?'

'Well, firstly, it would be a good opportunity for you to meet my family. Some of my siblings are around in the next couple of weeks. You could rekindle your relationship with Leo. Meet the others. It has to be done some time. My mother wouldn't be in attendance if that's what's worrying you,' she assured him when she saw that he'd gone a little pale. 'She's been in Argentina for the last month and, as far as I understand, is planning on staying there for the foreseeable future. On an estancia with a cattle billionaire. The best place for her, if you ask me. Nice and far away. Furthermore, it would be an opportunity to fix the mess you made by pre-empting our news. I could use the occasion to spin the idea that I've moved on from my past. From what Leo said, it doesn't sound as though you provided much in the way of detail about what's going on, so why couldn't we have reached a deeper understanding in the interim? It's a win-win on a number of levels, don't you agree?'

Olympia sat back, rather pleased with the robustness of her argument, until Alex leaned forward and gave his head a sharp shake. 'I couldn't agree less,' he said flatly. 'It's a no-win on every level. And none of it is happening.'

She blinked at the harshness of his tone. 'Why not?'

'I don't do parties.'

'That's not a problem. I do parties enough for the both of us. I excel at putting on a show. All you'd have to do is turn up.'

'No.'

'Don't you think you owe me?'

'I don't owe you anything,' he said, a muscle ticking in his jaw. 'I've already apologised for speaking to Leo. We're not throwing a party.'

Agh. Why was he such a control freak? 'Well, *I* might.'

'With the groom nowhere to be seen? Wouldn't that negate the object of the exercise? I'd think twice if I were you.'

He was right, dammit. It would totally negate the object of the exercise. 'Is there anything I can do to persuade you otherwise?'

'Not a thing. Now, you'll have to excuse me,' he said, giving her a wintry smile as he pushed his chair back and got to his feet. 'I have work to do.'

Given that he'd spent pretty much the entire afternoon in his study sitting at his desk, Alex had achieved precious little. On a Saturday, the markets were closed but there was still a tonne of research and analysis to do before they reopened first thing on Monday morning. He had meetings to prepare for. Investment strategies to define.

However, he'd been so unsettled by the events of today that he hadn't been able to concentrate. Reports lay untouched and files remained unread. In fact, it was a good thing he hadn't been able to trade because, if he had, he might well have made a careless mistake and lost millions. He was that distracted.

As if the morning hadn't been enough of an upheaval, he'd had to contend with lunch. He'd spent the first half of it dwelling on everything Olympia had flung at him in the kitchen. Quite apart from the irritating defiance she'd displayed and the fact that she was totally unintimidated by him, which, he was prepared to admit, piqued his vanity, he'd never met anyone so unafraid to voice the thoughts in their head. To so boldly and unashamedly state what they wanted and go for it. At least, not on a personal level, and he found it as confusing as hell. One minute she was seducing him in stairwells and planning to manipulate the truth for her own purposes—which indicated he shouldn't trust her—and the next she was unguardedly and transparently detailing her vulnerabilities and her desires—which suggested he could.

Which was the real her?

What should he believe?

He couldn't work it out.

Then she'd hit him with the engagement party. Where that idea had sprung from he had no clue, but he should have guessed she'd do something at some point to wreck his illusion of control because it happened all too often. Nothing big? Two hundred people? And to think he'd imagined she sometimes felt as lonely as he did. He must have lost his mind.

Quite honestly, there was nothing he'd rather do less than attend a party filled with Stanhopes. By managing his attendance at both corporate and social events, he'd succeeded in avoiding most of them these last twenty years. The thought of being confronted by a handful at once, and the memories he'd subsequently be battered with, made his brain bleed, which was why he'd put his foot down.

Besides, who would he invite to such a thing? Unlike her, he had no family and few friends. No doubt if he'd agreed she'd have pressed him for a guest list, which he wouldn't have been able to provide, and that would have led to questions about his past and how he felt about it that he never wanted to answer.

Such discombobulation had been behind his decision to hole up here until he got it all straight, not that he'd had any success. His brain simply refused to function. He was too wound up.

And then, a couple of hours ago, Olympia had pitched up at the pool, and soon after that he'd given up all pretence of work. When she'd removed her robe to reveal the stunning body beneath he'd nearly swallowed his tongue. Her gold bikini was barely there. Just four small triangles held together with what looked like string. Her limbs were long and toned, her curves spectacular, her stomach still flat, and in the light of the afternoon sun she seemed to glow.

All thoughts of parties and meetings and clients and IPOs had flown from his head. Transfixed, he'd watched her dive neatly into the water and had been walloped by the urge to join her. When she'd finished her swim, she'd dried off and then had twisted herself into a series of poses that might have been yogic, but definitely made him think of other situations where such flexibility might be a benefit.

Before settling down to sunbathe, she'd applied sunscreen and his fingers had itched to do it for her. He already knew the shape of her breasts and the softness of her skin, but his memory was sketchy. He wanted to reacquaint himself with those parts of her he'd once touched, and explore the rest. At length and with great thoroughness. He wanted to taste her again so badly that his mouth actually watered.

And now, as she stirred from what had looked like a nap and rose from the sun lounger to take another dip, he was wondering, suddenly, why shouldn't he? Why was he denying himself that pleasure when he didn't have to? He was soon to marry a confusing woman who caused him all kinds of grief, but to whom he was also insanely attracted, and he'd committed himself to a lifetime of celibacy because there was no way in hell *he* would break his marriage vows, even if they were merely a technicality.

What on earth had he been thinking? Why had he done that? Because he feared the desire he felt for her getting out of hand and somehow destroying him? It wouldn't. If anything, it would lessen. It always did. Most likely it would burn out within days and settle into something entirely manageable. So this relationship didn't have to be a crazed, lust-filled nightmare. Nor did it have to be sexless. And God, it would be novel to engage with her in an activity that he did understand.

Olympia emerged from the pool, a fluid movement of undulating curves, the water sluicing over her like a caress, and barely before he was aware of what he was doing, Alex was throwing his glasses onto his desk, leaping out of his chair and striding out of the study, across the hall and into the sitting room. He pushed open the French doors and stepped out onto the terrace, every cell of his body rigid with tension, his pulse hammering so hard he could hear it in his ears.

All he could think about as he stalked towards her was hauling her into his arms, crushing his mouth to hers and losing himself in the dynamite heat they generated together. The scent and taste of her had kept him awake all that night in Switzerland. Back in his suite, he'd lost count of the number of times he'd nearly caved in and stormed to her room to find out exactly what they could do in a bed.

Well, now was his chance.

When Olympia saw Alex bearing down on her like a thunderstorm, her heart gave a great lurch and then began to race. She'd been poolside for two hours now, and she'd been bordering on desperate, but now it looked as though Plan B might be working.

With his intransigence over the party, the only option he'd left her with to secure his commitment was seduction. To that end, having recalled from the morning's tour that his desk overlooked the pool, she'd decided on a swim. She'd been feeling hot and prickly anyway, but if he happened to spot her scantily clad body out of the study window, and found himself suddenly so helpless to resist the attraction he'd all but admitted he still felt that he ravished her on a sun lounger, wouldn't that represent the win she was after? Wouldn't she be strengthening his connection to their baby through her? And on a more personal level, wouldn't the collapse of his resistance and his surrender to temptation be empowering and satisfying and brilliant? As she'd stripped off her sundress and donned her bikini, Olympia had rather thought it would.

She hadn't expected it to take this long. His willpower was formidable indeed. But judging by the way his dark-as-night eyes were locked onto hers and the determination with which his jaw was set, it looked as though her bikini, yoga, sunscreen ruse might have worked. He was focusing on her so intently that she was rooted to the spot. He radiated such predatory intensity that she'd never felt so vindicated. Or so palpably excited. But she would be wise to exercise caution. He could be out here for any number of reasons, and he had a habit of behaving in ways she did not anticipate, so she wouldn't be taking anything for granted. He came to an abrupt stop a couple of feet in front of her and it was all she could do to carry on squeezing the water from her hair and stay where she was.

'What's happened?' she asked, trying to suppress the adrenaline that was flooding her system as hot thrills of anticipation shot down her spine. 'Is something wrong?'

His laser-like gaze roamed over her so slowly and thoroughly that it left a trail of fire across her skin and a muscle began to hammer in his jaw. 'Nothing's happened and there's nothing wrong,' he said, his voice edged with a roughness that made him sound as though he'd swallowed a bucket of gravel.

'You look a little unhinged,' she said, her nerve-endings quivering madly in response.

'I feel a little unhinged.'

'Then what is it?'

'It's you.'

Her heart almost stopped. Could this plan have succeeded where the party suggestion had failed? 'Me?'

His gaze landed on her mouth and darkened. 'I want you,' he practically growled while she thought, *Oh, thank God for that. It's worked.* 'I want to kiss you until neither of us can think straight. Then I intend to carry you up to my bed and keep you there for the next twenty-four hours. After that, we'll see. But as I recall you have two weeks off. I'm sure we can think of interesting ways to fill them.'

Olympia was sure they could. She'd spent the entire afternoon imagining exactly how the immediate future would play out if she had her way. 'What happened to sex complicating things?' she asked, as breathless as if she'd just run the two hundred metres. 'To what we did being a one-off? You were so resolute.'

'I've had a rethink. Sex isn't complicated. It's simply the physical representation of chemistry. It occurred to me that this marriage of ours will likely last years, and in actual fact I'm *not* a fan of celibacy. We're in it for the long haul, and as you pointed out only this morning, we need to make the best of it.'

'I'm delighted we're finally on the same page.'

'Not half as delighted as I am.'

'Then what are you waiting for?'

'I have absolutely no idea.'

With one quick move, he reached out and pulled her into his arms. As his mouth crashed down on hers,

Olympia threw her arms around his neck and sank into his powerful embrace. She closed her eyes and gave herself up to a sizzling kiss that lit a bonfire of desire inside her and instantly transported her to a plane where nothing existed but oblivion. His hands roamed over her back before settling, one between her shoulder blades, the other on her bottom, and he didn't need to pull her in because she was already plastered up against him, as close as she could get.

He was big and hard everywhere, which made her feel unbelievably soft and delicate, and she must be soaking him through but that didn't appear to bother him. All he seemed to care about as he lowered her to a sun lounger and eased her back—his body blotting out the sun so completely that all she could see was him—was getting her horizontal.

And why would she complain about that when the feel of his weight pressing down on her was so delicious? Why would she complain about anything when she was enveloped in such scorching heat and the rigidly controlled strength that she couldn't wait to unleash? When she felt so blisteringly fabulous?

She knew that the euphoria would fade once they'd satisfied their desire. It always did and always too soon. But the great thing about this particular situation was that she could just have another hit whenever she needed one. She could have this every day of the week if she wanted, because she would do her best to ensure that he was going nowhere.

And anyway, why was she even thinking about what

happened next? Why was she thinking at all? Shouldn't her brain be in bits? Shouldn't she be focusing on getting him as naked as he was trying to get her?

Why was she suddenly bothering about whether or not she might have coerced him into this, and what was that thing that had been niggling away at the back of her mind all afternoon and was now screeching through her thoughts like a claxon? Why couldn't she shake it?

It was something else she'd learned in rehab, she realised with a jolt as he wrenched his mouth from hers, dragging it down her neck to rain kisses along the slope of her right breast while one hand caressed her left, the other making quick work of the knot that held her bikini top in place. Something she'd completely forgotten about because, up until the mad half an hour with him in Switzerland, she'd been too focused on work for it to come up, and afterwards she'd been too wrapped up in rejection and shame to see it.

Her use of sex as a coping mechanism.

As a way of getting attention and feeling valued.

Of temporarily blocking the constant turmoil with which she lived, replacing it with a few blissful hours of wild abandon—her standard operating procedure for years.

She'd done it that night back in May, provoking him into giving her what she'd wanted because she equated sexual acceptance to personal acceptance, and she was doing it again. Right now. Not only had she engineered him into this, to secure his commitment and to make herself feel good, and a little less lonely, but she was also trying to change the way he felt about her, to get him to like her. And if she let this reach its natural conclusion it could mean undoing all the hard work she'd put into trying to understand that her value wasn't tied up in sex and other people. That it had to come from a solid sense of self and emotional independence, rather than an unreliable and unpredictable external source. Much of the progress she'd made would be gone, just like that.

So she had to put a stop to it, she thought dazedly, fighting for control even though she still shook with desire and her body screamed in protest. She had to reset the boundaries and continue to put the effort in now, for the sake of her future self. She didn't want to go back to the person she'd been before. She wanted to look and move forward. And she could not afford to jeopardise the precious new life she was carrying by careering down that slippery slope. So thank God she'd had this epiphany before it was too late.

Digging deep to silence the voice in her head insisting it didn't have to be this way—didn't she *need* to lock him in? Didn't she *want* to feel good?—Olympia opened her eyes and blinked away the fog. While she still had the ability to resist him, she summoned up every drop of physical and emotional strength she possessed.

She put her hands on his shoulders, gave him a little push, and panted, 'Stop, Alex. Stop.'

CHAPTER EIGHT

ALEX MIGHT HAVE been so addled with need that he'd lost his mind along with his control, but he wasn't so far gone that Olympia's tremulous but firm plea didn't pierce the haze in his brain. It did. And the second it did, his blood chilled and he froze. He jerked his head up as if she'd slapped him, shock ricocheting through him, his breathing fast and harsh.

'What's wrong?' he grated, scouring her face for some sort of clue as to what was going on. He couldn't read her expression, but the fierce heat had faded from her gaze, he just about managed to note. The pressure of her hands on his shoulders was light but firm. Unmistakable evidence that she was not as into this as he was. But she had been. He was sure of it. So what had changed?

'We need to stop.'

'Yes, I got that,' he said, perhaps a little sharply, but then he was confused, in physical pain and being battered by the concern that he was somehow at fault. 'But why? Is it the baby?'

'What? No. It's not the baby.' A faint frown creased her forehead. 'It's just that you're not the only one who's had a rethink.'

She pushed at him again, and with Herculean effort and a whole lot of discomfort, he lifted himself off her. Somehow, he made it to the sun lounger next to hers, watching uncomprehendingly as she picked up her robe and pulled it on. When she drew the sides together and tied the belt around her waist, hiding from sight the luscious body he'd planned to reacquaint himself with over the next two weeks, the disappointment that seared through him was like a punch to the gut. 'I don't understand.'

'I've changed my mind,' she said. 'You're right. Celibacy *is* the way forward. Maybe not for ever, but certainly for the time being.'

Denial careened through him fast and hard. Hadn't they dealt with this? 'It absolutely is *not* the way forward.'

'It is for me.'

'Why?'

'Because I can't engage in casual sex right now. Or any sex for that matter. It's not good for my recovery.'

He stilled and stared at her in bewilderment. What was she talking about? The sex, more intense and satisfying than any he'd ever known, and potentially continuing for years, would be anything but casual. And recovery? From what? 'What do you mean?'

'As I'm sure you're aware, not so long ago I spent three months in rehab.'

Somehow he managed to nod. He'd read about it in the press at the time. But... 'What does that have to do with this?'

'While I was there I underwent a lot of therapy, which, among many other things, taught me that I use sex as a coping mechanism. To make myself feel less empty and not quite so rubbish about myself. Not all that often,' she was quick to add. 'I wasn't nearly as promiscuous as the press made out. But enough for it to be a problem. And it never worked because the satisfaction was always fleeting. After the initial high wore off I would inevitably be back at square one.'

He frowned, shoved his hands through his hair and then rubbed them over his face, trying to compute what she was telling him, an almost impossible task right now. 'Is that what happened in Switzerland?' he asked, feeling slightly sick at the thought that sex with him might have had such an effect.

'Yes,' she confirmed, and his stomach turned harder, even though by deploying the few brain cells that were still functioning he could just about understand on an intellectual level that it wasn't him per se, although the way he'd dashed off that night couldn't have helped. 'You were right when you said that shouldn't have happened. It really shouldn't. I'd been so focused on work that I somehow managed to forget everything I learned on that front. And then afterwards, ironically, I was too preoccupied with the way it had made me feel to think about why. I only remembered it just now.'

'Your timing is terrible.'

'I know. I'm sorry. But I can't make the same mistake again. I need to break the habit and find my self-worth elsewhere. And that means steering clear of sex until I can value myself for being me. I apologise for giving you a different impression. I shouldn't have led you on. I'm a work in progress.'

'You didn't lead me on,' he said, thinking that it had been his decision to overturn his vow that there would be no sex in this relationship, no one else's. She hadn't forced him to abandon work and come out here. He'd done that totally voluntarily.

'I don't normally do yoga at the pool. That was purely for your benefit. It's clear you neither like me nor approve of me and I was feeling a little insecure about your commitment to our baby. I thought I could strengthen it with the party, and when that didn't work, through sex. But I shouldn't have done it. It was manipulative of me and wrong and I apologise for that too.'

Right.

God.

What was it about this woman that turned him into such an unsuspecting fool?

'You have no reason to doubt my commitment,' he said, sweating at the thought of how easily he'd been seduced once again. 'Thanks to your mother, I've witnessed first-hand the devastation the breakdown of a family can wreak, and there is no way on earth I would allow any child of mine to suffer like that. So we're in this together until he or she can fend for itself.'

'What happened?'

'It's not important.'

'I'd like to understand.'

'Yes, well, I'd like a cold shower.'

'Of course,' she said, reddening. 'I'm sorry.'

And now, unfathomably, he was the one to feel like a heel. 'Whatever your reasons for starting this, you never need to apologise for changing your mind.'

'Are you sure?'

'Quite sure,' he confirmed because, on that point at least, he was. What he was going to do about the crucifying sexual frustration, the continuing befuddlement and the frighteningly weak defences he had against her, however, he had no idea. Removing himself from her unsettling orbit seemed like a good place to start, so he got to his feet, gave her a nod and said, before turning on his heel and heading back into the house, 'Enjoy the rest of your afternoon.'

The relief that Olympia felt at Alex listening to and respecting her position on the subject of sex was immense. She hadn't been sure how he'd react. Other men of her acquaintance might not have been quite so accommodating, although to be fair she'd never put a stop to proceedings before so she couldn't say for sure. She felt that he, on the other hand, really was a man of strength and integrity and tolerance, because his disappointment had been obvious. And to take her confession that she'd been out to seduce him so lightly, well, that had been a relief too, although unexpected. But perhaps he appreciated her candidness.

However, over the course of the following day it became apparent that he was not handling the situation as well as she'd assumed. Her attempts at conversation were met with increasingly terse replies. Her enquiries into what effect her mother's affair with his father had had on him, something she just couldn't seem to let go, were stonewalled entirely. Eye contact deteriorated and he kept vanishing into his study.

On Monday morning she woke to an empty house and the petrifying thought that she'd pushed him too far. That—thanks to her bid to satisfy her insatiable curiosity about his past and her crippling insecurities, which meant she was now the one blowing hot and cold—he'd finally had enough.

Her heart thudded loudly in the eerie silence as she searched for him in vain. Where could he have gone? Had he been in such a hurry he couldn't even leave a note? What did that mean for her and the baby?

Back in the kitchen, but feeling too sick for breakfast, she brought up his number on her phone. Not altogether surprisingly, the call went to voicemail. So she sent him a text, and after thirty agonising minutes of pacing up and down, wondering whether she'd blown things for good with her reckless impulsivity and persistence, her phone pinged with a reply.

He was at the office. Apparently, because of a truncated Friday afternoon and disrupted weekend, he'd had a mountain of work to get through before the markets had opened this morning. He wasn't sure when he'd be back. Tuesday, perhaps, or Wednesday. He would mostly likely be uncontactable for much of the time, but his housekeeper was on hand for anything she required.

That all sounded very much like an excuse, Olympia

thought, her hands shaking a little as she filled a glass with water. He'd spent much of the weekend holed up in his study here, precisely for the purpose of catching up. And Athens wasn't so far it necessitated an overnight stay. He was avoiding her. That much was obvious. Because he was having second thoughts? Or could he be after a woman who wouldn't lead him on and then change her mind? None of that bore thinking about.

So what was she going to do?

Well, she could follow him into the city and demand to know what he was playing at, which was what her instincts were urging her to do. On the other hand, the more circumspect voice in her head—which sounded a lot like one of her therapists in rehab—insisted that she might be wise to exercise caution. Patience wasn't something she'd ever been particularly good at, but look at where a lack of it had got her. Fretting and stressing and potentially abandoned. Applying more pressure to an already fragile situation could turn out to be a terrible idea. She couldn't blame him if he needed some time to get his head around everything that had happened recently. She did too. It had been pretty intense. Hard to be believe it had been only three days, really. And she knew she was a handful.

So as much as it went against her natural inclination to track him down, she would give him the space he needed and trust that he wasn't wrapped around some uncomplicated woman who he didn't dislike. She'd keep herself occupied for the next day or two—somehow—and if he hadn't reappeared by the middle of the week, she'd reassess. She'd use the time to revisit everything she'd learned in rehab with a view to the future. She'd call her brother and see if he had any insight into the impact of the affair. She'd turn her thoughts to how she'd like to raise her baby, and consider the extent to which her mother was, in fact, going to be a problem. She'd take it easy and refuse to catastrophise.

It was thirty-six hours max, she told herself, concentrating on breathing slowly and deeply until the panic subsided. Not long at all. How hard could it be?

Despite innumerable cold showers and many frustratingly futile hours locked away in his study, by Sunday night Alex had known that he couldn't stick around at the villa any longer.

To his intense frustration, he was unable to get his response to Olympia under control. His dreams were filled with alternative endings to Saturday afternoon by the pool, visions that had her not pushing him away but pulling him in. Fielding her increasingly probing questions had become so stressful that his muscles ached with tension.

His nerves were fraying. The constant wariness and the unassuaged desire made him feel tense and on edge. He had tried to keep his distance, but she'd drawn him like a magnet nonetheless. The air had seemed to be filled with her scent. He'd been aware of her even when he couldn't see her.

And, as if managing that wasn't enough of a challenge, he couldn't get to grips with various aspects of her personality and his inability to read any of them. She tied him in knots, which no one had ever done before. It was draining and bewildering.

His self-control had never felt so under threat. He hadn't liked any of it, which was why he'd got up at the crack of dawn, having barely slept a wink anyway, and driven back to Athens. But he might as well not have bothered because, by late Tuesday afternoon, restlessness was kicking in and his conscience was giving him grief. He'd worked precisely nothing out and he still dreamed of her, he was still obsessing over the questions she'd thrown at him, so what had been the purpose of escape? Didn't avoiding her like this smack of cowardice? And what was he planning to do? Stay out of her way for ever? Well, that wasn't going to work. At some point he was going to have to face her again and he'd never been one to procrastinate.

He had to get over himself, he thought grimly as he snatched up his phone and keys and stalked out of the office because staying here in the city was no longer feasible. He had no choice. He couldn't keep dashing off whenever she hurled him off balance. Where would that leave their child? He had to make his relationship with Olympia work, and he'd come to the conclusion that the only way to achieve that was to find out what made her tick. Only by knowing her would he understand her, and only by understanding her would he be able to anticipate her moves and regain control.

Of course, by embarking on such an enterprise he'd probably end up learning far more about the Stanhopes than he'd ever be comfortable with. Containing how he felt about her mother might be tricky. But it wasn't as if he'd be sucked into any sort of emotional connection with her, and he was in a permanent state of discomfort anyway. If push came to shove he could answer any questions she may have about him with the baldest of facts. He needn't disclose anything of importance. They needn't discuss him at all. This course of action would be one hundred per cent about her. He would unravel her secrets if it was the last thing he did. He wasn't used to failing and he wouldn't in this.

By Tuesday evening, Olympia was practically climbing the walls. She'd discovered that patience was far harder to implement than she'd anticipated. There was only so much taking it easy she could stand. Leo had had no insight into anything. Within hours she'd been itching to hop in the car and drive to Alex's office to demand to know what was going on.

However, by drumming up the strategies she'd learned in rehab to curb her impulses, she'd resisted. She'd swum so many lengths of the pool she could practically have reached Crete. Every time her thoughts turned to what he was getting up to and who with, or what he might be planning, she closed her eyes and practised the mindfulness that would stop them spinning out of control. No good would come of second-guessing his intentions. Confronting him in person could make matters worse. All she could do was wait. For a little while longer, at least.

But it hadn't been easy. Her nerves were stretched to their absolute limit. And, when she heard the slam of the front door, shattering the silence, the tension drained from her body so fast she went dizzy.

God, it was good to see him, she thought when a few moments later he appeared on the terrace, where she sat trying to concentrate on a book while the sun set in front of her. He looked so handsome in a dark suit and white shirt, which was unbuttoned at the top to reveal a tantalising wedge of chest. A light stubble covered his jaw and his hair was dishevelled as if he'd been ploughing his hands through it.

And she'd missed him, she was surprised to realise. Which was ridiculous when she'd only moved in five days ago, but what a rollercoaster of a ride those five days had been. The first three had been so energising and thrilling—the last two so flat and dull.

However, how he looked and how she felt about it was irrelevant. All that mattered was that he'd returned. And from now on, she vowed, she would do her level best not to rock the boat further. She would shove a lid on her insecurities and bury the attraction that hadn't diminished one bit. She'd draw a line under everything that had happened to date and start again. She'd be cool and composed, as compliant as she could manage, and channel the mature, responsible adult she was trying to become. The security of her baby depended on it.

'You're back,' she said, reduced to stating the obvious from the sheer relief that perhaps she hadn't screwed up after all. 'How was the city?'

'Busy,' he said, as he pulled out a chair and sat down opposite her.

'Did you get done what you needed to get done?'

'In a manner of speaking.'

'What does that mean?'

'We need to talk.'

At that, Olympia stilled. Her heart plummeted and she briefly thought she might throw up, because that was a phrase no one ever wanted to hear. But she swallowed down the flare of panic that threatened her control, and she fought back the urge to throw herself at him and beg for forgiveness. 'I apologise for my behaviour on Saturday,' she said, just about managing to keep her emotions contained. 'I'll endeavour to do better in future. You have my word.'

His eyebrows rose. 'Do I?'

'Absolutely.'

'Good to know.' He sat back and studied her for a moment with his dark glittering gaze, as if the self-doubt she was riddled with was written all over her face. 'I thought we could start with you.'

She stared at him blankly. 'What?'

'I'm interested in hearing more about those family dynamics you mentioned.'

Her heart skipped a beat. Now *her* eyebrows were the ones to shoot up. 'You actually want to talk?'

'Yes. That's what I said.' He frowned. 'Why? What did you think I meant?'

'Nothing,' she said, getting a grip and silently cursing the low self-esteem that made her immediately imagine the worst. 'Ignore me. Pregnancy hormones making me a little loopy, that's all. I just feared you might have given me up as a lost cause, that's all.'

'I would never abandon my child.'

She flushed. 'No, of course not.'

'And talking was your idea in the first place, as I recall.' He sat back and stretched out his legs. 'So shoot.'

'Now?'

'You advocated getting a move on.'

Yes, she'd done that too. So why was she hesitating? Nothing about her life to date was a secret, and she still believed that them getting to know each other was the best chance their relationship had of success. Once she'd answered his questions, he could finally answer hers, and they could move forward. There was no cause for concern.

'Right,' she said, reminding herself that she'd been through it a dozen times in therapy and this would be no different. 'Well. As you must know, I'm the youngest of six. Leo's ten years older than me. Zander, Thalia, Atticus and Daphne are in between. Our parents weren't exactly what you might call nurturing. To be honest, they were so negligent that, if they hadn't had money and status, they'd probably have been in jail. My mother is selfishness personified and my father was the stiff-upper-lip type who believed that children should be seen and not heard. Apart from Leo, of course, who he was grooming to take over the family business. The rest of us were mainly brought up by nannies.'

'That must have been difficult.'

'I didn't know any different at the time,' she said with a shrug that belied just how traumatic it had been. 'And materially we wanted for nothing, of course, so I'm aware I'm playing the world's tiniest violin. Nevertheless, as the baby of the family, I got virtually no attention from anyone. I was always overshadowed by my older siblings. I could never work out where I fitted in. None of my accomplishments were original. Things like learning to ride a bike or swim—the others had done it all before. No one was ever impressed by anything I did. Or even vaguely interested. I was virtually invisible.'

'I find that hard to believe,' he murmured, running his gaze slowly over her before returning it to hers.

She ignored the flush of heat his perusal had provoked and forced herself to concentrate. 'Nevertheless, it's true.'

'You don't lack attention now.'

'No, well, I've devoted a lot of time and effort to getting it.'

'How?'

'It's not a pretty story,' she said with a wince.

'Let me be the judge of that.'

But that was what she feared. Him sizing her up and finding her lacking. It was bad enough when people she didn't know did it, but how would she handle the father of her child, her husband-to-be, thinking her even more shallow and pointless than he already did? 'Why don't we talk about your upbringing instead?'

'Because mine wasn't very interesting.'

'I doubt that very much,' she said, her curiosity piqued by the metaphorical doors slamming shut around him. 'You implied that my mother caused the breakdown of your family. What happened? I'd like to know.'

'Maybe later,' he said vaguely. 'Right now, however, I'd like to know more about *you*.'

Her heart gave a little jump, but she managed to keep it under control. 'For the baby's sake.'

He shook his head. 'For my sake. I can't work you out. You repeatedly confound me. It's been driving me mad. That's why I left. And why I've come back. To find out what makes you tick.'

This time, her control was no match for her emotions. This attention he was paying her was for her. Not for the baby, but for her. She'd had so little of it in her life, how could she possibly resist telling him everything he wanted to know? She might never get another chance to be the sole object of his focus, and the need to string it out for as long as possible drummed hard and fast inside her.

'I guess we do have to be open and honest with each other if we're going to make a success of this,' she said, her chest so tight it was making her dizzy.

'Exactly.'

'And you'll keep an open mind?'

'Yes.'

All right, then. She drew in a couple of deep steady breaths to ease the pressure on her lungs and braced herself. 'I must have realised at quite an early age that if I didn't want to disappear entirely I'd have to make myself visible, so I started acting up.'

'In what way?'

'The usual look-at-me things,' she said, recalling fragments of behaviour that had begun innocently enough but had become increasing self-destructive. 'When I was a kid, I was always putting on shows for anyone who would watch. Plays, musicals, anything really. I was the ultimate extrovert. Lots of friends, the leader of the gang, that sort of thing. But that didn't work—my family still more or less ignored me—so as I got older I devoted myself to accomplishments that *were* original.'

'Such as?'

'I began shoplifting. Not for the money, obviously. Not even for the high. I think I wanted someone to catch me, although no one ever did. I skipped school and disappeared for hours. Occasionally the alarm was raised, but by the time I was born the nannies had pretty much given up on discipline altogether so nothing ever came of it.'

'You were pushing against boundaries that weren't even there.'

'Right,' she said, marvelling a little at his perceptiveness. 'I had no one to build me up or set me straight. No one who cared. It was a confusing time. And then it got worse.'

'How?'

'When I was twelve and she was thirteen, Daphne was diagnosed with cancer.'

He frowned. 'I didn't know that.'

'It was kept out of the press. It shook us all up. Even our parents managed to put aside some of their self-interest until she went into remission. And I'm really not proud of this,' she said, swallowing down the hot lump of shame that had lodged in her throat, still crushing after all these years, 'but it occurred to me that if I wanted the attention she'd had I'd have to get ill, which was when I really went off the rails.'

'What happened?'

'I developed a mild eating disorder, and when that didn't achieve the desired result I started drinking and dabbling in drugs. Again nothing too serious. Just enough to blot the pain, I guess, because that seemed to make things better. It made me stop caring quite so much. From then on, I gave up trying to attract the attention of my family and dedicated myself to having fun, something I got very good at indeed.'

'Did no one seriously know what was going on?' Alex asked, his tone even, giving nothing away. 'Not even one of your siblings?'

Olympia shook her head, knowing that they weren't to blame. 'I masked what I was really feeling exceptionally well. But even if they had, it had to be me who wanted to change. That's how I ended up in rehab. One of my friends was hospitalised after an overdose. She was fine but it pulled me up short. I saw how my life might turn out if I didn't do something to fix it, so I checked into the clinic in Arizona, and the rest, as they say, is history.'

Done with her story, she stopped, but Alex seemed

to have nothing further to say and a heavy silence fell. She searched his face, unable to tell what he was thinking. But she hoped to God it wasn't appal. Or disgust. She hoped he'd kept that mind open and could understand that, despite its inauspicious beginnings, she was trying to turn her life around.

Because what if he didn't? What if he thought her a complete narcissist like her mother, or believed she presented some sort of danger to their child? Might he try and take it away from her? Could he even do that?

Perhaps she'd made a massive mistake in involving him and agreeing to this marriage. Perhaps she ought to leave and find support elsewhere. Surely *one* of her siblings could give her the help she would need?

But no. She was being ridiculous. That would never happen. Of course he wouldn't take her baby away. This wasn't Victorian England. What was she thinking? What she'd told him was a lot to take in, that was all. She'd needed three months to work it through, and still hadn't fully. He'd had it dumped on him in less than five minutes. It was bound to take time to process.

'So there you go,' she prompted when the silence became too thick to bear. 'That's me and my mad family dynamics. Quite something, right?'

CHAPTER NINE

'QUITE SOMETHING' WAS one way to describe it, Alex reflected darkly as everything Olympia had told him flashed around his head like lightning. He didn't know what he'd expected when he'd asked her to expand on her upbringing. He hadn't given it much thought. But it had turned out to be far more complex than he could ever have envisaged. And so—he was coming to realise—was she.

The press had always made her out to be shallow and flighty and, more often than not, a contemptible waste of space. And if he was being brutally honest, that was how he'd seen her too, at least initially. But as the details of her childhood had unfolded, even the most cynical of people would have been disabused of any those assumptions, and that included him.

He was the first to admit he was no expert when it came to siblings, but he excelled in applying logic to a situation and, the more he thought about it, the more he felt that she'd simply reacted to a set of circumstances beyond her control. Her most basic emotional needs had not been met. She'd never had any support. No one had ever cared enough to recognise what was going on and address it. Her parents, her siblings, everyone had failed her, and it was therefore no wonder she'd been so troubled. No wonder her self-esteem was on the floor and she struggled to locate her value. And he now completely understood why she'd wanted to spin the story of their relationship, which meant he would probably have to reconsider the idea of the engagement party she'd proposed.

What did come as a surprise, however, was his reaction to her many and varied revelations. An intense wave of anger, frustration and offence on her behalf was sweeping through him. He wanted to shake her siblings and throttle her mother, and not because of what she'd done to him. He wanted to erase from this world every scathing article the press had ever written about her and fire the people responsible.

Most of all, though, he felt a pressing urge to fix the way she viewed herself. He wasn't sure quite why. He wasn't remotely altruistic and, as much as he wanted her in his bed, her efforts to turn her life around deserved his respect and he would never deliberately try to thwart them by falsely building her up.

Perhaps, then, he had in mind their child and its need for stability. His own mother had been anything but emotionally robust, and she'd become even more fragile after his father's sudden death, which was why he'd had to step up to the plate even though he'd been a little more than a kid himself. He'd witnessed the misery self-doubt could cause and he wouldn't wish it on anyone apart from Selene Stanhope. Their child would certainly benefit from two strong secure parents, so yes, that was most likely it.

'I agree that crazy is one way of looking at it,' he said, not much liking the way Olympia had paled and was biting her lip, as if she feared his verdict, which for some unfathomable reason made him want to hit something hard. 'Through no fault of your own you didn't have it easy, and I can understand how and why you made some unwise choices. But we're all shaped by the past and there's nothing any of us can do to change that.'

'Even you?'

'We're not talking about me.'

'Yet.'

'My point is,' he continued, vowing to keep his past private for as long as he possibly could, 'you can reframe the way you perceive it. What you've been through has made you resilient and tough, a survivor. It shows you're open to new and unconventional experiences. You're adventurous and a risk-taker. You're self-aware. You identified a problem and you took action. Decisively. These things are positives, not negatives, and they come from you. No one else. You.'

By the time he'd finished speaking, Olympia was looking a little shell-shocked, which wasn't far off how he was feeling right now. Where all this was coming from he had no clue, and God knew he was no therapist, but it seemed as though he wasn't done, because apparently he had more observations on the subject that were clamouring to be voiced.

'When you started working for Stanhope's,' he said, having shuffled them into some sort of order, 'I thought your appointment an absurd affront to the industry. I didn't think you'd last five minutes—as you know. But I underestimated you. You've proved yourself to be determined and tenacious. You don't give up. You go for what you want and don't stop until you get it. You take no prisoners. I've witnessed that myself on a number of occasions. Even though I disapprove of you trying to steal my number one client, and I wasn't at all happy about being seduced in a stairwell or by the pool, I can't deny you're impressive. You have charm and charisma in abundance. The way you're turning your failures into success is admirable. You should give yourself more credit, Olympia, and believe in your abilities. Because they're not insignificant. They're not insignificant at all.'

Now he really was done, which was just as well, because if his heart beat any harder it would be in danger of cracking a rib. And if her eyes widened any further they'd likely pop out of her head.

'Do you really think all that?' she said breathlessly, clearly stunned.

'I do,' he replied, because in the end it hadn't been hard to identify her strengths, of which, he'd come to realise as she'd shared the details of her upbringing, there were many. He hadn't had to embellish or invent a thing. He did genuinely believe that she was in possession of every trait he'd described. Objectively, it was nothing less than the truth.

'I don't know what to say.'

No, well, in all honesty, he was just as confused as she was. Not by her this time, which made a change, but by himself, because there was nothing objective about the tightness of his chest and the fire powering through his veins. Or about the other adjectives rattling around his head that described her—magnificent, unique, fascinating. He didn't understand what he was doing or what he was feeling, so the rumble his stomach suddenly gave could not have come at a better time.

'Are you hungry?' he asked as, with some relief, he switched his focus from the insanely complicated to the very simple. 'I am. We should eat.'

Olympia followed Alex into the kitchen in something of a daze. He shrugged off his jacket, hunting down some equipment and ingredients while she struggled to make sense of everything he'd said. Her offer to help with the slicing and dicing of the salad vegetables was declined, which on reflection was a good thing. She'd never chopped a tomato in her life and now, with the way her hands seemed to be trembling, was probably not the time to start.

She didn't much follow the conversation over supper. She answered his questions about Daphne's illness automatically, and elaborated on some of the other things she'd got up to as an out-of-control adolescent, but she was so distracted by his alternative view of her character that she hadn't been able to give him or the conversation her full concentration.

She ate the chicken souvlaki and salad without really tasting it. The elderflower pressé she drank slipped down largely unnoticed. She was fleetingly diverted by the flickering candles that cast dancing shadows across the handsome planes of his face, but within moments she was back in her thoughts, trying to get her head around the value he saw in her.

The process was not an easy one. Worthlessness had been entrenched in her for so long that denial was her default setting. It had never occurred to her to find anything constructive in the chaos that had been her life. She'd only ever focused on the destructive, which had been so impactful, and which for the last decade the headlines had reinforced at every available opportunity.

But now she was being forced to give it some thought, to fight through the denial and try to consider herself in the light that Alex had shone on her. Was she really everything he'd described? Well, yes, perhaps she was. She *was* determined and tough. Persistent and focused. She only had to look at the last year or so to see that. But even before then she'd thrown herself into every decision she'd made. They might not necessarily have been wise ones, but she'd always had a plan and gone with it. She'd always given everything one hundred per cent. And, as he'd pointed out, she was trying her best to put her failures behind her and seek success.

So maybe he wasn't the only one to underestimate her, she thought, as all the revelations he'd unearthed began pinging around her head and zapping the nuggets of self-doubt that plagued her. She'd underestimated herself, and not just on an emotional level. Because she was a dropout who didn't have a clutch of academic qualifications she'd always thought of herself as somehow lesser than her siblings. Deep down she'd considered herself a loser. But that wasn't necessarily the case. The lack of a certificate or two didn't mean anything. She might not have passed any exams but perhaps the charm and charisma he'd identified made up for that deficiency. A piece of paper certainly wouldn't have helped smash the targets Zander had set.

She had to start believing that her worth lay in herself, in her work and in her plans for the future. She got a thrill out of her brother telling her she'd done well. When she signed another new client, the high she felt was because of something *she'd* achieved. She was stronger and more confident than she'd imagined. Whatever her motives for seeking a good time, she was fun to be around and a loyal friend. And in the last few days, she'd been called impressive—twice.

It had all been there, she thought a little giddily as a wave of acceptance swept away the last vestiges of denial, and she was filled with a strange sense of calm. She'd just needed a nudge in the right direction to realise it, and Alex—clever man that he was—had given her that nudge. For the first time in her life, she could allow herself to take pride in what she was good at rather than wallow in shame over what she wasn't. She could believe that she didn't have to be defined by the past, and that she did have something to offer the world.

And it was all because of him, she thought, her heart rate picking up as she watched him from across the table. He'd been unexpectedly fierce in his defence of her. He'd seen things in her that no one else ever had. To have someone on her side, in her corner, was such an overwhelming concept that she could barely breathe with the force of it. If he protected and looked out for their child in the same steadfast way, it would never have to question its self-worth. It would never make bad decisions and wind up dancing in fountains. It truly would be blessed.

And so perhaps she should start looking for the positives in her relationship with Alex too. Now they were talking, this marriage had a real chance of success. Now she could accept herself as he saw her, there was no reason to hold back. Nothing was stopping her from taking what she wanted, and right now, with hot heady desire suddenly crashing through her, she wanted him.

Alex was fighting a number of internal battles when he noticed a shift in the air that prickled his senses and sent a rash of goosebumps skittering across his skin.

First, there was his suggestion that Olympia reframe her perception of the past, which had somehow lodged in his head and which, no matter how hard he tried, he couldn't shake off. He didn't know where that insight had originated but it had unhelpfully occurred to him since that he could equally apply it to himself. Which made no sense, because his situation was entirely different. His past hadn't had nearly such an impact on him. Up until his father and her mother had had their affair, his life had been uneventful. He'd lacked for nothing either materially or emotionally. He hadn't had to go off the rails to get attention or push at non-existent boundaries. As an only child he'd been doted on.

And yes, things had irrevocably changed once his family had fallen apart, the comfort that he'd taken for granted evaporating virtually overnight. But while he could easily have descended into a boiling pit of anger and resentment, he hadn't. Instead, he'd channelled how he'd felt into restoring the family's fortunes, and once he'd achieved that he'd devoted himself to chasing the success that would make him invincible. He was more than happy with the way that had turned out, so he couldn't for the life of him work out why he was suddenly dwelling on it.

Then there was the desire that burned as brightly as ever. Olympia looked impossibly sexy in her white strapless dress with her dark shining hair tumbling around her shoulders. As supper progressed, increasingly all he'd wanted to do was realise the dreams that had tormented him these past two nights, even though such a course of action was obviously out of the question.

He'd eaten the chicken that had tasted of nothing with gloomy despondency. How long it would take for her to see what he saw? Presumably, that sort of thing took months of contemplation. If he sourced the very best therapists the world had to offer, might that speed the process up? And what if she never reached the point at which she could bring herself to sleep with him? How would he bear it?

But now, suddenly, the night seemed to be crackling with electricity, as if a storm had enveloped them, and when he glanced up to find her gaze on him—intense, hot, shimmering—every cell of his body stilled.

A surge of adrenaline dried his mouth and kickstarted his pulse.

What was going on?

'Why are you looking at me like that?' he asked, his voice thick and strained, even to his own ears.

'Like what?'

'As if you're thinking about kissing me.'

Her gaze dropped to his mouth and darkened and the world seemed to glide to a halt. 'Because I am,' she said with a huskiness that tightened his stomach and sent all his blood straight to his groin. 'And it's not just kissing you that's running through my mind.'

'Oh?'

'I want to finish what I started by the pool.'

Images from that afternoon flashed through his mind. How good she'd felt. How crazed he'd been. Instinct urged him to leap to his feet, grab her by the hand and haul her up the stairs, but his head was yelling *no!* Despite their earlier conversation, he still had little understanding of how she operated. This could be another attempt to manipulate him. Or it might give rise to another about turn when her insecurities took over.

'What's brought this on?' he asked, doing his best to suppress the urgent response of his body because he didn't think he could face another cold shower. 'I thought you were embracing celibacy.'

She shook her head. 'Not any more. And it's you who's brought this on. With all those things you said about me. Your reframing of the past worked. You've made me recognise the value I have and realise what I'm capable of.'

He swallowed hard. 'That was quick.'

'I know. But it was all there. I just needed a push in the right direction, which you gave me. If fund management doesn't work out you could make a fortune as a therapist. Mine never even suggested it. I'm very grateful. I'd like to show you exactly how much.'

'Is that right?'

'It couldn't be more right. I know I have many faults, and I know the incident by the pool may suggest otherwise, but prick teasing has never been my thing.' She tilted her head and gave him a smile that, for some reason, struck him square in the chest. 'There's no reason sex can't be just sex, right?'

Well, yes. That was what he'd always believed and a policy he'd always followed. But this would not be the short-term affair he usually favoured. This would be something that would likely tangle him up for years, with an outcome that was anything but clear.

On the other hand, it was entirely possible he was overthinking things. He could understand how her many insecurities might lead to a need for control that he'd misread as deliberate manipulation. The real her might well be transparent and honest. Why shouldn't he trust that it was? And who was he to question her decision anyway? Hadn't he just pointed out her capabilities in that area?

He wanted her with a desperation that was turning him inside out and he could see no reason to deny it. Once the chemistry was addressed the tension between them would vanish. The insatiable lust he had for her would lessen. And what better way to distract her whenever she asked him a question he'd rather not have to answer? The benefits of taking her up on her offer would be many indeed.

'You see,' he said, sitting back, watching her closely as his blood thickened and his body hardened even more. 'Determined and tenacious. You go for what you want.'

'I want you.'

'Are you sure?'

'Absolutely.'

'Then come and get me.'

Olympia regarded him for one heart-stopping moment and then, without taking her eyes off his, rose from her chair in a move that could only be described as sinuous. His pulse thudded heavily as she lifted the hem of her dress and slipped off her underwear. Then she sidled over to him and pushed his legs apart. She dropped to her knees and his temperature rocketed. She unbuckled his belt and tugged down his zip to free him, and when she leaned forward to take him first in her hand and then in her mouth, he nearly passed out with pleasure.

Shuddering, unable to hold back a rough groan, he tangled his hands in her hair and closed his eyes, thinking that if this was the way she showed her gratitude he'd make more of an effort in future to deserve it.

The ministrations of her soft hands and warm wet mouth were sending molten currents through his body, into his head and destroying his brain cells. Tension gripped his muscles, tightening them to the point of pain, and he could feel the need for release swelling fast and hard—but it was too soon. He wanted to de-molish her control, as she did his. One part of him, a part he didn't wish to analyse too closely, wanted to make her pay for the torment she'd put him through these past few days.

'Enough,' he grated before he reached the point of no return.

Ignoring her faint mewl of protest, he pulled her up and settled her on his lap. He clamped his hands to her hips, shifting her so that the straining length of his erection pressed against the softness of her centre. Winding her arms around his neck, she lowered her mouth to his and kissed him with such heat that the blood in his veins turned to fire. It spread through his body like a fever, incinerating his bones and draining the strength from his limbs. When they came up for air her breathing was as ragged as his.

'You have no idea how hard it's been resisting you,' he muttered hoarsely as she lifted her hips urgently and he moved one hand between them. 'I thought it would simply be a question of mind over matter. I was wrong. You've been killing me. Another reason I had to leave.'

'I'm glad you're back.'

'So am I.'

She gave a soft moan when he slipped his fingers inside her, trembling in his arms. She writhed against him, panting a little, and their mouths met again, but within seconds there seemed to be an urgency in her that matched the growing desperation in him. Then she moved, he moved and, a moment later, she was sinking onto him, taking him as deep as she could, and everything but her disappeared.

His senses reeled. Her skin was as soft and smooth as satin. Her scent was in his head and her hair felt like silk. Her eyes were dark and wild and locked to his with such heat that surely he was about to combust. She arched her back and breathed 'Unzip me' and he had no issue with that when it meant he could take her nipple in his mouth and tease it until she was begging him for release.

But he was in no mind to grant her wish, so he held her in place and focused on learning the shape and taste of her, every muscle he possessed coiling tighter every time she sighed or gasped or twitched.

Her breathing was shallow and choppy. Her head fell back. He moved his hand down her body, letting it linger for a moment where their baby grew, and then lower, to where they were joined—and with a cry she shattered so powerfully that it triggered his own roaring release. She clung onto him and shook and he hauled her close, pulsating into her hard and deep in a blaze of ecstasy that left him limp and dazed.

When the heat faded and the world swam back into focus, he tipped her off his lap and set her on her feet. Somehow he found the strength to get up himself.

'Follow me,' he muttered, grabbing her hand for support, although whether he was providing it or taking it he wasn't sure.

'Where are we going?'

'I seem to recall you wanting to find out what we could do in a bed.'

CHAPTER TEN

THE FOLLOWING MORNING, Olympia floated down the stairs and into the kitchen as if she was lighter than air.

What a night, she thought, a wide smile spreading across her face as she located a couple of cups, then popped a capsule into the coffee machine and turned it on. She couldn't recall one like it. She'd lost count of the number of times she and Alex had shattered in each other's arms before falling into an exhausted sleep at some time around dawn.

There wasn't an inch of his magnificent body that she hadn't explored. The things he'd done to her—not just in the bed, but also in the shower and on the balcony—would be imprinted for ever on her memory. His muscles were like velvet encased steel. The smattering of coarse dark hair that covered his chest had tickled her skin and electrified her nerve-endings. When he'd set his mouth between her legs and lingered there a while she'd practically jack-knifed off the bed.

Not for one moment did she regret any of it. It had been so empowering. So deliriously thrilling. And not in the least bit reckless because, unlike on such occasions in the past, she'd given it her full consideration before taking what she wanted.

When he'd told her to go over and get him she could have simply succumbed to the predatory gleam that had appeared in his eye without a second thought. But she hadn't. She'd paused. She'd looked at him across the table, her heart pounding, the excitement whipping through her more stimulating than any drug she'd ever taken, and had asked herself whether she was sure she was doing the right thing. Whether she was really ready to take this step.

Well, she was, she'd decided a moment later, because she'd spent the whole of supper realising that her self-worth *didn't* lie in sex, so she had nothing to fear from it. She wasn't being rash and impulsive. She was making a choice based on a number of well thought through arguments—and what a spectacular choice it had been. Her self-esteem was sky high, and not just because he couldn't get enough of her body. The euphoria she'd experienced had been dazzling but not manic. She really felt as though they were making progress. The concept of being a team was no longer some pipe dream but a very real possibility.

She still had a lot to learn about him of course. Almost everything, in fact, because while she'd spilled practically the entirety of her soul to him last night he'd been frustratingly reticent in return. But now they'd taken the edge off their desire, there'd be more opportunity for conversation this morning, she was sure. The emotional connection she wanted with the father of her child was growing. Trust, even in its nascent form, truly was a wonderful thing.

A knock at the front door jolted Olympia out of her dreamy thoughts and she abandoned the coffee for the hall. Two minutes later she'd signed for two envelopes, one addressed to Alex, the other addressed to her. She placed his on the round marble table that dominated the space. Hers she took back to the kitchen to open, and shook out the sheaf of papers. It looked to be documentation relating to their marriage and that made her frown. Hadn't he informed her in no uncertain terms that they were going to wait?

Maybe he'd reflected on the point she'd made the morning she'd moved in about implementing their plans right away and changed his mind. That could only be a good thing. Whatever the reason behind it, it proved his commitment to their baby. And to her? Well, it was early days for them and she mustn't get ahead of herself, but the signs were there.

So did he have any ideas in mind about what format the wedding might take, and where? Or would he give her free rein? She'd have to ask. Not that she knew what she wanted. She'd never dreamed she'd ever marry. Although, they'd better do it quickly, because she wasn't sure she wanted to wear a white dress with a massive bump on display.

But hang on. What was this?

Setting aside the contract, Olympia frowned down at the second document in the pack. It appeared to be a prenuptial agreement, which was bizarre when he'd never mentioned one, and money would never be an issue. Even more curiously, there seemed to be only one clause.

Bemused, she scanned it once.

Then again.

And it was on the third reading that everything fell apart.

In the event she messed up in some unspecified way, Alex would divorce her and seek sole custody of their child. She would rescind visitation rights. She would only see her child under a number of very specific circumstances and never on her own. Every decision to be made from there on in would be his.

It was very clear. Very concise. And absolutely brutal.

Olympia's vision blurred and her heart was suddenly beating too fast and too hard. Somehow, she found a stool and managed to sit on it before her legs gave way.

The nightmare scenario she'd told herself couldn't possibly happen the night before had materialised. He *was* planning on taking her child away from her. He didn't trust her at all, she realised, beginning to shake from head to toe as the implications of the prenup sank in and she was filled with roaring emotion. He never had and likely never would. They weren't a team. They weren't anything. He'd even warned her he'd use any weapon at his disposal to get what he wanted, so she didn't know why she was so surprised.

He still thought of her as the wild child she'd once been. She'd never leave her past behind. It would follow her, tainting everything she did, for ever, no matter how much progress she made. And to think that last night she'd actually imagined they'd turned a corner. Just how big a fool was she?

She knew the only person to blame for what had happened here was her. She'd allowed herself to believe that he valued her as an individual rather than just the mother of his child. And a white wedding? *Really?* What had she been *thinking?*

But God it hurt. Her throat was sore and tight. Every cell of her body ached and her heart felt as though it had cleaved in two. She wanted to curl up and cry and then to hit the city. To find the nearest twenty-four-hour club and lose herself in the music. To obliterate the pain with champagne and a line or two. But she couldn't, because she was pregnant and she didn't do that anymore and she would never give him any cause to enact the prenup even if she did sign it.

So she was going to have to deal with this bruising development in a different way. And while it would be the easiest thing in the world to walk out on Alex and his lack of trust, to take her chances and go it alone, her baby needed her to meet the challenges she faced head on. She would *not* let herself revert to her old ways and descend into a seething pit of misery and self-doubt. She could drive herself mad second-guessing what he'd been thinking with this prenup, and those days were over.

Instead, she would bury the anger and pain, channel the determination and tenacity she didn't need him to tell her she had, and find out what he had to say.

* * *

Upstairs in the ensuite bathroom, Alex stood beneath the shower, the hot water going some way to ease the pleasant ache in his muscles, and thought that taking Olympia at her word had absolutely been the right thing to do. Twelve hours ago he'd been a man at the end of his tether but now, the mad lust having been dampened, he was back on an even keel. He had no doubt that from here on in the desire would be manageable.

Furthermore, while she'd slumbered beside him, he'd revisited their conversation before supper, finally managing to apply the analysis he was supposedly famed for. He now understood her a whole lot better than he had before. He could see where her insecurities and vulnerabilities stemmed from, and he had renewed admiration for the way she'd pulled herself back from the abyss. Going forward, he would be able to handle whatever she threw at him calmly and objectively. He was back in control of this relationship—and himself—and that was the way things would stay.

Satisfied that he'd one hundred per cent succeeded in the mission he'd embarked upon the night before, and indescribably relieved that she'd sorted out her issues with self-worth, Alex switched off the shower and reached for a towel. He rubbed it over his head, then tied it round his waist and returned to the bedroom— where he found Olympia, sitting on the edge of the bed instead of in it, disappointingly clothed and wearing a blank expression that sent a shiver down his spine.

'What's wrong?' he asked with a frown. When she'd

announced she was off to make some coffee she'd had a smile on her face. He was sure of it. He'd put it there only five minutes before.

'While you were in the shower, the paperwork for our marriage was delivered.' Her voice was cold and flat and her body was rigid. 'The contract and your prenup. I gather you've changed your mind about the timeframe. Not that it particularly matters, because I'm signing neither.'

Alex stilled. White noise rushed in his ears and his stomach clenched. He recalled the instructions he'd given to his lawyers back when he'd considered her a loose cannon, and he knew instinctively that this could be bad. Very bad indeed.

'I'd forgotten all about that.'

She stared at him for a moment, pale, stunned, and then her eyes blazed and she shot her feet. 'You forgot that you've decided to weaponise our child?' she asked, blasting him with the full force of her hurt and anger. 'To cut me out of the picture if I make a mistake? How could you be so cruel? What sort of man does that?' She gave her head a sharp furious shake, no longer pale and stunned, but incandescent. 'I can't believe I actually thought we were in this together. I can't believe I thought you trusted me. You even told me you wouldn't hesitate to use my past against me if I dared to defy you. I really am the biggest idiot alive.'

'No,' he said abruptly. 'Stop that. I can explain.'

'How?' She planted her hands on her hips as her chin

shot up. 'How can you *possibly* explain what you've done?'

'I ordered the prenup to be drawn up the morning you showed up here and turned my life even more upside down than it already was. At the time it made sense. You'd just told me how vulnerable you were, and the security of our child was my number one priority. You'd said you recognised the danger of relapse. I couldn't risk you taking off on a whim or cutting me out for good.'

'I would never have done that. I told you I needed your support. And I'm well aware of the importance of a stable environment for a child to grow up in.'

'I didn't know that then.'

Her eyebrows arched. 'And you do now?'

'After everything you told me last night, yes.'

'Why should I believe you?'

'Because it's the truth. I meant every word of what I said.'

'No,' she snapped back. 'That's not good enough. You can't expect me to simply take your word for it and just accept your compliments, when for all I know you were just trying to flatter me into bed.'

His jaw clenched. 'I would not do that.'

'So *you* say. But look at it from my perspective. You know practically everything there is to know about me, and all I know about you is that you own and control a billion-euro empire and you're all alone in this world. You've told me nothing about yourself and I've asked time and time again. Your need for control puts your wishes so far above mine they're on another planet. And I realise that I am nothing more to you than the mother of your child, but I won't be able to live like that. I *refuse* to live like that. I deserve respect. So does our child. So if you can't give us that we'd be better off on our own.'

At the thought of Olympia turning on her heel and walking out of his house and his life, something fierce and primitive roared inside him. That wasn't happening. He had to fix this. He had to acknowledge that she had a point. With his reluctance to dive into the trauma of his past he *had* been thinking only of himself. He'd feared an emotional connection developing. Getting in too deep. But he was already up to his neck and that wasn't going to change, so he had to accept he was fighting a losing battle.

She had every right to be angry and hurt. He'd caused her distress, unforgivably if unintentionally triggering her self-esteem issues, and he did not wish to exacerbate it further. He would do whatever it took to prevent her from leaving and taking his future with her, and if that meant talking to her as she had to him, then so be it.

'All right,' he said, folding his arms over his chest and steeling himself for an unpleasant trip down memory lane. 'You wanted to know what the impact of our parents' affair had on me, well, it was, devastating. My upbringing wasn't like yours. It was conventional and uneventful. Until I introduced your mother to my father one school sports day and unleashed carnage.

The divorce bankrupted my parents. The stress of it brought on the heart attack that killed my father and reduced my mother to a wreck. I was the one who had to pick up the pieces. I gave up my place at university and took a job that would make me a lot of money fast. Which I did. But it wasn't enough to save the home that had been in my family for generations. And it wasn't enough to stop the cancer that killed my mother two years later.'

'The repercussions lasted years,' he continued, noting that the fire was fading from her gaze, the tension ebbing from her shoulders as he pressed home his advantage. 'I've spent two decades repairing the damage that was done and I won't let history repeat itself by allowing our child to suffer the same fate because of us. So I'll tell you more, Olympia. I'll tell you everything. I'll rip up the prenup and prove to you that you do have my respect. You can have your party and spin it how you wish. You can have whatever you want. But in order for all that to happen, you need to stay.'

What Olympia badly wanted right now was to cling on to the hurt and anger that she'd been wearing like a shield and tell him to get lost. She wanted to protect her damaged self-esteem and convince herself that his opinion of her didn't matter, and that she and her baby really would be fine on their own. She hated and feared the volatility of these feelings that, if she weakened, could have her careening towards a destination she never wanted to revisit.

But she couldn't just selfishly turn round and walk out. She still remained absolutely certain that their baby deserved two functioning parents. And try as she might, she had no argument against his claim that he'd simply arranged the prenup in response to what she herself had told him. She'd have done the same in his position.

In truth, his explanation had taken some of the heat out of her emotions the minute he'd given it. She had to grudgingly admit it had made sense. Now, she'd cooled down enough to realise that by opening the door to his past he'd heard her and afforded her the respect she'd demanded. Whether or not he meant what he said about having whatever she wanted remained to be seen, but he'd seemed to be serious about the party.

So she may have overreacted. She didn't really think he'd flattered her into bed. He'd never given her any reason to doubt the truth of what he said. She had to focus on the last couple of days of this relationship, not the first, and let it go.

They were both taking major steps to make this thing work and she wasn't going to give up the chance to further the emotional connection between them. On the contrary, she was going to do everything in her power to cement it. He'd opened the door to himself and she was going to stride on through.

'Fine.'

CHAPTER ELEVEN

OF COURSE GETTING Alex to open up wasn't that easy. He clearly hadn't talked about his past before. Olympia's questions about his childhood and the fallout of the divorce, as well as the fact that her mother was going to be their child's grandmother, were met with long pauses and deep scowls and he had trouble articulating how he felt about it all. But at least he was trying. And if he resorted to sex whenever she tried to get him to dig deep and expand on his feelings, then that was all right with her, for now. Things were on the right track. They had plenty of time to finesse the conversation.

Now, this Thursday morning, they were travelling by boat to Alex's private island in the Saronic Gulf. He might have agreed to the party, but he'd also told her that he was damned if he was going to have God knew how many Stanhopes invading his home and traipsing across his garden, so it would not be happening there.

As they docked alongside the jetty an hour after departing Piraeus, Olympia looked round and thought that she had no objection whatsoever to his establishing some sort of control over the proceedings. Who would complain about holding a party in such an idyllic spot?

The tiny, isolated landmass was ringed by a beach of golden sand. The water surrounding it shimmered and sparkled in the setting sun, a mesmerising combination of jade, turquoise and azure. Nestled in a forest of trees—at the top of a series of terraces that rose up from the beach—was the house. It was stepped into the lush hillside and had clearly been designed to take full advantage of the views. With its three storeys of clean lines and crisp angles that were held together by acres of sparkling glass, it was a beautiful, very contemporary retreat.

'This is a great venue for the party,' she said, popping on her sunglasses, shading her eyes from the sun's intense reflection, as she disembarked with his help. 'What a house. Modern yet somehow it blends in with the landscape. It's remarkably lovely. Did you build it?'

'I did.' He lifted their luggage out of the boat with barely any effort at all, dumping it on the jetty. 'Or rather, I had it built. Five years ago.'

'Do you entertain here a lot?'

'No.'

'Why not?'

'One, I don't have the time. And two, when I do, I come here to escape the noise of the city. I come here for the peace.'

Alex alighted and picked up their cases, while Olympia ogled the bunch and flex of his muscles and went weak at the knees.

'I can see the appeal of that,' she said, giving herself a quick shake before they then set off towards land. 'I always adored being surrounded by people. I was hardly ever on my own, but I suspect that was just so I didn't have to think. A distraction from my inner turmoil, if you will.'

'How's your inner turmoil these days?'

'Lessening by the minute. Enough now for me to be able to appreciate peace. How's yours?'

'I don't have any.'

'Are you sure about that?'

'Quite sure. You've therapied it out of me.'

Hmm. She didn't think she had just yet. Still waters ran deep, but she'd get to the bottom of them eventually—for the baby's sake, naturally.

'Well, our guests are going to love this,' she said as the jetty ended and the steps up to the house began. 'Mine will, at least. I'm thinking we can hire a private ferry for the occasion. They could be greeted by fire eaters and raspberry and passion fruit martinis. That should get things going with a bang.'

'I'll have to take your word for it.'

'Do you really not like parties?'

'Not ones filled with Stanhopes.'

'Don't worry, I'll protect you. Someone once told me I'm tough and determined.'

'So I recall.'

'The parties I used to throw were wild,' she said, recalling with a faint wince some of the craziest. 'Once, in Rome, three hundred of us danced the night away in a room with a ceiling painted by Leonardo da Vinci, until one guy started swinging on a chandelier and we got thrown out. I didn't even know half of them. I've been much more ruthless with my guestlist for this party. For a start, I've culled everyone who tried to convince me I didn't need to go rehab. I can't have people like that in my life anymore.'

'No,' he said shortly. 'You can't.'

At his depth of feeling on the subject, she bristled. 'There's no need to be quite so judgemental.'

'I'm not. I simply meant that if anyone so much as dared to try and set you back I'd give them cause to regret it.'

Oh. Right. A curl of warmth unfurled inside her and she inwardly sighed with what felt a lot like envy. 'Our baby is lucky indeed to have such a caring and attentive father.'

For a moment he didn't say anything, just frowned up at the house. 'Are you sure a party is a good idea?'

'It'll be fine,' she reassured him, ignoring the strange ache in her chest and pulling herself together. 'My issues were minor ones and I've been totally sober for months. And don't forget, I'm pregnant. I have an added incentive to steer clear of the booze. But you're sweet to be concerned.'

At that descriptor, his eyebrows shot up. *'Sweet?'* he echoed, clearly appalled.

'Well, perhaps not sweet,' she demurred, thinking of the companies he'd told her he'd taken down and the people who'd crossed him that he'd buried. Back when he'd seethed with hatred and resentment for anyone with her surname, he'd apparently even toyed with the idea of ruining the Stanhope Kallis shipping and banking empire—until he'd realised that its three hundred year history and power that spanned the globe made it frustratingly untouchable. 'I didn't mean to offend. But your concern is misplaced. It's good for my recovery to be in situations that in the past may have caused me grief. I can't avoid social occasions for ever. Nor can you if you're going to be married to me. It'll be fun.'

He emitted a strangled sound that suggested he'd rather chew his own toenails, and she couldn't prevent a small grin. 'So who are you planning to invite?'

'The sort who'll appreciate fire eaters and martinis but wouldn't swing from the chandeliers even if I had any. Assuming they're available with only three days' notice.'

'I've arranged parties with far less than that. Even if people aren't free, they generally become so. My reputation does have some uses. Any potential gatecrashers I need to be worried about?'

'Such as?'

'Business rivals?'

'No.'

'Spurned girlfriends with a grudge?'

'No girlfriends at all.'

What? Seriously? 'How is that possible?' she asked, unable to keep the incredulity from her voice as they reached the top of the steps, circumnavigating the enormous, very inviting infinity pool. 'I mean, you're handsome and successful, not to mention principled and insightful. You have a protective streak a mile wide, you take your responsibilities seriously and you fight for what's yours. How you have you stayed single all this time?'

'Just lucky I guess.'

At the dry cynicism she could hear in his voice, Olympia frowned. 'Is that really how you view commitment?'

'Up until the afternoon you appeared in my office and forced me to reconsider, yes. I generally work ten hours a day, six, sometimes seven days a week. I'm responsible for eight offices around the world and a thousand staff. My company doesn't run itself. It requires my full attention and always has.'

'It sounds as though I'm not the only one in need of distraction.'

'You couldn't be more wrong,' he countered smoothly. 'There is nothing I need distracting from.'

'Not even loneliness?'

'I don't have time for loneliness. Ask your brother about the pressures of running a global business and the workload. His company is ten times the size of mine.'

'He's also married with a child. He seems to manage.'

'And so will I when the time comes. What was your view of commitment before all this?'

'Oh, I've always been far too much of a handful for anyone to take on for any length of time. I'm only good for one night, two at the most.'

'Don't be ridiculous,' he said as he opened the front door and stood aside to let her in. 'I'm taking you on. Potentially for years.'

'Only because of the baby,' she observed, because it felt necessary to think and say it repeatedly. 'That's who you're really taking on, not me. There's a difference.'

Alex dropped the bags on the pale limestone floor and stared at her for one long moment. His dark eyes glittered as they roamed over her, and quite suddenly Olympia didn't want to talk any more. She didn't want to think about everything that had happened since Friday and why she was here. All she wanted was him.

Her pulse was racing and her mouth was dry, and it seemed too long since there'd been nothing between them but heat and desire.

'This conversation is over, isn't it?' she asked, her voice thick with the need that she could see reflected in his gaze.

'Yes.'

'Will you show me around?'

'We'll start with the bedroom,' he said, then grabbed her hand and led her up the stairs.

Alex didn't get round to giving Olympia a tour of the rest of the house until later that afternoon, when she told him that her body needed a break and the sex bubble he'd deliberately created to avoid having to think about their conversation on the jetty popped.

How had she managed to stir up so much trouble

for him in such a short space of time? he wondered darkly as he left her by the pool and went inside to make the call he could scarcely believe he was about to make. Caring and attentive weren't words he'd ever use to describe himself. And as for friends, commitment, inner turmoil and work as a distraction, well, he didn't tend to dwell on any of that if he could help it. What was the point?

He'd always accepted that he was better off without friends, and the investment of time and energy they'd require with no quantifiable return. Thanks to the breakdown of his parents' marriage he'd spent his entire adult life avoiding commitment like the plague. He'd never been one for navel-gazing. His job required all his attention. And the last thing he wanted to think about was how comprehensively his peace was going to be shattered on Saturday night at eight.

Besides, he'd already come to terms with the ins and outs of throwing this party. He'd have to meet her family at some point, and at least this way he could ensure it happened on his turf, in a place where the air was fresh and he could breathe. He could knock on the head the catchup that Leo had been so keen on, and stamp out the niggle of guilt that he still felt over going behind Olympia's back and calling him up in the first place. In the absence of friends and family he'd invite his clients, both current and prospective, and the useful acquaintances he'd made over the years. He would treat the event as a business opportunity. An occasion to strengthen his connections and therefore his company. Her mother was on the other side of the world, so that was one nightmare he wouldn't have to face just yet, and with any luck, if Olympia was busy organising a party, she wouldn't have time to keep trying to probe into his feelings about the past.

Much to his amazement, sharing with her the details of his life that he'd never shared with anyone before wasn't as traumatic as he'd feared. It was only when she tilted her head and asked him questions such as 'what were some things you liked about that situation?' or 'how do you think you could have handled that differently?' that he froze up. He wasn't used to talking about his emotions, and with her it felt insanely risky to do so.

Luckily, she didn't seem to mind when he distracted her with sex, but he sensed he couldn't put her off for ever. Alarmingly, he increasingly didn't want to. The unfathomable urge to correct her every time she insisted that he was only interested in her because of the baby was growing too.

She wasn't the only loose cannon in this situation, he thought as he brought up the number of Georgiou's, Athens' most exclusive, most discreet jewellers and wondered whether he could actually be losing his mind. She'd upended his life. She tied him in knots. And the truly unsettling thing was that he was beginning to wonder whether part of him actually liked it.

Olympia was on the phone to the event planner the next morning when she heard the rapid *whoop-whoop* sound of an approaching helicopter. Shading her eyes, she looked up to see it pass by overhead—a small metallic dot in a vast expanse of blue—and then turned her attention back to the conversation.

With money no object, arrangements for the party were progressing apace. The DJ, the florist and the pyrotechnician were all booked and on their way. Zander's wife, Mia, a caterer with a flair for the original, was insisting on doing the food despite being on maternity leave, and the world's number one mixologist was being flown in from New York.

Yesterday, when Alex had left her by the pool muttering something about a call, she'd turned her attention to how she might use the party to further her career. When he'd returned, whipping off his T-shirt and stretching beside her on the double sun lounger, she'd wasted no time in outlining his role in her plans.

'I'm looking forward to you meeting Zander,' she'd said, resisting the urge to climb on top of him and assuage the desire that seemed to be getting hotter instead of cooler. 'You can extol my virtues and persuade him to give me the job I really want.'

'What job is that?' he'd said with an oddly inscrutable look in her direction.

'I want to do what you do. I want to manage funds and investments on behalf of other people.'

'Why?'

'I had a lot of time on my hands in the three months I spent in the Arizona desert. I filled it by reading anything I could get hold of, and much of that was material that focused on business. I have no idea why that was the favoured subject matter, but as a result I developed a wholly unexpected interest in finance. I studied market trends and fluctuations. I even identified the sector I found most fascinating—hotels and real estate, weirdly—and devoured as much analysis on it as I could.'

'Identifying the sector one finds the most fascinating and then devouring it seems like a very good idea,' he'd murmured, running his gaze over her bikini-clad body and letting it linger on the parts she knew he liked best.

Olympia had ignored the sizzle of heat that encouraged her to plaster her mouth to his and forced herself to concentrate. 'I have no idea why the idea of making money out of nothing appeals so much, but I came across a programme that allows simulated trading and discovered I have a talent for it. I've been working on gaining the necessary regulatory qualifications and am desperate to put what I've learned into practice. But Zander doesn't think that either I or our clients are quite ready for that. He's insisting I complete a full year drumming up new business before I can move on. A casual word in his ear, telling him how capable I am, repeating all those things you said about me on Tuesday night, wouldn't go amiss. I was also hoping you might share with me everything you know, so that when the time comes I can hit the ground running.'

'You must be mad if you think I'd enable a rival like that.'

'I'm flattered you'd see me as a rival.'

'Stop fishing for compliments. I've already paid you plenty.'

She'd stretched like a cat and given him her most seductive smile. 'I'd make it worth your while.'

'How?'

She'd told him and within seconds he'd leapt off the lounger and dragged her to his study, to share with her some of the finer details of his job. He'd described the speed with which she got to grips with spreads and returns on investments as remarkable. Her ability to correctly apply external events to market movements was apparently uncanny. They hadn't got round to discussing client management, because by that point she'd been overcome with the need to express her appreciation, and he'd had her flat on her back on his desk a moment later.

Fifteen minutes after she finished her conversation with the event planner, Alex materialised on the terrace where she sat, looming over her like a pillar at the Temple of Apollo, and said, 'You have a visitor.'

'The helicopter?'

He nodded and Olympia frowned, sitting up a little straighter in her chair. In approximately thirty-six hours the island would be a hive of activity, but everyone involved in the setting up of the party would be arriving by boat, and she wasn't expecting anyone else.

'Who?' she asked, squinting up at him and hoping to God it wasn't her mother, who was supposed to be on the other side of the world, but with Selene, one never quite knew.

'It occurred to me that if you want to put on a show on Saturday night, you'll need an engagement ring. So I've had a selection flown over from Athens from which you can take your pick.'

Before she could react, he turned abruptly and gave a short nod. A man in an immaculately tailored pale grey suit, holding a silver briefcase, stepped into her line of sight. Behind him moved two other taller and bulkier men, both wearing black suits, sunglasses and earpieces. 'This is Aristotle Georgiou.'

Olympia recognised the name if not the face, and as he and Alex sat down beside her, her heart began to beat unnaturally fast. A ring? From one of the world's most prestigious jewellers? For her?

'How very thoughtful,' she murmured, trying to contain the dangerous thrills that were suddenly shooting through her.

'Hmm.'

Aristotle Georgiou set the case on the table and unlocked it. When he opened the lid she couldn't help but gasp. In front of her was the most dazzling array of diamonds, sapphires, rubies and emeralds she'd ever seen. She was no stranger to wealth and extravagance. Her mother's jewellery collection was allegedly worth billions. But these pieces were something else. Stones the size of coins flashed in the sun with a brilliance that was blinding. The gold and platinum in which they were set had been polished to a shine that gleamed. Each one was an exquisite work of art that for some bizarre reason brought tears to her eyes.

And she would have assumed that it would be easy to choose one because it wasn't as if the ring meant anything. It was simply for show and she knew that. So in theory all she had to do was close her eyes, pick one out at random and then put it on her finger.

But she couldn't. She couldn't move. She could barely even breathe. The only thought now banging around her head was, what if this were for real? What if Alex loved her and she loved him and this—the first piece of jewellery she'd ever been given—mattered?

For one electrifying moment the world tilted on its axis. The terrace beneath her feet disappeared. She'd never wanted anything so badly. To be loved and valued and the centre of someone's world—the idea of it made her head spin like a top and her heart ache so hard that she was in pain.

But she had to get a grip, she told herself frantically, fighting for control before she mortified herself by blubbing. That wasn't for her. She must never make the mistake of thinking any of what was happening here was for real. This relationship had been born out of necessity and that was all. Alex didn't want *her*. He didn't love her and she wasn't the centre of his world. By providing her with a ring, he was merely doing her a favour. It *didn't* matter, and she must not forget that.

'This one will do,' he said, his voice slicing through the thundering haze in her head as he plucked a ring from the case, evidently fed up with her inability to decide. 'It suits your colouring and passionate personality.'

'An emerald-cut red diamond solitaire set in a band of twenty-four-carat gold,' intoned the jeweller as Alex unceremoniously took her left hand and stuck it on her finger. 'Simple yet stunning. Very rare. An excellent choice.'

It was, Olympia thought, swallowing hard as she stared down at the ring, turned her hand this way and that, and tried not to like it too much. It fitted her finger perfectly. It sparkled like fire. She couldn't have chosen better herself.

But she must not overthink his reasons for choosing it, which, although hardly romantic, weren't random at all. She must not let herself be overtaken by what-ifs. Because if she did, if she wasn't careful and started to read more into this than there was, she could find herself in a whole heap of trouble.

CHAPTER TWELVE

AT TEN ON Saturday evening, Olympia stood at the top of the steps, in the flickering shadows, and gazed out over the terraces that cascaded down to the beach. She might be a screwup, she thought as she surveyed the scene with a warm ripple of pleasure, but she did know how to throw a party.

The event planner, who'd been working his socks off since first thing this morning, was worth every cent of his extortionate fee. Torches lined the jetty and the steps up to the house. Strings of lights edged the beach and draped through the trees. The pool shimmered like liquid jade, and around it sat tubs of myrtle perfuming the air. A DJ was playing music that had a sultry samba beat, which had the guests swaying, and the delicious food that her sister-in-law had provided was going down a treat.

For all Alex's misgivings, she wasn't tempted by any of the free-flowing alcohol. Once upon a time she'd got through a bottle of champagne a night with no problem at all, but she hadn't touched a drop of anything stronger than tonic water in a year, pregnant or not. She was perfectly happy with a margarita mocktail, especially since he'd rejected raspberry and passion fruit in favour of an alcohol-free beer, in what he'd described as a sign of solidarity. And that wasn't the only difference about this party. She was genuinely enjoying herself. She wasn't pretending to have a good time to mask the fact that she was miserable. In fact, the whole vibe of the evening was giving her a lovely warm glow.

Or perhaps that was the ring that she'd hardly been able to take her eyes off since he'd put it on her finger. Every time she looked at it she caught some new spark of fire, some new hue to its colour. With the sun on it, the stone shone light and clear. Now, as night fell and the stars came out, its rich dark tones made her think of intoxicating sensuality and heady desire. Of the twisted sheets and ragged breathing and wild abandonment she'd experienced with him last night, which had somehow felt more intense than before.

Beneath the moonlight, in between catching their breath and the rise of relentless desire, he'd told her about his need for financial security as a result of his parents' ruinous divorce. About how he'd been given a position in a bank by a sympathetic family friend and had turned out to have a knack for investment. The foreign markets in particular had become his playground, and within a year he'd made a cool five million. A decade later, he'd established his own funds, which traded a wide range of products on behalf of some of the richest people in the world.

He'd elaborated on his friendship with her brother, and the affair. Finally able to talk a little about his feelings, he'd confessed to the guilt he felt about introducing her mother to his father and the anger and resentment that had combined with the grief of losing both his parents. Olympia had tried to convince him that it wasn't his fault, but she didn't know if she'd succeeded. Nor did she have any further insight into how he felt now about her mother. He must have hated her at the time, and he obviously still harboured some ill will towards her, but to what extent? She'd asked but he'd prevaricated and she wondered if, perhaps, he didn't know either.

Now, instinctively, she sought him out, and her gaze landed on him almost immediately, because all evening she'd been aware of where he was. He was wearing a dark suit and an open-necked white shirt, and he looked so stunningly handsome that her breath caught in her throat for so long she went a little dizzy.

A moment ago, he'd been chatting to her brother, Leo, and before that, Zander. But now he was on his own once again, standing at the edge of the section of the beach that had been converted into a dancefloor, hands in his pockets, staring out to sea, and it struck her suddenly how very much alone he really was.

Most of the guests here were hers—friends, colleagues, all five of her siblings with their respective spouses. The few he'd invited seemed to be related to his business in some way. Even the Sheikh had put in a brief appearance, before being whisked away by his security detail. But when she'd subtly probed—while they'd all lauded his business acumen and success—

none of them had been able to shed any light on him personally.

She knew he had no family, and that was hardly his fault, but why did he have no friends? Why would anyone want to live like that? What was the real reason behind his avoidance of commitment? Surely it couldn't just be the demands of his job. And how did he actually feel about marrying her and fathering a child if he genuinely preferred his own company?

'Great party.'

These words, delivered in a familiar drawl, jolted Olympia out of her tumbling thoughts and she determinedly shook them off because tonight wasn't a night for such weighty ruminations. Tonight was a celebration. Or rather, she speedily amended as she turned to see that Zander had joined her at the balustrade, a *performance*.

'It is, isn't it?' she asked, the pride and pleasure with which she'd been regarding the proceedings faltering a fraction, before she forced herself to rally.

'Of course, I'd expect nothing less,' Zander said dryly. 'I thought I was a party animal, but you took it to a whole other level.'

'Not any more. You can't deny this is eminently civilised.'

'I wouldn't dream of it. It's the height of sophistication.' He looked at her shrewdly. 'So how are you coping?'

'Absolutely fine,' she said, slightly surprised by the question, which indicated a level of interest she'd learned not to expect. But then she hadn't envisaged all siblings plus in-laws turning up here tonight either, so who knew what was going on. 'Most of what I used to get up to was for show anyway. Rehab was more of a reset than a cure.'

'It did you good.'

'I know.'

Zander's expression turned unusually thoughtful as he folded his arms across his chest and leaned back against the balustrade. 'I was cornered by your new fiancé earlier.'

'I saw.'

'His reputation for ruthlessness precedes him, and I wouldn't want to get on the wrong side of him businesswise, but he seems like a decent enough guy. He can't sing your praises highly enough.'

At that, her eyebrows shot up and her heart skipped a quick beat. 'Oh?'

'I've been hearing all about your skill and tenacity, and the work you've been putting in to passing your exams. I understand he's shared with you all the trading tips he's picked up over the years. He's your biggest fan. He said that I was an idiot for not deploying your many talents in a more productive role, and that if I didn't give you the asset management job you want, he would.'

For a moment Olympia couldn't believe what she was hearing. Yes, she'd asked Alex to put in a good word for her, but she hadn't actually thought he'd do it. Was he simply holding up his side of the bargain, or did he genuinely believe her capable of doing the job she so badly wanted? Had he *fought* for her?

'Can you imagine the optics of that?' she said lightly while her mind raced, trying but failing to work out what it meant. 'The press would have a field day. It was bad enough when you hired me.'

'You may have a point,' Zander agreed with a nod. 'But he does too. You've done really well these past few months. I'm impressed. I should have seen it sooner, and I probably would have without the severe sleep deprivation a newborn baby brings. You'll find that out soon enough. Call me on Monday and we'll talk about your next move.'

'That would be great,' she said, noting not only the shadows beneath her brother's eyes but also the quiet way he seemed to light up at the mention of his tiny son, and wondering how Alex would feel when the time came. 'Thank you, Zander. I won't let you down.'

'You're welcome. I know you won't. But, although I'd like to take the credit, it's not me you should be thanking.'

Two hours into the party, Alex had to admit that it wasn't nearly as grim as he'd initially feared, but that was probably because he wasn't giving it his full attention. Even the endless stream of congratulations, which he'd assumed would have brought him out in hives, had failed to make much of an impression. He was too busy contemplating the ring.

If he'd ever thought that the outcome of selecting a

purely functional engagement ring merited any consideration, prior to Aristotle Georgiou's trip to his island, he would have assumed that once he'd dispatched the jeweller back to Athens that would have been that. He'd decided Olympia needed a prop and he'd got her one. Job done. He would not have anticipated it still playing on his mind some thirty-six hours later, yet it did.

Why, when she'd dithered and he'd had to step in before they both ossified where they sat—or worse, she made the wrong choice—had his involvement in the selection felt somehow portentous? Why, when instinct had told him, *this one*, had he for one mad moment wondered whether that instinct referred to the ring or the woman who'd be wearing it? And why did he feel such deep satisfaction whenever he caught her looking at it?

Initially, he'd simply pushed these frustratingly baffling questions from his head and forced himself to think instead about how brewing political unrest in various corners of the globe might affect his vast portfolio of funds. When the event organisers had shown up, and he'd immediately felt the beginnings of a headache, he'd escaped to the gym to sweat out his tension on the treadmill.

But later he'd taken her to bed, and for some reason the bloody ring had flashed like a beacon all sodding night, loosening his inhibitions and his tongue, and he might as well not have bothered with any of it. Had he had to share with her his innermost feelings about pretty much everything under the sun? No, he had not. But, as if she'd spiked him with some sort of truth drug, he'd barely been able to stop talking at all.

The insane disruption of the last day and a half had transformed his estate into some sort of dark twinkly flickering wonderland. With lights festooned about the place and artfully positioned pieces of furniture and random greenery, the gardens had never looked so appealing.

Nor had Olympia.

In a red knee-length halter-neck dress that she'd had sent over first thing this morning—because it apparently went with the ring that was causing him so much grief—she looked so stunning she took his breath away. Every time he caught sight of her he thought that his architecturally significant house wasn't the only remarkably lovely thing on the island.

As life and soul of the party, she was also in her element, chatting and laughing and making sure that everyone was having a good time, while attracting attention like moths to a flame. How she knew so many people he had no idea. She obviously collected them, and the thought that this might be his life from now on made him feel faint.

But at least the dreaded bombardment of memories hadn't materialised. All five of her siblings were here, which was a surprise when she'd implied that three of them would be unable to attend, but talking to them had been so uneventful he'd found himself wondering what on earth he'd been thinking all these years. There was nothing monstrous about any of them. They were all as perfectly normal as the next ultra-rich person. Zander had taken on board his observations about Olympia's many talents and how they might be of benefit to him with no problem at all.

In fact, the only conversation that had proved bothersome so far was the one he'd had with the Sheikh. 'Many congratulations on your forthcoming nuptials to Miss Stanhope,' Abdul Karim had said with a smile that had then turned disconcertingly knowing. 'I sensed something was up in Switzerland. Such sparks. I knew instantly that no one would be having dinner with her but you. I am never wrong about these things.'

Alex didn't know what exactly the Sheikh thought he could see. Although their chemistry was still pretty volatile, despite their very best efforts to dampen it, so perhaps that was the giveaway. But thankfully he hadn't been able to give the matter any further thought because Leo had then appeared at his side for the catchup he'd mentioned on the phone.

'Good to see you,' had been his former best friend's opening salvo as he'd clapped him on the back and shaken his hand. 'It's been a while.'

'Twenty years.'

'How have you been?'

'Good. You?'

'Great. Happy on Santorini building boats. Married. Two daughters. Hard to believe when you think about the things we used to get up to.'

'I'm sorry I cut you off so abruptly back then,' Alex had said with a frown, as Olympia's censure of how he'd handled the situation came back to him. 'But Selene destroyed my family. It left us all broken. I did what I had to do.'

Leo had looked at him shrewdly. 'I get that. Although it took me some time to work it out. I was sorry to hear about your parents.'

'I was sorry to hear about your father.'

'I could have done with a friend then,' Leo had said with a shrug. 'As could you, no doubt. But I've never seen much point in regret.'

'Nor me.'

'So you and Olympia… It's not just a convenience thing, is it?'

'What makes you say that?'

'You can't keep your eyes off each other.'

First the Sheikh, now Leo. What could they see that he couldn't?

'It's complicated,' Alex had muttered by way of prevarication.

'It always is.'

They'd chatted for a while longer, catching up on the last twenty years, and then Leo had sauntered off to find his wife, leaving Alex to ruminate on what his friend had said about the nature of his relationship with Olympia. It had changed over the last couple of days, he thought as he rubbed a hand along his jaw. He'd started talking about his feelings and the world hadn't imploded, even though he'd found it impossible to accept her perspective. So perhaps it was developing into one that went beyond mere convenience.

How he felt about that, however, he'd have to park for later analysis, because Olympia was making a bee-line for him with a determined yet dreamy look on her face, which he couldn't understand, but nevertheless it tightened his chest and constricted his lungs. The wave of emotion that he couldn't even begin to identify swept through him like a river bursting its banks, and nearly took out his knees.

But then something over his shoulder caught her eye and she stopped dead in her tracks, the dreaminess turning first to shock and then to appal. He glanced round to see what was causing her such consternation, fully prepared to come to her rescue if required, and then it was his turn to freeze.

Because coming to a whiplash of a stop at the end of the jetty, sending waves tumbling to the shore, was a speedboat. And being helped off that speedboat a moment later was a woman, swathed in gold lamé and draped in diamonds, a woman who looked not a day over forty even though she had to be in her mid-sixties.

Her mother.

His nemesis.

The very much uninvited, deeply unwelcome Selene Stanhope.

CHAPTER THIRTEEN

OH, DEAR GOD, thought Olympia, watching in abject horror as her mother sashayed along the jetty as if she were on the red carpet at some international film premiere. What the hell was she doing here? Why wasn't she in Argentina with her cattle billionaire? And how on earth had she found out about the party?

More pressingly how was she—Olympia—going to handle it? Unsurprisingly, in a crowd of two hundred, Leo and Zander—who were more used to dealing with this than she was—were nowhere to be seen. But a quick glance at Alex, standing there on the beach, frozen to the spot, his jaw so tight it looked as though it might be about to shatter, told her that despite his claims to the contrary, he evidently wasn't as blasé about the affair as he'd tried to make out. And, therefore, she knew without the shadow of a doubt that her mother could not stay.

Having no time to ponder the fact that her loyalty fell so unquestionably in his camp, or to wonder what that might mean, she galvanised into action, hurried down the steps and onto the jetty, to intercept Selene before she could do too much damage.

'Darling,' cried her mother expansively, as she threw open her arms for a hug that she had never earned and was never going to get. 'I heard you were having a party to celebrate your engagement. The last of my children to fly the nest. My littlest one. I've come to offer you my congratulations. A whirlwind engagement and a baby on the way. Quick work. That's my girl. I'm so proud. And to think I was worried you'd become boring.'

This outpouring of maternal interest—all for show, of course—did not faze Olympia in the slightest. Nor did the dig about the changes she'd made to her life, or the suggestion that they were alike. The only thing she was interested in was containing the chaos that Selene whipped up wherever she went, and then finding out if Alex was all right.

'You need to leave,' she said, taking her mother by the arm and wheeling her back in the direction she'd come.

'But I've only just arrived.'

'You weren't invited.'

'I assumed it was an oversight.'

'It wasn't.'

'Well, this wasn't the welcome I was expecting, I must say,' protested her mother with a pout. She broke free and tried to bypass Olympia to join the party. 'But no matter. I'm here now to liven things up.'

'Get back on the boat and off my island, Selene.'

The sudden appreciative gleam in her mother's eyes, as much as the cold clipped tones, told Olympia that

Alex was behind her. A fierce streak of protectiveness swept through her and she instinctively inched
closer to him.

'Are you the groom?' asked Selene, running her gaze
over him with such outrageously blatant interest that
Olympia wanted to push her into the sea. 'Well done,
Olympia. He's very handsome. In fact,' she said, tilting her head suddenly and giving him as thoughtful a
look as her overly Botoxed face would allow, 'he looks
like someone I used to know a long time ago. Let me
think…'

'I really wouldn't,' Olympia warned, glancing at
Alex, noting both the ice-cold fury burning in his eyes
and the seething tension he radiated.

'Nikolas Andino, I believe it was,' said Selene,
blithely blind to the danger she was in. 'Any relation?'

'I'm his son.'

'Ah, yes. Now I remember. Weren't you once a friend
of Leo's?'

'Until you blew my family apart.'

'Did I? Well, these things happen,' she said with
a dismissiveness that was shocking, even for her.
'But goodness,' she added, a hideously inappropriate
twinkle now lighting her eyes, 'if I were twenty years
younger and you weren't marrying my daughter and
I didn't have scruples… Now, who's going to get me
a drink?'

'No one,' he said. 'You are not staying.'

'That's what I said,' Olympia put in, feeling sick to
her stomach at her mother's callousness and her flirt-

ing. *Scruples? If only.* 'I'm having trouble making her listen.'

'No problem.'

Without preamble, he stepped forward and picked Selene up in his arms and then dumped her back in the boat. 'Take her back,' he said to the driver, in a tone that had the man nodding frantically and hastily loosening the lines. 'Do not return.'

'Well. I don't think I've ever been treated so rudely,' Selene exclaimed as he pulled in the fenders and fired the engine. 'Do not expect my presence at the wedding.'

'We won't.'

Heart pounding and head spinning, Olympia watched the boat disappear into the distance, then turned to the big angry man beside her, whose opinion of her mother was now blindingly obvious.

'So that was clearly as horrendous for you as it was for me,' she said, awash with concern for him—for them—and the need to do whatever it took to make this right. 'Are you OK?'

'I'm fine,' he said, and off he stalked.

But Alex wasn't fine. He wasn't fine at all. He felt as if he was about to throw up. Pass out. As if he were having an out of body experience. Somehow he managed to hold it together as he weaved his way through the guests, smiling here, muttering a suitable response there. But the minute he reached his study, all semblance of composure disappeared.

With shaking hands, he cracked open a bottle of

whisky he'd swiped from the kitchen en route through the house. He filled a glass and knocked it back, but the alcohol that burned down his throat and hit his stomach did nothing to numb the shock of seeing the woman who'd destroyed his parents' marriage and wrecked his life.

The second he'd laid eyes on her he'd been slammed back to the past, to the arguments and the tears, the giving up of his place at university, the devastating re-alisation that his father was human, just as susceptible to all the frailties that implied as anyone else. He was filled with the fiery cocktail of emotions that he'd told Olympia about but hadn't experienced in years—guilt, anger, resentment, fear. If he'd had any doubt whatso-ever about how he still felt about Selene Stanhope, it had gone. He seethed with rage. He loathed her with a passion. Twenty years seemed to have vanished, just like that.

The door opened. He first stiffened, then jerked his head round to see Olympia walk in.

'I'm so sorry about that,' she said before he could tell her to get out and leave him alone. 'I had no idea she was going to turn up. I genuinely thought she was safely several thousand miles away.'

He poured himself another measure and downed that in one too. 'I don't want to talk about it.'

'I know you don't,' she said, the concern he detected in her voice as unwanted and unwelcome as the pity he could see on her face. 'But I think you should.'

'No.'

'Please. Tell me how you feel. You need to deal with this.'

He did not need to deal with this, he had too many feelings to manage, and he did not need her telling him what to do. 'Stop it,' he said, his pulse hammering at his temple so loudly he could hear it. 'Stop trying to get inside my head.'

'I want to help.'

But he didn't want her help. Not now. Not ever. He never had, yet somehow she'd demolished every one of his carefully erected barriers so that he was doing everything she asked of him. Suddenly it was all too much. He was being thwacked over the head with the terrible realisation that history was repeating itself. Everything he'd feared had come to pass. Look at how swiftly he'd fallen under her spell. How easily he'd been seduced. She'd wrapped him around her finger with no trouble at all, even though he'd sworn that that would never happen, and he'd been so overwhelmed by lust, by her, he'd just let it all happen. He'd even told her she could have whatever she wanted. What the hell had he been doing this past week?

'I'm done dancing to your tune,' he said, suddenly feeling very cold and numb.

She paled. 'What do you mean?'

'Your mother implied that you were like her, and she was right. You have the same allure, the same power. Just as she trapped my father in her web, you've caught me in yours. You've had me doing things I never had any intention of doing. You've turned me into someone I don't recognise, and I won't allow it to continue.'

For a moment, she appeared to have nothing to say. Her eyes swam with hurt and confusion, and he steeled himself not to care.

'Is that really what you think?'

'Yes.'

'Well, that's not very fair.'

His brows snapped together. 'What?'

'You don't strike me as a man who does anything he doesn't want to,' she said with a jut of her chin, the hurt and confusion morphing into resolve right in front of him. 'You're not passive in any way. You don't *let* things happen to you. If you go along with something it's because you want to. I admit to provoking you into action on occasion, but you didn't have to suggest marriage. You didn't have to buy me a ring. And you certainly didn't have to put in a good word with Zander, although I am grateful for that. I may resemble my mother, and I may have once behaved a bit like she does, but I'm not like her. I refuse to be. Not just for my own sense of self, but because I want my child to have a better start in life than I did. I want it to know love and security, to have a better mother than I do, and to never have to question its self-worth. We've moved way beyond this, Alex. So don't think I don't know what you're doing here.'

'What's that?'

'You're deflecting.'

He scowled at her. 'What makes you the expert?'

'I learned all about it in rehab. It's a defence mechanism. You're in shock, being battered by painful memories, and you're taking it out on me. And that's fine. For now. I understand. But you need to get over the issues you have with my mother. And you *must*,' she entreated. 'For the baby's sake. For my sake and yours and ours. I know she's a nightmare, and she's caused you untold misery, but we have a real shot at this. Neither of us needs to be lonely any more. We have a connection that goes beyond the baby, and we can build on that. So put your past behind you as I did mine. Look forwards, not backwards. It's been twenty years. Move on. Let it go.'

For a moment, Alex could do no more than reel. His breath was stuck in his throat. He felt as though he'd been hit with a hammer. *Let it go? Was she serious?*

'I can't *let it go*,' he said, so scathingly that she flinched. 'It's part of who I am and always will be. My entire adult life has been based on it. I never asked for an emotional connection and I certainly don't want one. I won't be enslaved by you, Olympia. I won't be spat out when you're done, as your mother did to my father. I hate the way you make me feel. The lust I have for you threatens my control and destroys my reason. That's why I snubbed you the night we met. Why I left you in the stairwell in Switzerland. You make me do things I'm not proud of. Believing I could control it was a mistake. *We* are a mistake.'

She was as white as a sheet. 'You can't mean that.'

'I do.' He'd never meant anything more in his life.

'But it's not unfixable. You can move out of my house and back to yours. In due course, we will call off the engagement. There's still plenty of time to come to some arrangement over the baby. There's no reason we can't be civilised about this. In the meantime, however, I'd like to be left alone.'

Stunned and shaken, Olympia left Alex's study and stumbled to the cloakroom, where she was violently sick. Somehow she made it up the stairs, into the bedroom they were sharing and sank down onto the bed. Outside, the party was in full swing, but how could return to it when her world had just fallen apart? How could she chat and smile and radiate happiness when inside she was in pieces?

He resented her allure.

He hated the way she made him feel.

He didn't want any sort of relationship with her.

How was she to stand it when, for her, with regards to all these points, the opposite was true?

She'd thought the prenup had caused her excruciating pain, but that was nothing compared with the indescribable agony she was feeling now. It was as if he'd reached into her chest and ripped out her heart. She'd never cried, not once, not even as a kid, yet now tears were leaking out of her eyes like the Haliacmon.

And it wasn't because her reputation would suffer from a broken engagement. Or because she feared for the future of their child.

It was because she'd fallen in love with him.

Over the last week, he'd come to mean everything to her. He'd given her all the things she'd been missing her entire life. He'd built up her self-esteem and uncovered her worth. He'd fought in her corner and shown her respect. The protectiveness he'd displayed towards their child had assured her that her upbringing hadn't been normal, and her response to it had not been her fault. He'd made her feel valued, special, cared for.

And to have it suddenly snatched away was like losing a limb.

He'd told her she could have whatever she wanted, but that wasn't true. She wanted him and he wasn't hers. But then why would he be? She was a bad return on investment and always had been. What had made her think she deserved to love and be loved anyway? To dream that, like Zander and Mia, she and Alex might find happiness after being brought together by an unexpected pregnancy? How could she have been so deluded?

But those were questions for later, she thought with a sniff and a blow of her nose. She could regret her loyalty, her defence of him and her stupidity another time. Right now, she had to figure out what to do. She couldn't stay here with a man who didn't want her. So she'd go back to the party and see it through. It wouldn't be the first time she'd put on a show while dying inside. And at the end of the night, mercifully soon, she'd pack up her things and stow away on one of the ferries returning the guests to the mainland. Once home she would lick her wounds in private and figure out how to proceed from there.

Giving herself a shake and taking a deep steadying breath, Olympia got to her feet. She powdered her nose, fluffed out her hair and practised her smile until it looked natural not manic. And then, summoning up every drop of strength and composure she possessed, calling on resources she hadn't had cause to use in a year, she headed downstairs.

CHAPTER FOURTEEN

ON AN INTELLECTUAL LEVEL, Alex knew that beyond the walls of his study the party was still going on, even if he couldn't hear it over the chaos screaming through his head. But it hardly registered. All he could focus on was the conversation that had just taken place and still thundered through his thoughts.

He'd been absolutely right to cool things down with Olympia, he assured himself grimly as, through the window, he watched a firework shoot into the sky and explode into a shower of glittering stars. They'd been moving too far and too fast. If he'd allowed the relationship to continue as it was, he had no doubt he would have been signing himself up for untold misery.

So why did he feel as though he'd been gutted like a fish? Why did he feel he'd be haunted for the rest of his days by the devastation on her face?

He couldn't seem to shake the points she'd made from his head. All he could think now was that the man he didn't recognise wasn't the one she'd turned him into, but the one he'd described as himself. That man sounded weak and powerless, and that *wasn't* him. So perhaps he *had* been lashing out at her, which *wasn't* fair.

And those observations weren't the only ones spinning through his thoughts on some torturous, relentless loop. No matter how hard he tried to shut it up, an irritating voice in his head demanded to know whether, despite the discouraging risk–reward ratio of friends, he was really content existing in isolation.

Might he in fact use work to stave off loneliness? Why had he wanted to refute her repeated declarations that he was only interested in their baby? Where had the shudder he'd always experienced at the thought of being connected to her for years gone? And if he was really so averse to romantic commitment, then why had Olympia's 'we's and 'our's given him such a kick these past few days?

Because he was in love with her.

The thought shot through his head like an arrow, and lodged in his brain. Every muscle in his body froze.

No. He couldn't be. It was impossible. He'd spent his entire life avoiding such a fate. He'd seen the damage love could do when it failed. He knew how fickle and treacherous the heart was. He'd sworn never to hand responsibility for his well-being and happiness to someone else for them to destroy.

But that insidious little voice was once again hammering him with questions and demanding answers. What if love didn't tear you apart but built you up? What if a heart could be steadfast and true? And what if that someone else didn't wreck your well-being and happiness, but treasured and nurtured it?

How Olympia had felt about him before he'd ruined

what had been developing he had no idea. Could she be in love with him too? Had the moment with the engagement ring been as significant for her as it had for him? She'd stood up for him. She'd convinced him that he could be the sort of father he was determined to be. He'd done the same for her, and he wasn't finished. He wanted to prove to her that she was worth more than one or two nights—that she might be a handful but she was his handful. He wanted her in his life for ever, stirring up his boring staid existence like a tornado. He wanted this child of theirs to be the first of many, to create a big noisy family of his own.

But, by needing to keep himself safe—by being completely blind to not only what the Sheikh and Leo had seen, but also in his violent reaction to the engagement ring—he'd destroyed any chance of it. He'd put his fears, his needs, above all else, which meant that he was no better than his father. History *was* repeating itself and he was at the root of it, so he was the only person who could do anything about it.

Olympia was right, he thought, his head spinning, his chest tight. He did have to get over the issues he had with his father and Selene. He did have to let it go and focus on the family he could have, rather than the one he'd lost. As she had, with the past and the prenup. She didn't dwell or stew. She moved on. She had more courage in her little finger than he did in his entire body. She was magnificent.

And he'd told her they were a mistake.

He'd told her she was just like her mother.

He was in love with her and he'd told her that he hated it.

What the hell had he done?

An image of her face, pale and wrecked, flashed before his eyes, and Alex felt an ice-cold sweat break out all over his skin. Nausea rolled up his throat. Whatever she felt for him, she cared enough to be hurt. He had to fix the mess he'd made. She was too important to lose. And to think that he'd assumed she'd be the one to screw up. How much more of a jackass could he be?

He surged to his feet and went in search of her. She wasn't in the house. Or on the terraces. He found her down on the beach, surrounded by a group of guests, and never had he wanted to get rid of a bunch of people more. To the untrained eye, the smile on her face would be blinding. But to him it looked like a struggle. There was a sheen to her eyes that suggested she'd been crying, and the realisation that he'd done that to her cut him to the bone.

'Olympia.'

'Ah, here he is,' she said smoothly, as if the conversation in his study had never happened. 'Everyone was wondering where you'd got to.'

'Just taking a moment to sort a few things out,' he said, regret and the need to put this right battering him hard. 'If you'll excuse us, I'd like a word with my fiancée.'

'We mustn't neglect our guests.'

'They can spare us for a few moments.'

'Maybe later.'

'This can't wait.'

Before she could protest further, he took her elbow and steered her away.

'Once again, you're wheeling me away from a party,' she said with a tonelessness that he didn't like one little bit, but for which he had only himself to blame. 'And look what happened the last time you did that.'

'Best move of my life.'

'What?'

Behind the tree he'd led her to, he let her go and rubbed his hands over his face, before thrusting them in the pockets of his trousers.

'I apologise for earlier,' he said gruffly. 'I didn't mean any of it. You were right. I was thrown by your mother showing up. I handled it badly. So very badly.'

She shrugged and stared at a point somewhere over his left shoulder. 'It's fine.'

'It's not fine. It's not fine at all.'

'It really doesn't matter.'

'It does. There's more. So much more I have to apologise for and tell you.'

'But I don't want to hear it,' she said, her gaze finally meeting his, shaking him to the core with its emptiness. 'In fact, I don't want to hear anything you have to say. I'm not interested in your apologies or anything else. I'm done, Alex. You wanted me gone and I'm going. The minute this party's over, I'm leaving. This is the last time we'll speak until the baby's born. We can communicate through our lawyers when necessary.'

She glanced over her shoulder. 'Now I really must get back to the party.'

She disappeared before he had time to blink, let alone think. He could barely breathe through the panic that gripped him at the thought that he'd blown it for good, let alone muster up a response. But as the fog in his head cleared, he was filled with the resolve that had made him a billionaire before he hit thirty.

If she thought this was the last time they spoke, she could think again. They would not be communicating through lawyers. She was leaving over his dead body. And she would absolutely hear what he had to say.

Back in the thick of things, Olympia took a surreptitious look at her watch. Half an hour to go. Half an hour until this ridiculously painful charade was over and she could go home.

If she'd known how difficult it was going to be to endure the congratulations and the increasing raucousness of the occasion she'd have remained holed up in the bedroom, because there was absolutely nothing to celebrate. But at least she'd stayed strong when Alex had dragged her off for a word. At least she hadn't broken down and begged him for a second chance. She'd never have got over the humiliation.

It was bad enough that she hurt so much, she thought, her throat aching from all the lumps she'd had to swallow down. She was so stupid for letting him get to her. For caring what he thought about her. She should have got used to rejection by now. She should have remembered that affection was never freely given. For years she'd avoided transferring her neediness onto a man for fear of the inevitable rejection, but she'd done it anyway. She was her own worst enemy in practically every way there was.

The music ground to a halt. Everyone hushed. She turned to see Alex behind the DJ's decks, holding the microphone and staring straight at her and, *oh, God,* what was going on now? Was he about to reveal that the engagement was off? Was her reputation once again about to be decimated? Where could she run? Where could she hide?

'I'd like to propose a toast,' he said, and she thought despairingly, to what? A lucky escape and freedom? The ruthless destruction of someone he hated? 'To my bride-to-be, Olympia Stanhope, with whom I'm head over heels in love.'

Her heart stopped. Her breath caught in her throat. All the blood rushed to her feet and she very nearly swooned. But these were just fine words, she reminded herself, and he wasn't to be trusted, not after the cruel things he'd hurled at her in his study. He wasn't in love with her. He couldn't be. It made no sense.

'She won't believe that,' he said, as if he could read her mind. 'I haven't made it easy. In fact, I may well have made it impossible. I've said some terrible things, and the apologies I owe her are too many to count. But I will address every single one of them, however long it takes, if she'll give me the chance.' He visibly swallowed and, when he continued, it was with a crack in his voice. 'Olympia, you are the strongest, bravest woman I've ever met. You are clever and resourceful and you don't give up. You have repeatedly blown me away with your willingness to face challenges head on, and our child will be so lucky to have you as its mother. I don't deserve you, I am aware of that, but if you'll forgive me for being such a self-centred jerk, I'll spend the rest of my life trying to. I will do everything in my power to make you love me as much as I love you. This is what I wanted to tell you. All this and how very sorry I am for screwing things up.'

He stopped and put down the mike, the silence deafening, and suddenly all eyes were on her. But she didn't know what to do. She didn't know what to think. Her heart was beating too fast in her chest and her head was spinning so wildly her vision blurred.

But her inner voice of reason, the one that had got her through the many struggles she'd had with her insecurities this past week, was trying to make its way through the chaos. It was insisting that maybe actions spoke louder than words. That maybe he'd been more thrown off balance by her mother's appearance than she'd thought. He was so supremely confident, such a tower of strength, that he appeared invincible. But he wasn't. No one was.

He'd just declared how he felt about her in front of two hundred people. He'd spun the party better than she ever could. He'd addressed her every fear and laid it to rest. All that envy for the baby who had his attention, and her siblings who'd found the happiness she'd never thought she deserved. Well, maybe she did. No. Not maybe. She *did*.

And suddenly, with the last of her defences crumbling to dust, Olympia couldn't stand being so far away from him any longer.

Her heart raced as she set off in his direction, the agog guests parting for her like the sea. He met her halfway and stopped. But she didn't. She walked right up to him, threw her arms around his neck and kissed him with every single thing she could now allow herself to feel for him, oblivious to the whoops and cheers around them.

He held her tight as if he never wanted to let her go, and she could feel the thundering of his heart against her own. 'I've never had anyone fight for me like that before,' she said dizzily when they broke for breath. 'I've never had anyone on my side.'

'I'll never leave it.' His eyes were dark, glazed with passion and emotion, but his expression was grave. 'I'll never stop fighting for you, *agape mou*. I'm so sorry for everything I said. I didn't mean any of it. You were right. I was lashing out. I was terrified. All my adult life I've feared the destruction love can cause. But not anymore. I don't want to be in hock to the past. I intend to make peace with Selene, who you are *nothing* like. It's beyond time. I want to look to the future, a future that includes you and our baby and hopefully many more. Since you came into it, my life has been so much more exciting, so much more everything. I love you. Very much.' He stared into her eyes, and she could see in his a flicker of uncertainty, a vulnerability that indicated his sincerity and intensified the emotion filling her up. 'Do you think in time you might be able to feel the same?'

'No,' she said, smiling up at him, leaning in for another kiss drenched in love. 'Because I already do.'

EPILOGUE

Eleven months later

ON A SATURDAY morning in early June, Olympia stood at the entrance to the Metropolitan Cathedral of Athens and took a moment to survey the achingly beautiful scene before her. The white columns, arches and gilded dome gleamed in the sunlight that streamed in through the windows. Flowers cascaded from urns, and the black and white marble of the floor shone.

Then her gaze landed on Alex. He stood at the other end of the aisle, in front of the altar, so tall, solid and handsome he took her breath away—and everything else simply disappeared.

Leo, his best man and the friend he'd reclaimed.

Elias, their four-month-old son, asleep in the arms of his doting Aunt Daphne.

The guests that filled the pews on both sides, because he'd opened himself up to the idea of friends and was no longer an island.

She could see nothing but him.

They'd come such a long way since the night of the engagement party, she thought, her heart filling with such joy she was surprised it hadn't burst. At work she'd moved into the role she'd wanted and was already outperforming the market. These days she hardly ever had a moment of self-doubt, and she knew her worth because Alex regularly reminded her of it.

As promised, he'd let go of his feelings towards her mother, although he'd made it very clear he'd be taking a zero-tolerance approach. Selene had a front-row seat this morning, and so far had demonstrated exemplary behaviour. Of course, it was still early, and who knew what might happen by nightfall, but she seemed to be just intimidated enough by her soon-to-be son-in-law to toe the line.

The day their son was born had been the happiest of her life. This, everything she'd never dreamed she could have—security, stability, the love of a man she adored—came a very close second.

'Ready?'

In response to Zander's question, Olympia nodded, her throat too thick to speak, because she'd never been readier for anything. The organ struck up, filling the church with music, and she threaded her arm through his. The congregation hushed. Everyone stood and turned. And with a smile that was wide and bright, barely able to contain the happiness swirling around inside her, she walked towards her future.

* * * * *

KIDNAPPED FOR HIS REVENGE

CAITLIN CREWS

MILLS & BOON

To Voltron, now and forever.

CHAPTER ONE

As KIDNAPS WENT, Irinka Scott-Day thought hers was rather civilized.

The London weather was hideous, which was to say, typical for an April morning. Irinka had left her sweetheart of a house in Notting Hill in a rush that morning. Normally she liked to stop and admire the eclectic bright colors of the houses and doors along the Portobello Road where she lived—guaranteed to lift the spirits even in the midst of the worst of Britain's gray doldrums—but not today. She was not a person who was easily frazzled, and would not describe herself that way even now, but she had been out entirely too late the night before.

On the job, naturally. Irinka had given up dating sometime during her university years—

Well.

She had never *dated*, exactly. And she knew precisely when and why she'd given it up after that summer that she would also not describe as *dating*—because what an insipid word that was and how little it applied to those hot, breathless months—but there was no point thinking about the epic mistakes of the past.

Forget the past and lose an eye, but dwell on the past and lose both eyes, as her mother liked to say, claiming it was a Russian proverb though, possibly, it was her own bloodthirstiness.

But Irinka did not want to think about her mother. She loved Roksana dearly, but her mother was not what anyone would call a *soothing influence*.

When Irinka dashed outside, doing a great impression of *frazzled*, she'd expected the typical sullen clouds and grim drizzle and had dressed accordingly. She was not prepared for the rain to be heaving it down, bucketing into the streets so that the tired old roads were almost immediately swamped.

It was the bloody great puddles that did it, in the end.

Because she rushed outside expecting to make her way to Notting Hill Gate to either hail a black cab— because she was supernaturally capable of summoning cabs at will, an unimaginable feat in the press and clamor of Central London, especially when it was pissing it down—or take her chances on the Tube. But it was so wet that she paused at the curb outside her own brightly painted door, debating whether or not she ought to go and change the exquisite leather boots she was wearing, produced by the finest Italian craftsmen in a little-known Milanese shop because she liked an artisan, for her proper wellies.

She didn't notice the gleaming black SUV until it was right there in front of her. Maybe it had been there all along, idling and waiting for her to emerge. It was hard to tell in the downpour and in any case, what she was focused on was the fact she was soaked where she stood.

"You look like you need a ride, ma'am," came a solicitous female voice, and the truth was that Irinka *did* need a ride.

All she saw was the black vehicle, and perhaps her need of it, and so she gratefully climbed inside, expecting it to be a minicab or an Uber or the like. It didn't surprise her at all that one should simply *appear* because she needed it. It was her single magical trick, after all. She settled back, sighing a little at the inescapable fact that magic or no magic, she was sopping wet after standing outside all of ten seconds.

Then the SUV started moving. And the locks engaged, a soft but insistent *click*.

Her intuition kicked in, sending a little jolt down her spine.

There were no licenses on display on the console and as she looked for them, an interior window went up and created a barrier between her and the driver. She had the urge to try the door handle nearest her, but restrained herself.

Because if Irinka knew one thing in this life, it was that the appearance of unconcern and ease—or of sheer indifference, whatever worked—was often the only weapon required in most situations.

So she folded her hands, gazed serenely out the window, and made herself wait as the vehicle that was very obviously not a taxi of any kind made its way out of Central London and was soon enough on a motorway, heading away from the city.

That was worrisome.

This was when she decided that she was, in fact, being kidnapped.

Irinka considered pulling out her mobile and texting an SOS to her best friends, who also happened to be her business partners. But what could they do other than make calls that might or might not help when she had no identifying features of the vehicle to share and didn't know where they were headed? Together, she and her friends ran His Girl Friday, an agency of requirement, as Irinka liked to call it. They catered toward unconventional solutions to certain problems for the very wealthy. A niche market, perhaps. Luckily enough, there was no shortage of wealthy people with entirely too much money on their hands, happy to outsource whenever possible.

Irinka and her friends had found an opportunity, gone after it, and made it theirs.

They had all gone to university together. Lynna cooked for tremendously wealthy people who liked to have gourmet meals on call. Auggie was the queen of PR, rescuing the reputations of those who probably didn't deserve it, but could certainly afford it. Maude was something of a forest creature, which was helpful as she did groundskeeping on grand old estates and made the ancient gardens she found there nothing short of enchanted.

Irinka's contribution was the one they never advertised. What she did was only whispered about in certain exalted circles. Word of mouth was the only way that a particular sort of wealthy man with a specific, thorny problem knew to reach out to her—or would consider doing so in the first place. Because otherwise, she simply looked like the typical bored heiress like so many of the girls she'd known her whole life, made up of pedigrees and impressive parentage, some fame and some notoriety. All of them kicking around the Big Smoke, marking time while they waited for the various trust funds and inheritances to kick in.

To the outside world, Irinka was merely the secretary of His Girl Friday, general dogsbody, and office manager. And she wasn't half bad at those things—she considered herself a dab hand at a spreadsheet, as it happened—but the truth was that really, the office didn't need much managing or secretarial support. The four of them did more work in their group chat than many of the billionaires Irinka had spent time with did in the course of their endless board meetings and tedious rolling phone calls.

The truth was, first, that she had no trust funds or incoming grand inheritances. She was not an heiress, not in the way that people assumed she was. She was, through no fault of her own, the infamous illegitimate daughter of an extremely high-in-the-instep duke, however. That was a fact. And it was true that he had settled something of a fortune upon her in the hopes that she would go away.

There are fortunes and then there are dukedoms, Roksana had said dismissively when the papers had all screeched to the world the settlement details she'd won for her daughter in court. *Trust a duke to throw a few crumbs and pretend it's a castle.*

That was what happened when a stodgy old duke had an illicit affair with an extremely spiteful Russian supermodel—the mononymous Roksana, beloved in all fashion circles as much for her cutting remarks as for the vicious blades of her cheekbones—and then imagined that he could walk away from her and face no repercussions.

It had taken a great deal of tabloid attention and several court cases to not only prove Irinka's paternity beyond any legal or biological doubt, but to force the Duke to provide for her in a comparable fashion to the way he provided for the children he'd had with his long-suffering blue-blooded wife. Irinka had thus learned early on that the best way to get men to do what she wanted was to smile prettily, threaten vaguely, and invoke her mother's name whenever necessary.

She had been a fixture of the society pages since she was a teenager, sometimes because she sought attention and sometimes because she couldn't escape it. That was when she'd learned that people—sometimes a whole lot of people—preferred the idea of her to the reality of her, at least according to the sneering press. Irinka had adjusted accordingly, and had become mysterious. This was useful when she was at the same absurd functions that her legitimate half siblings attended, where they could all bare their teeth at each other and try to outdo one another's level of icy, vicious courtesy—and then Irinka would disappear.

It was one of Irinka's favorite games, if she was honest. They were mean, she was mysterious, and this was how her reputation was built.

And it was important that she kept it up even now that she was older and supposedly wiser on this side of her university days, because it was important that most of the largely inbred European society viewed her with the same vague mix of distaste and weaponized pity that her half siblings did. Oh, sure, it was buried under jolly laughter and endless invitations to this party or that. But at the end of the day they would all whisper behind their hands that it was *lucky* Irinka was so pretty, because there was certain to be someone blue-blooded and broke—or cluelessly American—who would be more than happy to take her on.

Eventually.

But it would never make her anything but the discarded by-blow of a duke. In those circles, that was still a stain.

And the sort of pitiable, socially questionable creature Irinka was widely held to be by a certain strata of high society could be expected to do no better than to maintain a pointless secretarial job with her university mates, waiting for her pedigreed prince—or some nouveau riche Wall Street banker, the more likely bet—to arrive.

The reality was that Irinka had learned early in life that it was best to hide in plain sight. In fact, she'd become an expert at it.

And that was why some of the wealthiest men in the world hired her. They could count on her discretion, because she was excellent at disguises. Not only her appearance, but her voice, adopting any accent she pleased. She could change her mannerisms and even how she held her body, so that even people who knew her would not recognize her if she didn't want them to.

She had become the most sought-after breakup artist in Europe.

Irinka was the one who appeared when a man needed to end a relationship and needed to make certain that there would be no attempts on the part of the woman that he was scraping off to chase after him, begging for second thoughts and third chances. She had played wounded wives and furious girlfriends, as well as slinky other women, too many times to count.

Sometimes she was the woman at the bar who the man in question couldn't seem to look away from, infuriating his date into losing his number. Sometimes she walked into hotel rooms, "surprising" an intimate scene. Sometimes she arranged herself in a bed in the same hotel rooms, claiming to be the significant other who'd come as a surprise and who, pray, was the woman on her man's arm?

Being so good at these performances of hers was a great way to drum up business.

What it was not, she reflected as the SUV drove on, taking her farther and farther away from London, was a decent way to make sure she had no enemies.

All the ways and whys a person might take against a woman who did the job she did clattered about in her head as she sat there, locked up tight in the back seat. She kept gazing out the window, looking as if, perhaps, she might have lapsed off into a spot of meditation. Or so she hoped.

But she was not entirely surprised to find that when the SUV turned off the motorway, it was to head toward a private airfield.

Truthfully, it was not *completely* unexpected that

someone might wish to kidnap her. It did not *beggar belief* that she might have upset a person to this degree.

Irinka supposed that meant she lived a life of drama, the very sort Roksana had lived, still lived, and always warned her daughter to avoid. In dark and dramatic tones. But it was significantly less dramatic than her childhood, which had involved being chased by paparazzi and fielding abuse hurled at her on the streets by those who took umbrage against her mother's tactics and temerity.

Really, a pleasant ride in the back of a lovely vehicle and the prospect of a plane ride was a bit of a holiday compared to all that.

But in an abundance of caution, she took her mobile and stuffed it into her boot, where it pressed against her shin and was not exactly comfortable—but was less likely to be confiscated straight off. Then she waited as serenely as possible as the SUV drove straight out onto the tarmac and pulled up next to a waiting jet.

The window went down between her and her driver and the woman looked back through the rearview mirror with a particular, assessing sort of look that told Irinka many things. Most importantly, that this woman worked for someone else. She had that look of smooth, hired muscle. There was that blankness around the eyes.

Not, in other words, the person she really had to worry about. Not the person engineering this. So there was really no point attempting to extricate herself, because a look at the woman made it clear that she would suppress all such efforts. And quickly.

"Are you going to walk onto that plane or am I going to have to carry you?" the woman asked.

A glance at her biceps made Irinka believed that she could do this. And without much difficulty.

"Are those my only options?" Irinka asked, languidly. "Because I was headed to the spa. This does seem like rather an interruption."

The woman didn't laugh. She didn't really respond at all. She just continued to stare, dead-eyed, through the rearview mirror and it occurred to Irinka that perhaps she should be slightly more concerned than she was. That this was becoming less of a lark and more of a problem by the moment.

She wasn't sure that hysterics would work, however, which was a pity. She was excellent at hysterics. She could turn them on and off, complete with tears, at will and often did. "May I ask where I'm going?" she asked brightly. "I do hope it's a holiday. It's exhausting to be kidnapped. I'm afraid I'm going to need quite a bit of recovery."

"My employer will explain everything to you when you arrive in Italy," the woman told her.

"*Amo l'Italia!*" Irinka cried. Theatrically. "How I long to gaze upon the waters of Lake Como. Or wander the ruins of so many centuries of civilization in the Eternal City, *la bella Roma*. Or *immerse myself* in the grandeur of Firenze's art and culture—"

"You are going to Venice," the driver said curtly.

Venice.

Irinka felt the usual deep lurch inside of her that she always did when she heard the name of that city, but she shoved it aside. She inclined her head in acquiescence and the woman got out of the vehicle, then opened her door. Irinka climbed out, not sure if she was happy or offended that the rain had settled down to a faint mist. Sheets of rain might have helped now. At least, where her mood was concerned.

As she stood there, contemplating the vagaries of the weather, the woman held out her hand. It was not an encouraging sort of gesture. Not from this tall, muscled woman who looked like she ate CrossFit gyms for breakfast.

"Your bag, please," the woman said.

"A girl doesn't simply hand over her purse to any passing ruffian." Irinka laughed as if this was a cocktail party, not a kidnapping. "Have you done this before? I think if you had, you would know that."

She stared back, impassive. "Your bag, please."

"Are you going to hurt me?" she asked.

The woman frowned, but only slightly. "My orders are to deliver you safely to your final destination. But I will do what is necessary to achieve my objectives."

"Noted." Irinka handed over her bag. And was immediately glad that she'd moved her mobile when she rifled through it, then handed it back.

"Empty your pockets," the woman said.

Irinka made a show of producing her empty coat pockets for review, but shrunk back when she moved too close. "This is a Burberry," she said with a bit of a shriek, as if the other woman's proximity was an assault. "It is to be *gently handled* with *respect* and *reverence*."

At that, the woman actually sighed in exasperation and Irinka felt a bit of relief wash right through her.

Because exasperation was a human reaction. An assassin wouldn't crack, but someone's security detail might. Only a little, sure. But it made Irinka significantly more convinced that violence wasn't the objective here.

Before the woman could ask, she unzipped her coat and patted each of her pockets on the skinny jeans she wore tucked into her poor, sodden boots.

"I don't know what you're looking for, but I am not packing explosives on my person. Isn't that what airport security is worried about?"

"Let's go," muttered her captor, and then Irinka was being escorted up the steps and onto the waiting jet.

Once inside, she took a look around, noting all the details and flourishes that indicated that this was a high-end jet. And not the sort that was normally rented out. There were personal touches here. She had flown all over the world on private jets, for work and pleasure. She could tell the difference.

The moment she boarded, she shared a bright, fake smile with a waiting flight attendant, and asked for the bathroom. Once inside, she pulled out her mobile and typed a quick text to her friends.

Looks like I'm going on a bit of an unexpected holiday, she told them. *If you don't hear from me in three days, initiate the emergency protocol.*

I'm sorry, "the emergency protocol?" Auggie replied almost at once. *That's all you're going to say? No details? You must be joking.*

There is a bit of a time crunch, Irinka typed back. *Just track my mobile. You know you do anyway.*

I thought you said that no one would dare do anything to you any longer, Lynna responded. *That your reputation precedes you and even the billionaire class is helpless before your power, or something.*

This might be a case of my reputation preceding me, now that you mention it, Irinka replied. *I don't feel that I'm in danger. Not yet.*

Thank you, replied Maude. *That's not at all concerning.*

But Irinka didn't dare take any more time in the bathroom. She didn't want to invite anyone to come crashing back in. She slid her mobile back into her boot, wiggling her leg so that it went down and rested snugly against one calf. She eyed the boot critically, now that she wasn't being observed. The leather was supple but had its own structural integrity, so the fact that she'd chucked something down there wasn't obvious.

You must spoil before you spin, Roksana always muttered. Practice might not make perfect here, but it was working.

Irinka flushed so that her captors would hear it, then washed her hands and checked her appearance automatically. That was what her mother had always taught her to do.

Beauty is a commodity, Roksana had always told her, with the intensity she reserved for life lessons. *That makes it a weapon. And you must always make certain your blade is sharp.*

Irinka smoothed her hair slightly and fixed what she could of her face with only a bit of water in the mirror.

Then she sailed back out to find the flight attendant waiting for her, beckoning her to a seat. Of course, they took her coat, politely. And, of course, she saw Ms. Thug herself sitting opposite her seat, and tracked the way she swept her gaze all over Irinka now that there was no coat to block the view.

Irinka was braced for the woman to call out the mobile in her boot, but she didn't. So Irinka sat down in the seat they'd designated, buckled herself in, and smiled widely as the plane began to taxi.

"This is very exciting," she said. "I do love surprises. Will there be snacks?"

Once again, she saw exasperation move all over the woman's face, mixed with the slightest bit of something almost dazed. As if she couldn't believe that Irinka was reacting this way and didn't quite know what to do about it.

Excellent, Irinka thought.

Because she'd made quite a study of reading people in her lifetime. Initially because it was necessary. There were her mother's many lovers, a fact of life Irinka supposed she'd gotten used to before she'd even entered the world. Since Roksana had married pretty quickly after her relationship with the Duke deteriorated, to great tabloid furor. Whether her temporary husband had at any point believed that the baby Roksana carried was his was unknown. Either way, Roksana had wasted no time divorcing him after Irinka was born.

Roksana had bestowed the Duke's surname upon

their daughter as a shot across the bow. A warning and a proclamation, despite his rages. And Irinka had kept the name all this time, long after Roksana had decided that the Duke—having paid up—was beneath her notice, out of spite.

Later she'd learned how to read the Duke himself, her ever-indignant biological father, on the few-and-far-between occasions she'd met with him, providing him a receptacle for his enduring outrage that his actions had indeed had consequences. She could read her unfriendly siblings, two half brothers and one half sister, from across ballrooms and knew without ever having to discuss it that they were all *filled with umbrage* over the fact that Irinka got all the attention.

Later, this ability of hers had become the foundation of her job.

Because, of course, there were her clients. She could read them easily. The bulk of them were repeat customers because they much preferred it when she handled the unpleasantness of the end of their love affairs. So she knew things about them that perhaps only their ex-lovers did.

It was almost intimate.

A lot like being kidnapped, it turned out. Irinka felt confident now that Ms. Thug wasn't going to hurt her. Or really do anything but deliver her, like a parcel.

That was comforting enough as long as Irinka stayed in the moment and didn't think too much about the future.

The plane took off. Snacks were, in fact, provided.

And as the plane rose into the air, leaving the thick,

dark clouds of England behind, she tried to think of who she knew in Venice.

It was difficult, as the sort of men she worked for had properties everywhere. Any one of them could have a property in Venice. Many of them were unaware of how many properties they actually had, as that was the province of the money people they employed, who talked endlessly about *portfolios* and were absentee landlords.

Irinka began to wonder how much of her bravado was actually shock as it began to wear off.

The truth was, civil or not, she'd been flown off to God knows where and although no one had hurt her, she thought it had been very clear that if necessary, the blank-eyed woman across from her would have manhandled her onto this plane.

Woman-handled, she corrected herself.

And it was a lot like how she operated in the world, now that she thought about it. The threat was always implied. It didn't have to be explicit.

It turned out it was far more unpleasant than she realized. She would have to make a mental note.

Then again, maybe the threat was Venice. Maybe that was the only threat that worked.

Soon enough the plane began its descent. Once they landed into the blues and deep greens of Italy, Irinka was gently encouraged to get into yet another car. This one drove her to a dock, where it was suggested that she get into a boat.

By this point, the only languid thing about her was the smile she kept on her face the whole time, because she knew that people who wanted her intimidated found it irritating. She'd been told so often enough.

She made herself sit bonelessly. She fairly lounged on her seat in the little jet boat as it chugged along, took a turn, and then there they were. On the Grand Canal in Venice, the city of mystery.

And memory.

Irinka had only been here once before. That summer directly after university when she had discovered, once and for all, that recklessness and heedlessness—and being *seen* and *known*—were not for her.

She was not nostalgic. She refused to let those memories pull at her. But she felt tendrils all the same—whispers in the dark that she'd thought she'd extinguished. Scraps of touch, of heat—

Nothing that needed to be dug up again, she told herself briskly. No one liked the dead coming back to life.

And so she was already feeling something like bittersweet, and something a good deal darker than nostalgia, when the boat began to slow. She looked up and it took considerable effort to school her expression.

Because she knew the house they were approaching. Not that it was a *house*.

It was one of Venice's oldest palazzos, set back from the Grand Canal with a garden in between, thanks to a fire in some bygone century that had turned its fifteenth-century facade to ash. What remained was a lovely old house that managed to convey the same air of genteel exhaustion as the rest of the city, having long since been repaired and renovated.

Her heart picked up in her chest. She could feel the

effect of this place, everywhere, and the thudding of the blood in her veins made it remarkably difficult to smile serenely at her captors as they docked the boat and then waited for her to climb out.

But she did it.

No matter what dead things were rising here, most notably inside her.

And she could pretend that she'd heard dire things about the brackish water in Venetian canals. She could pretend that she was worried about all the other boats and how easy it would be to be swept up and run down while splashing around out there.

But that wasn't why she didn't turn and run, then swim for it.

It was the same thing it had always been. That deep and unfortunate pull that dragged her here whether she wanted to come or not.

That madness she had only ever experienced once before.

She told herself that this time it was nothing but curiosity.

It was warmer in Venice. Brighter, though still the skies were a touch moody. She followed where she was led—because she had to know, now—marching up the central pathway that led to the grand front entrance of the palazzo.

With every step, it wasn't just her heart that reacted but every other part of her. She could feel a tightness in her throat as if there were still words unsaid when she knew better. She could feel her chest constrict as if she would finally let herself sob, but she refused.

She still refused.

And then it all seemed to be happening too quickly. She was marched inside, into dim, grand rooms. She was ushered through the palazzo's high-ceilinged, exquisitely wrought spaces that flowed one into another, up the stairs from the water line, and then into what she knew too well was the main living area on the second floor.

She was delivered inside, the door was closed behind her, and then...

There he was.

He stood out on one of the balconies, a study in male elegance. He did not turn to look at her, but Irinka had no doubt whatsoever that he knew she was there.

She supposed that he was probably drawing out the tension of this moment, but she was grateful for it.

Because she had never intended to lay eyes on him again. And she wasn't prepared now.

He was looking out toward the canal and she understood with a sort of *winnowing* sensation inside her that he'd watched her approach.

Irinka tried to make sense of what was happening instead of simply *reacting* to it. Why, years later, would he go to the trouble of having her picked up off the London street and transported across Europe? Why now? What could he want?

But she refused to ask.

And her brain refused to cooperate, anyway. All it wanted to do was dig up old graves and let the ghosts dance free.

He took his time straightening. And, for a moment,

she was staring at the long, finely molded line of his back. His shoulders were wide, his waist narrow. Everything he wore was exquisite, tailored specifically to his body and his preferences. And so while all he appeared to be wearing was a shirt and trousers, the effect was mouthwatering.

It turned out she was still susceptible to him. This was not information she'd wanted to learn.

Even with his back to her, everything about him was ferociously masculine and astonishingly sophisticated. She had seen so many men who should have been like him in the years since. All of these wealthy, powerful men, who were somehow incapable of sorting out their own relationships.

It only occurred to her now that perhaps her excellence in her profession had been her way of trying to convince herself that he was just like all of them.

But he wasn't.

He turned, then, and it was as if he'd thrown open windows in a dark room and let the morning light in.

Because there was no one like this man.

There never had been. They never would be.

His back was poetry rendered in finely muscled male flesh. She knew that already. But looking at him, face-to-face after all this time, she found herself unprepared for the impact of him. Memory had dulled the sheer brutal thrust of his beauty.

Or perhaps time had honed it.

If Irinka's beauty was a weapon she'd been taught to wield, his was something else entirely. Looking at him was like stepping into an ancient cathedral, like the very famous one not far from his palazzo. It was an experience of soaring, everything drawn up into the force of him by something outside human comprehension.

His hair was dark and close-cropped. His eyes looked black. He was sculpted to perfection, formed by generations of beautiful Venetian men, tall and dark-haired and with flashing eyes, and the stunning women they had married as if it was no more than their due.

She had studied all of them in the portraits that hung on the walls in this place, sitting cheek by jowl with Picassos, Caravaggios, and Titians.

Irinka told herself that she was deliberately standing still, her head up and her eyes on him. But the truth was that she felt frozen into place.

She felt his eyes all over her the way his hands had been, once. The way his mouth had followed, teaching her complicated lessons about immolation.

And she didn't know why he had brought her here. But that hardly mattered. Because she wasn't the girl she'd been that summer. She never had been before, and never had been since. That was the important thing.

So she smiled her patented languid smile, the one she hadn't perfected yet when she'd been here last. And she tilted her head to the side as she regarded him, as if he was the captured animal in the zoo here, not her.

"Hello, Zago," she said, and she hadn't said his name in so long that she could taste it on her tongue, rich and decadent. "What an extraordinary invitation. I've never received one quite like it. Your standards must be slipping."

But Zago Baldissera only smiled, sending a dark shiver down the length of her spine.

"It was not an invitation," he replied, in that voice that she understood, now, had haunted her all these years. In her dreams, just out of reach. "That time is long past. What you are here for is a reckoning."

CHAPTER TWO

ZAGO BALDISSERA HAD waited a long time for this moment.

Irinka Scott-Day, out of her element. Back here in this palazzo as if there had been no time at all between that fateful summer and now. As if that handful of years—that he could remember living through all too well—had been a blank, after all.

It felt like a *victory*.

And yet he never would have engineered this moment into being, however, had it not been for his sister.

He reminded himself that Nicolosa was the point of this. That it was Nicolosa, who had been crying for the last month straight, who deserved that revenge be taken in her name.

As her older brother and protector, he would have done what was necessary no matter what. It was simply a stroke of good luck that when he'd gone digging into the individuals who had been involved in his sister's heartbreak, he'd found Irinka.

Of all people.

He was tempted to consider it fate.

Hers, that was.

"A reckoning?"

Irinka drifted farther into the room, looking utterly unconcerned. This was the Palazzo delle Sospira. Even if it burned, and it had, it did not change. And his role in life was to make certain it never did. To fight as best he could to preserve the history and legacy of his family until the palazzo sank beneath the waters of the lagoon, as they all would, in time.

That eventuality came closer every day, but Zago thought of himself as a man who straddled time. It took, it gave, and he did what he must in between.

And what he needed to do today was this.

"Does the idea of a reckoning frighten you?" he asked when she seemed content enough to do nothing more than drift from a statue some claimed was an unknown Donatello liberated from Florence in the 1400s, to the Murano glass bowls on a side table, to the small figurines his great-grandmother had collected, all made for her by well-regarded artists of the time. "I suppose it should. Where would you even begin to tally up your sins? Do you even know *which* sin it is that I feel requires your penance, or do they all blend together?"

"I'm sure you have a laundry list."

She didn't sound *bored*, exactly. But, of course, she was too good at what she did for that.

Zago had spent the last month learning everything there was to know about this baffling creature that Irinka had become. There had been nothing but glowing reviews from the otherwise extraordinarily picky and private men that he'd contacted under the guise of seeking the sort of woman who would do the kind of job for him that had been done to his sister.

He had found nothing but rapturous praise and he'd had to read between the lines. She was entirely professional. *Cold straight through,* one man had said admiringly. *All business.* Scenarios were discussed, then at least two top picks were selected in the event that circumstances required a change midstream. The date was picked out and agreed upon.

And then Irinka would appear—looking nothing like herself but still very much like a woman the man in question might actually be involved with, a critical detail—and would then do what needed to be done.

And the thing about her is that she's good at it, another man had confided. *A proper actress, in the end. Absolutely sells the scene and never the* same *scene twice. She is a national treasure.*

Zago intended to tarnish this treasure.

Or possibly wreck it entirely. He had yet to decide how this would go. It rather depended on her.

He watched as Irinka found a seat and then sank into it, looking entirely at her ease.

And the trouble was, even though he'd braced himself, he really hadn't been prepared for that same electric shock that he'd always felt in her presence. He wasn't prepared to find her even more compelling than he had three years ago.

He would have told himself that was impossible.

She looked as if she inhabited her body more now than she had then. As if every part of her was fully controlled, and he couldn't help but find that attractive. More than attractive. But then, she had always been beautiful. He had thought it the least interesting thing about her, in the end, but there was no denying it. No pretending that she was not her famously stunning mother's daughter in every regard.

In *every* regard, he reminded himself.

Irinka's thick black hair was clipped back at her nape, the long tail of it flipped over one shoulder. Her eyes were that blue that he'd liked to tell himself, in retrospect, were nothing but icy and cold, but they never had been. Not really. And they weren't now.

The only blue he had ever seen to compare was the water of Venice at dawn, mysterious and inviting.

He needed to vanquish the part of him that allowed her to haunt him even here, in this place where his ancestors had been traced to the ninth century, in one form or another.

Perhaps what he needed to do was dwell on the person she'd decided to become after leaving him. Because it was difficult not to assume that a woman who was that good at putting on all her different masks had put one on for him, too.

Maybe this squalid thing she did was who she really was. And maybe she had done it to him first.

A truth that sat unpleasantly in his gut.

"You have no questions, then." Zago watched her, telling himself he did not know why his chest was too tight, a sensation that did not make his gut feel any better about this woman and her masks and lies. Unless it was the righteous fury of a brother avenging his sister, that was. And what else could it be? "I suppose it is an everyday occurrence for you, is it?"

"To be kidnapped?" Irinka shook her head, and he

could remember the silk of her hair against his skin. Like a taunt. "This is my first time. I'll be certain to review the experience later with the authorities, but I don't really know that I could possibly predict what you might do, Zago." When her blue gaze met his, then, it was direct. Not the least bit *airy*. "I was certain that after the last time we saw each other, you would never wish to lay eyes on me again."

That was an alarmingly reductive take on what had happened between them, but he supposed that was the point. He had no intention of wading into her take on that mess of a summer. Zago doubted very much that he would be impressed with the spin she'd put on it.

Particularly because she had snuck out in the night like some kind of thief and had never looked back.

He refused to give her the satisfaction of bringing any of that up.

It would give the impression that he had held on to all of it, and he had not.

He had *not*.

"Indeed, I did not wish to see you again," he agreed. "Or even think of you, Irinka. You cannot imagine how little I wish these measures were necessary."

She smiled again, as if he had said something droll and amusing at the sort of cocktail parties that wearied him. Then she waved her hand, taking in the room all around them. The frescoed walls, antiques dating back to any number of fallen empires, and the Grand Canal beyond, whispering its silken threats and seductive invitations as it went. That it had taken so many, that it would take them all, that this was no more than the price of beauty in so small a life.

He normally found this comforting.

Or, at the very least, a commentary on the sort of pressure a Baldissera heir must be prepared to withstand as long as he—and the family legacy, embodied in this palazzo—stayed above the waterline. His life's work was to make certain he did.

There was less solace in it today, he found. He blamed Irinka for that, too.

"I assume you are meandering about in the direction of telling me why I am here?" she asked, though she did not sound as worried about that as he'd expected. As, perhaps, he'd wanted. If anything, she sounded like all that blue blood in her veins had finally taken hold and frozen her as solid as the country she came from. "The palazzo is looking lovely. You're maintaining it beautifully. I'm sure that your father would be proud."

And he was glad she'd said that. *Fiercely* glad.

Because she was reminding him, in the most subtle way possible—another hallmark of the way she did her dirty business, he'd been given to understand—that she was not afraid to use the weapons she had. So there was no need for *him* to hold back, either.

His father had been absolutely certain that no one, living or dead, could care more for the palazzo and the Baldissera name than himself. He had died of heart failure when Zago was twenty-eight. And Zago had still been reeling from that loss, and from the mess it had been to excavate all of his father's secrets and plans and mistakes, a year later when he'd met Irinka.

He had shared too much with her and he had regretted it ever since.

But today it was a gift.

Because she was reminding him that there was no need to play nicely.

"You have a very interesting line of business, do you not?" Zago moved farther into the room and seated himself opposite her. He could have called for his staff to bring refreshments, but this wasn't a social visit and there was no need to worry about her comfort.

This was business. Family business.

"I do," she agreed, in that same pleasant tone with a whole *dukedom* of not-quite-expressed disdain beneath.

Zago could see why so many of her clients, who worked for their money—or at least had, once—and were easily bewitched by crumbling old ruins and the odd castle, were enamored of her. She was likely the only woman they ever encountered who quietly asserted the fact that she was *better* than them. Then refused to sleep with them, by all accounts.

They loved her for it.

He, personally, did not care to speculate about who she did or did not sleep with.

"I'm sure you remember me talking about my friends from university," she was saying, another dangerous nod toward their past. Because remembering anything could mean remembering everything, and he doubted she wanted that.

It occurred to him, then, that she was trying to minimize it—and there would be no need to do that if it wasn't as large and unwieldy a memory for her as it was for him, would there?

He told himself what he felt at that thought was mere interest, nothing more. It was *interesting*, that was all.

And she was still talking, chattering as if they were acquaintances at a brunch, the sort of event Zago would never attend. "We started a specialty sort of agency. My friends go off into the world and provide services for wealthy individuals who require them. One is a world-class chef. Another can pretty much fix any reputation, no matter what. Another one can take any family pile and transform it into a garden oasis. These are all very specialized skills. Meanwhile, I hold down the fort in our office."

Zago studied her lovely face for a long moment, but she seemed prepared to gaze back at him like that forever. Guileless. At her ease.

Deceitful to her core.

"That will be the last lie you tell me, Irinka," he said, with enough quiet fury that he saw her sit a little bit straighter. "Do you understand me? I know perfectly well you are not a receptionist."

"I'm an excellent receptionist."

"I'm more interested in your other pursuits." He settled back in his seat and told himself his heart beat faster only with the thrill of this chase reaching its end. There could be no other reason. "For example, I believe you are familiar with a certain Peruvian financier. Felipe De Osma."

She looked wholly unbothered by this line of questioning, but he didn't believe that, either. Surely it was her job to look unconcerned, and she was clearly an excellent actress. "Of course. He has contracted the services of our agency many times."

"And what services does he require of you?"

Her smile never wavered. "I'm afraid that the one thing we promise our clientele above all else is privacy. I can't tell you what it is we do for him or anyone else we may or may not do work for. Just as, if you were our client, I wouldn't tell anyone what we did for you, either."

Zago studied her. "I already know what you do."

She shrugged, and it made her hair move while another memory scraped over him. "How marvelous. Then I don't need to feel all *cloak and dagger* that I'm not telling you."

"Tell me about the events of about a month ago," he invited her. Though it was more of an order. "You walked into the luxury flat of Felipe De Osma despite the security measures in place, found him in a compromising position with a woman, and threw a glass of wine in his face." He thought he saw a trace of amusement in her blue eyes, but it was gone in a flash. "While he was mopping himself up, you launched into a spate of blistering, outraged Spanish, claiming that you were his lover. Are you?"

"What an indelicate question." But her eyes gleamed. "Even if it was remotely your concern, which it isn't, I can't imagine why I would answer you."

It was his turn to very obliquely look around the room, as if measuring the thickness of the walls and therefore the parameters of her cell here. "I'm certain I can convince you that it's in your best interest."

"I'm sure you think you can," Irinka said, which was not quite agreement. "What I'm more interested in is how you know what was said in the middle of an altercation in someone else's flat. Are you stalking Felipe? Whatever for?"

"I am not stalking anyone."

"Oh." And her expression was innocent enough, though Zago could see that gleam in her gaze intensify. "Do you outsource that the way you do kidnappers?"

And it didn't help to see that spark in her. To remember how he had ignited it and where it had taken them. Just as it did not help anything to find that he was not nearly as immune to her as he had expected he would be.

After all, he had offered her the world, and she had turned him down flat.

What was there to be susceptible to after that?

Especially when her behavior since proved that really, she had done him a favor.

Irinka kept her gaze trained on him, as if she could read him too easily. There was a part of him that was very much worried that she could.

But he told himself that was unlikely. "Speaking of outsourcing, how often do you go about interfering in other people's relationships and making women you don't even know cry?" he asked instead.

The strangest expression moved over her face then, and he told himself that it was an improvement, anyway, from her attempts at innocence. Whatever it was, it was more *real*. He was sure of it—even though it disappeared almost as quickly as it came.

"I'm sure I don't know what you mean."

"What I mean, Irinka, is that you are widely known as the breakup artist that every man of a certain sort needs on speed dial. If a man doesn't have the stomach to handle his own mess, you come and do it for him. Are you pretending that you don't? What other reason would you have for storming into Felipe De Osma's flat and disrupting the intimate evening he was having with another woman?"

"I still don't know what you're talking about."

"I wonder what would happen to your business if I were to have a frank and far-reaching discussion with, say, a selection of tabloids about what it is you actually do at that agency of yours." He settled back against the ancient settee and gazed at the frescoed ceiling. "I can't help but notice that you've taken a great deal of trouble to make yourself seem toothless. Unremarkable. Everyone thinks of you as little more than a dilettante, wafting around Europe and pretending that you're some kind of party girl, when everyone knows that your father—*His Grace*—wants nothing to do with you. That must be painful." He watched her lift her chin a bit at that, as if it was a blow that landed. And he told himself that the searing sensation that moved through him then was a triumph. "Perhaps it is unsurprising that you choose to translate that kind of pain into preying on others. That is the sort of thing that rolls downhill, does it not?"

"That's a bit rich coming from the hereditary heir to an ancient Venetian fortune that was not exactly built on good vibes and sunshine, as I recall."

That was also a blow that landed. Zago didn't like it.

The truth, as far as he knew, was that no family that could trace itself into antiquity and yet still hold on tight to some of its spoils—like the palazzo they sat in now—

could do so without what his father had always referred to as *uno brutto momento*. A bad moment.

In a family like theirs, there had been many. Some matched up with the wars that had made and destroyed and remade Europe. Some were of their own, personal making. Zago could remember his father's rants all throughout his childhood, increasing in intensity as the years went by, as if he could reach back through time and lecture his ancestors on the duties and legacies they had periodically neglected.

We must be the paragons our bloodline needs in the future to make up for the past, his father had liked to say in his later years, usually when Zago had dared interrupt him in his study. The place he liked to go to hide away from the world in general and his children in particular, leaving them to their own devices.

Sometimes Zago thought that he had been raised as a ghost, left to haunt the halls of the palazzo with all the rest.

He deeply regretted telling Irinka these things over the course of that summer.

And he could not forgive himself for trusting her with the stories—good and bad—of those who had come before him, not to mention with his father's obsessions.

He abandoned you, she had said once. *Without committing to actually leaving. That's quite a feat.*

And then she had abandoned him, too. But she had also made sure to leave, just to make sure that knife was stuck in deep. Zago thought he could feel it still, buried deep between his shoulder blades.

"The choice is yours," he told her now, and absolutely

did not shift his position to relieve the bite of a knife that wasn't there.

He had long since decided that the burdens his father had bequeathed to him—like the weight of this palazzo and its history and the legacy that he was expected to tend and nurture into a future that expanded far beyond him, to say nothing of his family's ancient reputation all the social expectations that went with that in certain quarters of this country—were a gift.

No one ever said a gift had to *feel* good all the time.

A distinction he intended to make clear to Irinka this time around.

"A choice?" Irinka said that with mock delight and no little astonishment. "Am I truly being offered a choice? That's the first time all day."

He opted to ignore that. "The choice is very simple. Answer my questions or lose your little agency. It will take two phone calls, at most. Is that what you want?"

She sat across from him, as impossibly perfect as ever. Impenetrable, unknowable. It was difficult for him to imagine, now, how desperate he had been to hurl himself against those walls she put up around her and find his way inside.

Just as it was difficult to accept that he had failed.

"I'm not saying that I know what you're talking about," she said after a moment. "But it would seem to me that if a man was such a coward that he required a *service* to end a relationship, that any woman he chose to do that to was better off for it."

"That's a remarkable take, and interestingly enough,

absolves you of any culpability." He smiled. "How curious."

"I wouldn't know," she replied, carefully. "But I have to think that if such a service existed, it would profit off the men involved while providing a kind of rescue to the women. Because what decent, honorable man would do such a thing in the first place?"

"Do you think that this argument will work?" He found himself leaning forward, thinking of fragile, sweet Nicolosa's inability to get out of bed. Of that look on her face, as if she'd been kicked. Repeatedly. It was unbearable. "Do you suppose that if you were to go out there and locate all the women you did this to that they would applaud you?"

"Do you think that they wouldn't, in the fullness of time, understand that they dodged a bullet?" she shot back. Then smiled. "Not that I know anything about it, but even hearing about such a service, I have to ask— is wine thrown in their faces? Who is shouted at—the presumably cheating man or the woman he's with?"

And Zago had done his research. He had been on a mission to root out the perpetrators and bring them to some kind of justice since the night his sister had called him in hysterics. And once he'd found the identity of the woman who had come into the apartment that night— and had sat with that a minute—he had gone and found his way to other examples of her work.

For research purposes, naturally.

And it was true. All the drama was focused on the man. The woman he was with usually ran off, often in tears. But if anything was thrown or broken, it was either at the man or belonged to the man.

He hadn't noticed that. It seemed interesting, now, that he hadn't. But he told himself it didn't matter. It couldn't.

"You cannot possibly justify your actions," he told Irinka. "Even if you don't do what you do to the woman. Is a murder any better if it is painless?"

Her smile sharpened. "Comparing a breakup to murder seems a little over the top, doesn't it?"

He didn't think of his sister then. He didn't think of the way Nicolosa had wailed and told him that there was no possible way that Felipe was seeing anyone else.

I might be a fool, his sister had sobbed. *But I'm not that much of a fool. It's entirely possible that he was seeing other women, but if he was, it would have to have been a night here, a night there. There simply wasn't time for him to have the kind of in-depth relationship that woman was screaming about. You have to believe me, Zago. You* have *to.*

And he had believed her. But that wasn't what he thought about now.

It was *this* woman, of all people, telling *him* how a breakup ought to feel.

"I was not at all surprised that the woman who would do these things was you, Irinka," he said after a moment. "Because, as we both know, you have no qualm whatsoever reaching into the chest of another, ripping his heart out, and tossing it to the carrion crows."

He did nothing to prevent the bitterness from coming

out in his voice. He did nothing to bank the fury that he could feel cover his face and no doubt take over his gaze.

For the first time in three years, he didn't pretend that the way she'd left was okay.

But this time, it wasn't his own face staring back at him from a mirror while he *didn't* think these things. She was right here.

And she was staring right back at him.

"Is that why you really brought me here?" Irinka asked softly. "All these years later, you want to sit here and conduct a postmortem on our breakup?" She laughed, almost ruefully. "I'll make it simple for you. I was very young. We had nothing in common. I'm no longer quite so young, but the second part still holds. Will I get the private jet back to London or will you be petty and have me find my own way?"

"You're not leaving," he gritted out. But when her brow rose, all cool challenge, he remembered that he was not a caveman. "What I meant to say is, you can leave at will. But I've already outlined the consequences. I would make very certain that you are ready for that. Because in case you've forgotten, I am not a man given to levity. This is not a joke."

"You don't say. And here I've been giggling to myself the whole time, from being swiped off the Portobello Road to being frog marched into this palazzo. The hilarity never ends with you, Zago."

"I don't recall you complaining about my intensity when it mattered." He was moving before he meant to, but then she was, too.

And suddenly they were both standing there in the

space between her chair and his settee, the Venetian light filtering in through the ancient windows, pale gold streaming everywhere.

But if there was any oxygen between them, he couldn't find it.

"I haven't complained about anything," she told him, her eyes blazing. "Then or now. I seem to recall that was you."

He laughed, and he hadn't known until that moment that he had sounds like that inside of him. Just as he wasn't sure he knew the man who reached over and slid his hand to take her jaw in his palm.

He didn't grip too hard. He didn't move her about. Zago simply held her there and then, almost fitfully, dragged his thumb over that wicked, tempting, dangerous mouth of hers.

"There you were," he all but crooned. "Parading around as the daughter of one of the most scandalous women alive and vamping it up in her shadow. And only you and I know the truth, don't we?" He leaned in, only a little. He lowered his voice. "It was all an act. Little games you played to keep people at a distance when the truth was, you were an untouched virgin. You played your games then. Now you play them on a dangerous stage. But at the end of the day, we both know that I'm the one who brought you alive. Who put my mouth on every inch of your body, and taught you who you are."

Zago had never said things like that out loud before. But that didn't make them any less true.

Her gaze glittered. "Your arrogance is breathtaking."

"It always was," he agreed. "And even now that I've

kidnapped you, brought you to Venice, and have showed myself arrogant once more, what do you think I would find if I slid my hand between your legs, Irinka?"

He shifted closer, until his mouth was nearly on hers. He could see the way her eyes dilated. He could see her pulse go wild in her neck. He could feel the heat of her skin, and later, perhaps, he would explore precisely how it felt to know that everything was as it had always been between them.

Because he was hard, ready, and aching for her as if he had only just had her.

As if there had been no time in between but a few scant minutes instead of years.

"Because between you and me," Zago whispered, "I think we both know that you're already wet. And ready. And hungry. For me, as always."

Something that wasn't as simple as temper, or as complicated as grief, flashed across her face. She lifted a hand to grip his wrist as if she wanted to tear his hand away, but she didn't.

Instead, she leaned closer. "If you wanted to ask me for a date, Zago, you could have texted. Like a normal person."

"Speaking of arrogance," he replied. He let go of her then, though he didn't step back. But then, she didn't, either. "This isn't about you, Irinka, as hard as that might be for you to believe."

"It is difficult, yes," she agreed. "Given the kidnap. And the fact that I'm currently being held in your palazzo, subject to attempts at intimidation. You can see how a person might jump to the conclusion that it was about them."

He ignored that. "This is about my sister. Do you remember her? She was only sixteen back then. And though she is nineteen now, and headed off to university as she should, she is sheltered. Naive." He shook his head. "Knowing this, I made it clear to her that she was to be careful around men, but all that did was keep her from telling me about him when she met him. She knew I wouldn't approve. It was only when he made so many declarations that she felt emboldened." Zago blew out a frustrated breath. "I found what she did tell me sufficiently alarming that I was already planning to go to London, but then instead, you turned up. She was spending the night in his apartment—not for the first time, I am to understand, little as I wish to know these details about my baby sister—and in came this woman making wild accusations and hurling crockery. Nicolosa, bless her, assumed that she and her lover would present a united front, laugh off these accusations, and call the police. But that's not what happened."

He didn't know what he expected her to do. All she did do was gaze back at him with a certain steadiness that suggested to him that she was taking this hard, though he had no evidence to support that. Just a feeling.

And too well did he know how little his feelings ever had to do with reality when it came to Irinka.

"Do you feel good about what you do when you actually know the woman you are paid to destroy?" he asked her. "Because since then, Nicolosa has dropped out of university. She has taken to her bed and refuses to leave her flat in London. She hardly sleeps or eats and if she is awake, she is likely crying."

And he could not bear it, though he did not say that out loud. Zago might have been a ghost in this house, but he had made certain that Nicolosa had a different sort of childhood. He had taken his role as her older brother seriously. Very seriously.

He had cared for her and played with her. As she grew, he had become her mentor, her protector. When there was nothing in these halls but the echoing silence of their father's interest in everything but them, he had told her stories about the people in all the paintings to redirect her attention.

That a man like de Osma had come along and crushed her like this had come terribly close to crushing Zago, too.

Though he did not intend to admit such a thing. Not to the woman who had been involved in his sister's heartbreak.

"I really am sorry for that," Irinka said quietly, after a moment or two. "I'm sorry that she is so upset. But I cannot be sorry to hear that she was liberated herself from the clutches of a man who has a vibrant reputation for preying upon girls just like her."

"And you are still convinced you are somehow the hero of this tale, are you not? Amazing."

"I notice you're not storming Felipe's residence to demand that he offer you reparation for your sister's broken heart," she retorted. "I'm not surprised that one outrageously wealthy man should find another outrageously wealthy man miraculously without responsibility for his own actions. It must, of course, be my fault."

He didn't point out that she'd essentially admitted it was her, at last. Not that he had been in any doubt.

"Once I knew it was you, I understood," he told her. "For only you, Irinka, are capable of such cruelty. It made all the sense in the world to me that you've made this your profession. After all, I was your first project."

"Is this what you kidnapped me to tell me?" she asked softly, though there was something almost wary in her gaze. "Once again, this really could have been a text." She actually dared roll her eyes at him then, as if this was little more than *an annoyance* to her. As if that's all he was, too. "And while we're on the subject of kidnaps, I told my friends that if they don't hear from me by teatime that they were to involve the authorities. So I hope you're planning on wrapping this up soon."

"I think you'd better call your friends," he said with quiet certainty. "And tell them that you're not coming home. Because we're going to experiment with a little accountability, you and I."

He could see the goose bumps rise along her neck, though she otherwise didn't react. "Are we now?" She dared to look at her watch, another version of a rolled eye. He knew perfectly well it was deliberate. "And how long do you think that will take?"

But when Zago laughed again, it felt more natural this time. "Oh, Irinka. Until we're finally done."

CHAPTER THREE

ALL HE HAD done was put his hand on her face.

It was nothing. *Nothing.*

She kept telling herself that, in the hope that might help her dial it back a bit. That it might counter the outsize reaction she was having to all of this. When it was nothing but a random touch on her chin. Basically like seeing a dentist.

But there'd been his thumb.

And the way he'd moved it across her lips, ragged and searing, igniting old memories she never normally let out in the light of day.

Irinka knew she couldn't let him see her react like this. He was right about one thing—she really had been playing games her whole life. He seemed to think she did that out of some Machiavellian need to manipulate people, which only went to show how little he knew her.

That's a good thing, she chided herself when thinking that made her ache.

She had let him know her well once and look how that had turned out. He had taught her to avoid that kind of intimacy like the plague. Because it hurt.

And in the end, familiarity really did breed contempt. She had watched that play out in real time between her mother and father. She knew better than to make that same mistake—only here, with Zago, had she ever tried to do the opposite and look how *that* had turned out.

But she did not intend to defend herself to him. He could make all the remarks he wanted about her character, and it wouldn't make any difference.

She knew what had happened here, between them that summer. She knew that *he* had not been one who'd been left broken. Or not the only one. And she also knew that she'd been right to leave while she could, before there was nothing left between them but contempt.

Something she might have told him under different circumstances, secure in the safety of all these years' distance.

Now she would say nothing. Holding his gaze, she made a small spectacle of bending over, reaching into her boot, and pulling out her phone. One of his dark brows rose, suggesting to her that Ms. Thug would be getting a talking-to.

She couldn't really say she minded that.

Irinka glared at him as she straightened. "Some privacy please?"

"There will be very little of that," he assured her.

She sighed and rolled her eyes again, because she'd seen him react the last time she'd done it. Then she simply opened up the group chat.

Her friends were not entertained by her absence. There were mounting cries for various dramatic responses from some quarters and rather more measured approaches from others, as always.

It's fine, she texted. I'm fine.

And she didn't wait for them to respond, which she knew they would, and likely rapidly. *I'm in Venice. It's lovely this time of year.*

Is this a cry for help? Maude asked.

Maybe it's code, Lynna added. *It doesn't surprise me that Irinka would have various codes, but she never shared any of them with me.*

Blink twice if this is really you, Irinka, Auggie added.

Really, I'm fine, Irinka texted back. *There's a small matter that needs some attention, that's all. I'll cancel my appointments.*

The mobile was snatched out of her hand. She glared up at Zago, outraged. "I beg your pardon."

He scrolled through the chat and slid a dark look her way. "How did three days become teatime?"

"Because it's felt like three years, actually. Give me my mobile back, please?"

He did not. *"Work wives?"* he asked, that cultured voice of his dripping with disdain.

It should not have dripped through her in turn, slow and sweet, like honey.

"That is what my friends and I call ourselves, yes," she told him, not quite matching his level of disdain, but she let her smile pick up the slack. "Do you have friends, Zago? If you did, you might also have funny nicknames that you use, shared histories, your own private language made up of anecdotes and memories. Alas."

"I'm fascinated that this is your approach." He apparently satisfied himself with her mobile and handed it back to her, looking as if she'd fallen short in some way. She assured herself that she didn't need him to validate her. It didn't matter what he thought about her friends, her group chat with said friends, or indeed any of her life choices.

What did matter was the fact that when she told herself that, it felt a bit hollow.

But she was in no mood to think about why that might be. "And by 'my approach' do you mean the part where I'm not wailing and lamenting at your feet, begging you to forgive me?" She laughed at that. "The thing is, Zago, I'm not ashamed of what I do. I prefer that you not broadcast it to the world only because that would make it very difficult to keep what I do under the radar, and it might also negatively affect my friends."

Predictably, he looked unmoved.

"If you think that you can lock me away in your little palace—" she began, maybe a little less calmly than she might have liked.

"It is not little, Irinka. I think you know that."

She stared at him. Because it almost sounded as if he meant—

But she refused to go there. "You could keep me locked up here for the rest of my life," she said, saying each word very deliberately. "It still won't make me believe that I'm not providing a necessary service. You might not like it. It might be something more like a mercy killing, if I'm being completely transparent. But every single one of those women who were encouraged to leave the men in question is one less daughter like me, who has had to sit in the presence of His Grace, the perpetually outraged Duke, and listen to him blame me for his inability to wear a condom."

"Seriously hurting innocent people is some kind of crusade, is that it?"

Irinka threw up her hands in the universal sign of exasperation and used that as an opportunity to retreat. She moved away from him, but didn't sit down again. That felt too risky. Instead, she moved almost restlessly toward that balcony, and went outside.

The afternoon was wearing on and the light was like magic, dancing and moving. The trouble with Venice was that it echoed back too well. The past. Her own longings. The things she'd said to him once that she wanted so desperately to deny, but couldn't.

She felt him come up behind her. "Irinka," he began.

But Zago was the most dangerous echo of all.

"Let's discuss the terms of confinement." She turned to face him, leaning back against the rail and crossing her arms. And she could remember too well the last time she'd stood here like this, gazing at him. The tragedy for her was that he had not gotten stooped and gnarled in the meantime. He was just as tall as she remembered him. Towering over her when she was five foot ten in her stocking feet. "Is there a dungeon? Will there be beatings? What is it going to look like?"

"It's the bravado," he murmured, almost as if he was whispering some kind of sweet nothing. "It just astonishes me. Is there nothing I can say to you to make you accept the gravity of the situation?"

Irinka tilted her head to one side as she gazed at him. "Is that really what you want, Zago? Me writhing about in abject terror that I might have put myself on the wrong side of your good opinion? Is that the kind of thing that excites you when you wake up from a dream in the middle of the night?"

"Even now, you attempt to provoke me." And there was something about the way he said it. It was calm, yes. That was alarming enough. Yet there was almost something like satisfaction in his voice. Like he had expected this. "But you forget that I know you."

She sighed at that. "You barely knew a girl that I haven't been for years."

What she did not say was that the girl he'd brought to this palazzo was not the girl who had left it only a few months later. He would probably love to hear that he had *made her a woman*, but not in the way people usually meant it when they said such things. It wasn't simply because he had taken her virginity. Or, more accurately, because she'd given him her virginity in an explosion of joy and heat and desire.

It was that walking away from him had changed her almost as profoundly as what happened between them had.

Irinka had never been the same.

And she had not had the option to cry for a month, not that she begrudged his sister her wallow. But Irinka hadn't had a benevolent father figure to look after her. She'd had to figure out a life for herself, one way or another.

And unless she wanted to tell her friends what had happened, she'd had to pretend that nothing had.

She'd gone for door number two. And only occasionally felt guilty about it.

But her experience here had made it clear to her that

no one could handle *all* of her, not even her friends. They benefited as much as anyone else from the way Irinka flitted in and out, never quite pinned down, allowing them to enjoy her without ever having to deal with the *too much* part.

She had learned that here.

There was no possible way that Zago could know the woman she'd become *because* of him.

"My sister has been wretched for an entire month," he told her now, that gleaming menace in his gaze that, sadly, only made him that much hotter. It was desperately unfair. "Thirty-some days is a long time. Why don't you and I start with a month."

It wasn't really a question. Much less an invitation.

"A month of what?" she asked, as if it really was some kind of invitation and she was mulling it over. "Why don't you lay out the parameters? Depending on what you say, I'll decide if I need to attempt to jump off this balcony right now."

Maybe Zago really did know her, because he took a moment to look over the side and then back at her, one dark eyebrow raised. "I wouldn't recommend it. It's steeper than it looks and it won't be a soft landing."

Irinka let her chin jut upward. "Don't threaten me with a good time." And then she made herself smile. "I mean it. Thirty days of what?"

"You can pick your labor." He said this as if he was granting her a great favor. "I've always fancied a personal housemaid. Perhaps you can cook and clean and wow me with your domestic prowess." That brow stayed lifted. "Or you could work it out in trade."

He said that lightly enough, but she couldn't be certain that he was kidding. Not with that look on his face, that dark promise that she knew he was fully capable of answering.

Too well did she know it.

She blew out a breath through pursed lips, then shook her head. "That does sound like labor. Housemaiding, that is."

"Irinka. Please. What do you know about cooking or cleaning?"

"I love that you really imagine that you're somehow the better choice. It must be truly spectacular to be a man." She waved her hand at him, taking in his whole… dark gold magnificence. She made herself look something like scornful. Taken aback. "I can get that anywhere, Zago. It gets thrown at me on the street, left and right. What do you think would compel me to sleep with a man who thinks as little of me as you do? What could be the possible benefit?"

"Very well, then," he said, not rising to debate the way she wanted him to do. "A new addition to the household staff. I will notify the *maggiordomo*."

What bothered Irinka was that he could be talking about *servitude* and she could still want him to so much. She had to question what exactly she was doing, and why it irked her that he was so *calm*. Did she want him to crack? Did she want him to boil over so that anything that happened after could be blamed on him? His temper, his overreach, his problem?

She was afraid she already knew the answer and it didn't exactly cover her in glory.

In that moment, she decided she *would* stay. It was all fun and games up to now—in the sense of not being fun at all and hating that she needed to play games in the first place—but she got the distinct impression that he expected her to…have a meltdown, perhaps? Rage at him that she could obviously not be expected to do either thing?

Irinka wondered what third option he had up his sleeve, and she refused to give him the opportunity to think that he was right about her. Or knew her.

At all.

Besides, as her mother always said, *Without hard work there is no getting fish from the pond.*

Meaning that the pain of the hard work got the necessary results.

Irinka could scrub a few floors if that would do the trick. Because proving Zago wrong would be its own reward. And if he exploded in the middle of it? Had a full-on temper tantrum and lost all access to this *calmness* of his? Even better.

Her mother wasn't the only one who only liked fishing when real fish weren't involved.

"I'm glad we worked that out," she said sweetly. "I can't wait to see what servants' quarters look like in a whole palazzo."

The last time she'd stayed here it had been in his vast, glorious bedroom that had made it clear that if this was a palace, he was its king. Today, he only laughed that dark, affecting laugh once more and then turned on his heel, beckoning her to follow him through the palazzo, but this time away from where she knew that bedroom was.

Irinka told herself she was *glad*.

He climbed the grand stair, then moved toward the back of the grand house, taking her all the way up to the very top where the roof was slanted and the rooms were tiny. The actual servants' quarters, just as she'd requested.

She supposed that he expected her to start weeping and wailing, begging to be taken down to some fancy part of the palazzo that better suited the daughter of a duke.

The joke was on him. She had been raised by Roksana, who liked to tell dark and disturbing stories about her childhood while simultaneously complaining that everyone in her adopted country was so *soft*. Squishy, even. Roksana was not a fan of coddling or anything else that might make life easy. She had been at great pains to make certain that her daughter was hardier than most.

Especially once her father had acknowledged her existence. And his paternity.

These are not gifts that he gives you, she would say. *These are your birthright. But they will also make you a soft target if you are not careful.*

The upshot of that was that Irinka had often slept on a pallet on the floor in their flat, her bed being deemed off-limits to her whenever her mother felt she was losing her edge.

The little room that Zago showed her into was a major upgrade from a pallet. It had a solid bed, a small chest of drawers, and a hanging rack for any clothes Irinka might have had with her if she hadn't been swiped up off the Portobello Road on a Tuesday morning.

"How homey," Irinka said brightly. She turned to him and beamed. "When do I report for duty?"

"I believe the kitchen feeds the staff in an hour," he replied stiffly. "I will inform the *maggiordomo* that you are to be put straight to work."

Again he paused, as if expecting pushback.

"Can't wait," she replied, smiling widely.

And then Irinka had the pleasure of seeing what she was pretty sure was temper on his face before he left her there, closing the door decisively behind him.

"Worth it," she murmured into the quiet of the little room.

She stood there a moment, listening to his footsteps retreat. Then she went and sat on the bed, wondering if that heartbeat of hers would ever slow down again. She put her hand on her chest and held it there, as if that could soothe her treacherous heart into behaving.

As if anything was going to be a balm on the wound that was Zago, when nothing ever had been.

Irinka felt that same buried sob in her chest. She felt a telltale kind of itch at the back of her eyes. But she stayed where she was, breathing steadily, until it went away.

Only then did she go to the window on the back side of the palazzo and look out. It wasn't the Grand Canal there before her. It was red-tiled roofs and church spires, domes and makeshift viewing platforms, narrow canals with gondolas aplenty and wooden walkways that ran alongside them.

She heard bells in the distance. The light changed constantly, dancing into the shadows of the old city, and seemed to come from a different sun that shone down elsewhere.

Maybe it was because everything here was doomed. Venice was sinking, everyone knew that. Maybe it was as magical as it was because it had never been meant to last.

Though thinking such things made the urge to sob come back, and she didn't want that.

Irinka pulled out her mobile again, canceled all of her pending appointments, and then opened her messages to find her three friends in a flurry of speculation.

Maybe I'm wrong, Auggie had texted, but didn't Irinka go to Venice the summer after we graduated from uni?

I think you know that she did, Lynna replied. And when she came back, she was oddly brittle.

Irinka took exception to that. Oddly brittle? She had been nothing of the sort. She had been marching around in the new life they were building together like a proper soldier with a broken heart, and none of them had been any the wiser.

She had *protected* them from her pain.

I gave her flowers of hope and plants of remembrance, Maude chimed in.

The funny thing was that Irinka remembered those flowers. They had been bright, happy peonies that she would never have bought for herself, too afraid of being *soft*. And the plants—bright, bold, green things she wouldn't have the slightest idea how to identify—were still in the office, still going strong, in complete defiance of Irinka's noted black thumb.

Do we suppose the sudden, pressing matter is in fact a boy? Auggie asked.

Irinka would be the absolute last person to share her private life even with her closest friends, Lynna replied. So I couldn't possibly speculate. By which I mean yes, clearly a boy.

Rose, hawthorn, and lemon balm for heartbreak, Maude added. It makes a lovely tea.

Irinka couldn't take it. Venice is actually one of the foremost holiday destinations on the planet, she found herself typing. Furiously. A person doesn't need a reason to go to Venice. Venice exists. That's reason enough.

Now she's a travelogue, Auggie observed.

Lynna sent a thumbs-up emoji. And then: This sudden love for Venice is more than I knew about Irinka five minutes ago, anyway.

It turns out that the brother of one of the women that Felipe was toying with took exception to the way his sister's relationship ended, Irinka wrote, hoping her frosty tone was making it into the text bubbles. We're discussing the moral ramifications.

...That sounds dangerous, Maude wrote.

It is not dangerous at all, Irinka assured them. It is actually very boring. I'm perfectly capable of handling men, as you might recall, given it is in fact MY JOB.

Is he hot? Auggie asked. Irinka decided that was enough texting for the day.

Also, it was a ridiculous question. Was Zago hot? Was the earth round? Was Venice the most achingly beautiful place she'd ever seen?

None of that was worth answering, because there was only one answer.

She decided to leave her room and take a wander down the hall, where she found a sitting room that looked softly lived in, and a lavatory that was clearly communal. That was fair enough. It reminded her of living in halls at university. Irinka splashed water on her face and wished that she had a toothbrush.

Then she wandered downstairs, even though she knew it wasn't quite time to present herself in the kitchens yet.

When she made it down to the bottom of the great stair, she stopped and looked toward the great door. She knew that if she raced through it, she'd be out in that courtyard. And if she wanted, she could flag someone down on the Grand Canal, maybe steal a boat if there was one at the dock, even take her chances with a swim—

But instead of doing any of that, she simply stood there.

It was almost as if she didn't want to leave.

And she didn't understand. Surely she should be itching at the chance. She should have heaved herself through the door and taken her chances.

But there was nothing in her that wanted to do that. It was like her body was protesting the very notion on a deep, bone level.

Irinka turned back toward the palazzo, away from her bid for freedom, and then went still.

Because Zago stood there at the top of the flight of grand, imposing stairs, watching her.

"Did you think I was going to run away?" she asked.

Though she sounded a good deal *throatier* than she'd intended.

"I'm wondering why you haven't," he replied.

She was too, despite her desire to go fishing earlier. But the moment he said that, she stopped caring about it and made herself shrug with as much nonchalance as she could manage.

"I've always wanted the opportunity to play Cinderella," she told him as if this really was nothing but a jolly lark. "I'm rather disappointed that there aren't cinders and ash in my little garret room." She held her arms away from her, indicating the clothes she'd put on for a rainy London morning. It seemed like a lifetime ago now. "I do hope you have some rags for me. That will really set the scene."

He shook his head, almost sadly, as he came down those wide steps and was once again standing in front of her. And she couldn't deny the heat between them, as wild as ever. Or that she recognized instantly that the scent that seemed to wind all around her was something she often thought she smelled in her dreams. Something like spice but unidentifiable.

She had never smelled anything like it.

When she dropped her hands back to her sides, she hit herself in the thighs a little harder than necessary, like that might snap her out of this.

"Still playing your games," he said, almost sorrowfully, but that heat in his gaze was more like temper. "I wonder what will happen when the gameplaying ends.

And it is only you and me, the truth of things, lying unvarnished between us."

"For that to happen, you would have to also stop playing games. And I don't think you're in any mood to do that, are you?" He looked as if he might respond, but she shook her head. "Don't kid yourself, Zago. I wasn't the only person in that relationship that summer. I was just the one who left before we burned ourselves alive."

Then she stepped around him, carefully, because the urge to simply melt into him was so strong that she was afraid that she might accidentally succumb to it. And then find herself in his arms without meaning to, and then what would she do?

Because one thing she knew entirely too well was that untangling herself from this man's touch, from the way he looked at her, not to mention how he made her *feel*, seemed impossible. Clearly she hadn't done a great job after the last time.

So she made her way around him almost gingerly— keeping her distance—and then headed off toward the kitchen to start playing her assigned role to perfection.

Because she was pretty sure that if she did, she might drive him mad.

A goal worth aiming for, she thought. So Irinka was smiling as she went.

CHAPTER FOUR

IT HAD NOT occurred to Zago that she would choose menial labor.

He thought that merely suggesting that she take to his bed to save her little business would lead to cracks in that armor of hers—because they both knew that whatever else that had happened between them, what had happened in his bed had been honest.

Scorchingly so.

Zago had certainly never intended to pressure her into his bed, not least because he did not think that *pressure* would be required. But he was also not averse to using whatever tools he could to come to a place that felt like justice when it came to her. And him. And Nicolosa most of all.

If he'd really thought she would sleep with him on demand, as some kind of payment, he would never have offered it as an option. Because in all his fantasies about what it might be like to have another night with Irinka— not that he admitted that such notions haunted him— in not a single one of them was the heat between them *transactional*.

He'd assumed that she would not wish to get intimate with him, because there had been too much honesty there and that had clearly been too much for her. He had intended to greatly enjoy watching her try to play one of her little roles with him, here.

There was no way she could do it. He was sure of it, and he'd intended to take great pleasure in watching her try.

Zago had rather thought that claiming she needed to spend a month in his bed was a bit of a taste of her own medicine. Strange things happened when a person messed around with other people's emotions. He had wanted to give her a much-needed object lesson.

Before she'd appeared at the palazzo, he may also have imagined that her power over him would be lessened, but still. He knew that in the end he was a man of honor.

He had never been anything else.

All Zago had wanted was to make her think twice about this role she played—the role that had led directly to his beloved sister's unhappiness.

He had thrown out the option for domestic service as more of a nuclear option, so perhaps he shouldn't have been surprised that the impossible woman chose it.

Then again, revenge could take many forms. Apparently she chose the menial route.

At first, he didn't think that she would really go through with it.

"Your expectation is that I put an Englishwoman of noble blood to work in the kitchens?" his *maggiordomo*, the austere Roderigo, asked in astonishment when Zago informed him of the addition to his staff. "Surely not. Surely I am misunderstanding your intent."

"That is exactly my intent," Zago told this man who had looked at him in the same exacting manner when Zago had been an unsupervised child and given to sliding down the banisters of ancient stairs in this place. "I think that daily chores will be just the thing *because* she is an Englishwoman of noble blood. Though half of her is quite Russian, if you are concerned."

He did not think it germane to mention that Roksana, who was still emblazoned on the covers of magazines with regularity, was no one's stereotype of any hardy Russian peasant, grimly tilling a field.

"With respect," Roderigo ventured. And he paused, as if considering the parameters of that respect. Or perhaps if he wished to show any respect at all in the face of such extraordinary events… But the man's lifetime of service to the Baldissera family clearly won the day. By a razor-thin margin. "It is only that I'm not certain you understand the care that goes into maintaining the palazzo. For anyone to be accepted to work here requires a great deal of training, no matter how menial the labor."

"I trust you," Zago said, his patience about as thin as that margin. And Roderigo immediately inclined his head, because he had not lowered himself to arguing with a member of the family in the span of anyone's memory. No matter the provocation.

He expected Roderigo to come back almost at once, Irinka in tow, because he could not imagine her working—*really working*—any more than Roderigo could.

Yet that night went by and there was no sign of her. The next morning, he woke early, expecting half the staff to be lined up outside his door with lists of their complaints about her princess behavior and inability to complete the tasks *they* did by rote, but the hallway was empty when he looked.

He was forced to demean himself and start skulking around until he could find her himself.

And when he did, he stopped in astonishment.

Because when she'd stayed here before, he didn't think she'd ever risen before noon. Partly because they had stayed up half the night, so perhaps that wasn't a fair assessment of how she normally greeted a new day. But still, it was barely six in the morning today. Early by any measure.

And the infamous socialite daughter of scandal and notoriety that was Irinka Scott-Day was not reclining in an eye mask somewhere. She was out with the rest of the maids, scrubbing the steps that led up into the palazzo. The way they did every morning, and much of the courtyard as well, to get the salt off from the canals' brackish water.

She didn't even look like herself. Someone had given her clothes and they were too baggy, and certainly not of the quality she generally preferred. Her hair was in two braids tight to her head in front and then woven together at the back. It was the sort of hairstyle that he thought would be better served under a tiara. In some ballroom somewhere.

Not scrubbing the steps.

Zago didn't like it. Though he could not have said why.

And he certainly shouldn't have found it appealing, despite his best efforts to quell it, that she seemed to take so easily to something that should have broken her. That had been engineered to break her, in fact.

But she was anything but broken. Irinka seemed to have no trouble whatsoever pitching in with the rest of them, as if she'd spent every day of her life doing absolutely nothing but scrubbing floors. When he knew that wasn't the case. Everyone knew it wasn't. Her manicure alone announced the truth of things without her having to say a word.

And yet even more strangely, the other maids seemed to have no trouble with her. There were no rolling eyes behind her back, no whispers, no quickly hidden smiles of disdain.

This was not at all how he'd planned this.

But if she could be so stubborn, then so too could he.

A few more days passed, and Zago continued to receive no bad reports about Irinka's tenure as a new staff member. He received no reports about Irinka at all, for that matter.

It had been a week when he finally caved and asked Roderigo.

"I keep expecting to hear complaints about your newest hirc," he said that evening, watching the sun set on the canal, a pageant of bright colors mixed into the water until it was all the same gleaming mystery.

It made him think of Irinka even more and he resented it.

"It is the most extraordinary thing," said Roderigo, sounding almost…overawed?

Zago looked at him, a bit narrowly. This from a man who had distinguished himself by failing to be impressed by anything, always. He had been running this house since before Zago was born and in all that time he had always remained resolutely under-awed by every person of means and consequence he'd encountered.

It was part of why Zago trusted him so implicitly.

"Don't tell me that you have fallen under her spell," Zago murmured. He swirled his *aperitivo* in its heavy crystal tumbler. "I am astounded at you, Roderigo."

The older man seemed as unimpressed with *him* as ever. He regarded Zago, his employer, with a cool eye. "Everyone knows precisely who she is, of course. Most of us remember when she was here before. And yet never could we have imagined that when put to the test, she would rise to meet it so beautifully."

"Beautifully," Zago repeated in disbelief.

"I suppose we are all of us given to our biases," the older man said then, in a philosophical tone of voice that Zago had never heard come from dour Roderigo in all his life. "I would expect a fine young lady such as the *signorina* to not only be emotionally unprepared to work as we do, but to be physically incapable as well. And yet she has been unflagging and enthusiastic in turn. She is the first one up in the morning and the last still working at night." He sighed, and appeared to remember himself, taking on his habitual *almost* frown. "I only wish this were not some bargain between the two of you, for I would hire her on the spot."

That was precisely what Zago did not wish to hear. He eyed the man who had in many ways raised him somewhat balefully. "I'm delighted to hear it."

The old man stopped pretending that he was polishing the statuary and fixed his employer with a narrow glare. "At the risk of overstepping—"

"Is that considered a risk in this house? I thought it was considered a perk of employment."

Roderigo ignored him. "There is a point at which a person can become blinded to the reality of things, too busy are they focusing on the past. Making it the present, when it cannot be. It can *never* be. And then it, too, is lost to time."

If his *maggiordomo* had hauled off and gut punched him, he would not have been any more surprised.

"Thank you," Zago replied after a moment, and even that was a challenge. "That will be all."

Roderigo inclined his head and withdrew so gracefully that it only made Zago feel churlish.

He had not bargained for this.

To be haunted by her even more than usual, because he knew that she was sleeping under this roof.

To think that at any moment he might turn a corner in his own home and find her there, shooting him an insolent look from those too-blue eyes and then carry on with some menial task as if he did not exist.

He had created the situation, he understood that. But it was still insupportable. It was *agony*.

And perhaps that was how he found himself moving through the house much later that night, telling himself that he did not wish to disturb anyone and that was why he remained so quiet.

Or perhaps that was simply a matter of plausible deniability.

If anyone had seen him, or heard him, then it was possible he might have thought better of what he was doing.

But no one did.

And Zago kept going, as if drawn through the house by a force outside his control.

He climbed the stairs in dim light until he found his way to the servants' quarters, and it was as if he was in a dream when he was, at last, standing at her door.

Drawn to her as he was when he slept, because he had certainly had a version of this dream before now. Many, many versions of it. More than he cared to admit. All of them with him standing outside a room, a house, and knowing she was within.

All of that longing and grief, despair and desire.

But he was awake this time, alive with this wanting—this need—that tore him inside out whether he indulged it or did not.

And he was aware that there were too many truths *just there*, simmering beneath the surface—

But Zago was not in the mood to sift through such detritus, so he put his hand to the door, opened it up, and stepped inside.

And Irinka, damn her, merely gazed back at him as if she had been expecting him all along.

As if his sudden appearance did not faze her in the least.

She was sitting on her bed, wearing something sloppy and oversize that both hid her figure and accentuated it. She set aside the book she was reading with every appearance of complete serenity and only the faintest hint of irritation, as if she had been having a pleasant evening and was preparing herself—bracing herself—for the excessively minor annoyance that was Zago.

And something in him, something doused in the fuel of that summer three years ago and the reckoning that so far wasn't...*ignited*.

That he should be haunted, pursued by her ghost through his own home, while she sat here so calmly. Reading a book. Completely at her ease and unbothered by all of this.

"I hope you are enjoying yourself," he managed to say, though his voice felt thick on his own tongue.

"I am," she replied with more of that perfect equanimity that made his skin feel six sizes too small. "I feel as if I'm on a spiritual retreat, Zago. Isn't that how a person transcends their ordinary little life? A bit of labor, a bit of chanting, a monastic cell, and ample time to interrogate one's thoughts? I'm certain I will achieve enlightenment at any moment."

It was that arch, amused voice of hers, and he hated it. That cocktail party version of her, brittle and witty in all the worst ways. It was the kind of wit that was too sharp, too unpredictable. The sort that created barriers, when his memories of her were all blurred boundaries, the two of them tangled and entwined in every possible way.

"Why are you looking at me like that?" Her eyebrows rose, and she made no attempt to soften the challenge in her expression. "Is this not what you wanted? A reckoning writ large upon my immortal soul while engaged in a good, old-fashioned mortification of the flesh? It's all so hair-shirted and Catholic. I must be in Italy."

And when he planned this, down to fetching her off the street in England, he had done so with great forethought. He had been careful, plotting it all out like a chess game. If this, then that. If not that, then this. He had allowed for every possible move and had arranged multiple countermoves to address each, or so he'd thought.

But he hadn't planned for *this*.

For her to be almost like a different person altogether. Colder. Harder.

"You have changed," he told her, darkly.

She regarded him coolly, which was at least some kind of improvement on *mild annoyance*. "You taught me a very important lesson, Zago. And don't think I'm not grateful. Before you, I had no idea that I was so susceptible to the kinds of nonsense that other girls indulge in. You showed me that I was no better than any of them. That there was no need to pretend otherwise. And once I accepted that part of myself, I found the true strength that my mother always tried to bring out in me." She smirked. "Kudos."

Something in him simply snapped.

Zago moved to the bed and he reached for her, hauling her into the air and then setting her on her feet before him.

"I cannot understand the game you're playing," he gritted out. "This is simply a role you're playing, like all the others. Because you know and I know that what happened between us was no silly girl's daydream. You know and I know *exactly* what this was."

"I have no idea what you're talking about," she threw at him, but there was a storm in her gaze.

He leaned closer, his hands curling around her shoulders to draw her closer. Or perhaps it was that he bent closer to her, he couldn't tell.

It hardly mattered.

"I told you not to lie to me," he said, so close that it was almost a kiss. "I warned you."

She made a sound of frustration, or perhaps it was the same need that shouted in him, and then she surged forward and up onto her toes to crash her mouth to his.

And the world shifted all around them once more.

This kaleidoscope, this catastrophe.

Every color in the world shattered and brought together, over and over again, every time her tongue touched his.

She angled her head and his hands moved so he could lift her into the air, because he knew what she would do even as she did it—wrapping her legs around his waist and hooking her arms around his neck.

There is nothing cold about *this* Irinka. There was nothing chilly, no barbed comments, no *serene irritation*.

There was only the impossible firestorm that had raged between them from the start.

He could remember it too well, especially now he had her in his arms once more.

He kissed her and kissed her, holding her up and reveling once again at how perfectly they fit together, how exquisitely their bodies seemed to know each other too well.

And he remembered.

That night at the beginning of that summer, looking up from a questionably modernized version of *La Traviata* at La Teatro Fenice, only to catch her eye during the interval.

And Zago had never believed in the kind of electric shock that could stop a man in his tracks, change his life, and make him over to someone new at a glance.

He had never believed that it was possible to look at a woman, feel hollowed out within, and never feel whole again unless he was with her.

And yet he had moved with single-minded purpose toward her, the very moment he'd seen her. He couldn't remember who she had been there with, or why. Nothing had existed for him but the girl with the blue eyes and the jet-black hair—and that look of shocked recognition that they had shared.

It all happened so fast.

He had left this very house that night one version of himself and had come back a different man entirely.

And in all these years since that night, since the summer that had followed it, he had questioned that feeling. He had almost convinced himself that it had been some kind of summer fever, not uncommon in Venice. And he had been something like relieved to discover it had shifted into a certain, driving coldness when he'd realized she was involved with Nicolosa's heartbreak.

But now the truth was here, in his arms, and he was changed anew.

Just as it had three years ago, everything escalated.

His hands moved, finding her bare skin beneath the baggy clothes she wore.

She moaned against his mouth and somehow they were moving, tangling up with each other on that tiny bed that barely fit her, much less the two of them.

But there was something about the situation that made it hotter.

Breathless and wild.

Neither one of them spoke. And there was no need to issue warnings, for surely the both of them were equally aware that most of the palazzo's staff slept nearby.

So it was all breath and hands, tongues and teeth. They wrestled and moved, relearning each other in a blistering rush of heat, moving with each other and against each other and into each other, until he found himself lying on his back with his hands wrapped around her hips.

He lifted her, his gaze finding her as the light neither one of them had bothered to turn off bathed them both in its glare.

Zago could see her perfectly—no dream, no blur—as Irinka pushed herself up on her knees, braced herself against the wall of his chest, and then lowered herself down on him—

And not slowly. She did not *ease* her way.

She was soft and wet, he was huge, and she made a whimpering sound as she took him in, hard and fast.

He pulled her down, smoothing his hand down the length of her spine and holding her face to his chest as she panted. That took some time. Then, slowly, she adjusted, moving her hips incrementally as she tried to accommodate him.

As she relearned him and how deep and wide he filled her.

It had taken a long time that first time, three years ago. It had taken him bringing her to pleasure with his mouth, his fingers. Testing her and teasing her until she was mindless and begging him and bargaining.

Only then did he press inside her body, and he'd done it slowly. It had been a sweet, exquisite torment.

But he had not hurt her.

"Why did you do that?" he asked, there at her ear.

"Maybe," she replied, her face still buried in his chest, "you are not the only one who wanted a reckoning."

Irinka pushed herself up then, and stunned him anew. Her hair was a wreck now, made messy by his hands. It flowed all around her and she still wore what he thought must be some discarded man's T-shirt someone in the house had donated to her, because it drooped off the side of her shoulder. But it gave him tantalizing glimpses of her breasts beneath. And he left it on because he could still slide his hands up and fill his palms with her. He could still pull her closer, and play with her nipples through the thin material with his mouth, because it drove her wild.

But she gazed down at him, and there was moisture in the corner of her eyes, and a tear or two on her cheek, wiped hastily away.

And something about her was so fierce that it made him ache.

Only then did she press her palms hard against his abdomen, and begin to move.

And the glory of this, the sheer, mad wonder, leveled him.

Ruined him.

"If I were you," he told her in a dark whisper, "I would hurry."

Then, at last, she was wholly and entirely the girl he'd known that summer. Her lips curved into something wicked and knowing.

And because she was Irinka, she immediately slowed.

Zago let her play. The way she lowered herself, the way she moved her hips. The way she rocked against him, bracing herself as she did it. He let her experiment with all of these things.

He let her set the pace, the rhythm.

But he also trailed a hand up and over her belly, beneath that shirt, and then tugged her down so she could play her games while his tongue was in her mouth, and he could meet that fire with fire of his own.

With his other hand, he reached between them and pressed down hard, just above the place where they were joined.

And Irinka shattered immediately.

She shattered and she screamed, but he swallowed the sound, taking all of it in his mouth and holding her as she shook and shook.

He kept thrusting into her, harder and harder, as she soared off one peak and then flew higher toward another.

Zago moved back, flipping her over and coming up to hold her close. Then he thrust deep, losing any rhythm save the one they made together, until she was thrown off that cliff once more.

And this time, as she began to calm down, he slowed and spent some time toying with her, too.

Because turnabout was fair play.

"You're a demon," she whispered, half a sigh and half a groan.

"You're welcome," he replied.

But the next time she shattered, he buried his face in her neck, and went with her.

CHAPTER FIVE

IRINKA TOLD HERSELF that one small, inconsequential slip didn't have to *mean* anything.

Zago had stayed in her room that night because neither one of them seemed able to move. They had slept together in that tiny, narrow bed and that had done her no good. She could admit that much. It was too much like all those dreams she'd had, except in a narrow bed like that there was no possibility that every part of her was not touching every part of him.

His scent was the only thing she could smell. He was every breath she took.

She slept and dreamed of him, woke and he was still there, and then it was so easy to simply turn in her sleep and meet him again. And feel him move deep inside of her.

And she had forgotten, that first time, that he really was that big. Long and thick and so hard it made her melt just thinking of it. But that did not mean she needed to slam herself onto him again and again in a kind of desperation that felt like the sharper edge of need.

In any case, he did not seem inclined to allow it.

So even in the dark, half-asleep in the middle of the night, he took his time. He moved his fingers through her slippery heat, making her bite down hard on his shoulder as she burst into flame, then shook all over him.

Only then did he find her molten core and push in, deep.

Only then did he set them both afire until, once again, there was little left of them but ash.

When Irinka woke again, it was morning. The very early morning, and her alarm was going off, and part of her thought that being with Zago was simply a dream. That same dream that she always had.

The dream that had taken her too long to wake up from, even when she'd limped back to England that summer, soft and bruised from the force of all those terrible emotions. Just as her mother had always warned her. She had slept on the floor for months to toughen herself up.

To make sure she would never be *soft* like that again.

But when she sat up, she could feel him all over her body. She was sore in a very specific, deeply satisfying way that made every nerve in her body feel more alive than she had in ages.

Her tiny little room was empty but she was naked in her bed, when Irinka never slept naked. And his shirt was one of the items of clothing strewn about on the floor.

Just in case she intended to keep telling herself she'd dreamed it all.

She went and picked up his shirt, betraying herself entirely when she held it to her face, breathing him in once more.

"Like a bloody addict," she muttered to herself.

Not that thinking that stopped her.

But time was moving along and so she made herself head down the hall to the shower just the same, having learned quickly enough that if she set her alarm just a half hour earlier than everyone else's, she could take her time. Today, she needed it.

And by the time she emerged from all that hot water, she was resolute once more.

There was no denying that she and Zago had chemistry. There was a part of her that was grateful to discover that they still did, that she hadn't been *quite* so foolish a girl as she liked to remember when she thought of that summer. If anything, that chemistry was even stronger now than it had been then.

But *Chemistry is what makes bombs,* Roksana liked to say.

And so Irinka did not go and find him, despite the minor ruckus in her body that urged her to do just that. Instead, she marched herself back down to the kitchen and went back to work.

She worked all day, the way she always did here. And while she had certainly enjoyed needling Zago about the *mortification of her flesh*, such as it was, the truth was that there really was something about this work that she liked.

Irinka was fully aware that part of her ability to enjoy it was because this wasn't actually her life. She was not doomed to scrub floors and steps and clean some rich man's antiques forever. And she knew herself well enough to know that if it had been her life, she would have been far less enamored of it.

But as a break from her life, it was amazing how satisfying it was. She was given concrete tasks and all she had to do was complete them. And when she was finished, she had either achieved what she'd been asked to do or she had not. There was no wiggle room—something was either dusted or dirty. There was no intense problem-solving. No inhabiting roles and gauging every room she walked into so that she could adjust her performance accordingly, and quickly.

No one in this house expected her to be anything but what she was: *il padrone*'s one-time lover back here playing Cinderella games.

It was remarkably freeing.

So much so that it was causing her to think about her life back in London in a way she hadn't in years. To ask herself if what she was doing was sustainable, especially now that all of her friends had found happiness with their new loves in ways that Irinka applauded—for them—but certainly did not understand.

Because the changes her friends had gone through lately raised an interesting question that she kept finding herself pondering as she scrubbed and dusted and polished. She was the one who had made a great many of the contacts that had kept His Girl Friday solvent all these years. But if all of her friends were set for life now, and could work not to survive, but to please themselves...was it necessary for Irinka to continue *her* work, too?

Did she do it because she liked it? Or because the agency needed it?

Or maybe, something in her whispered, *it has a bit*

more to do with the horrible wealthy man who treated your mother—and you—like actual rubbish to be tossed aside in the street, and you thought you might as well go in where smarter heads might fear to tread and help cut a bit of that waste removal *off at the pass?*

She couldn't answer that—or she didn't want to, because what did that say about her and her childhood trauma, how embarrassing that she'd never thought about that before—so while she mulled it all over she let the housework soothe her. On her lunch break she huddled at the back of the palazzo near the narrower canal used for deliveries and frowned out at the water and the steep sides of ancient buildings that rose all around. There were no walkways here, only steep sides and no boats, or she might have felt honor bound to attempt an escape no matter how *soothing* it was to make glass gleam.

Irinka was not foolish enough to tell her friends any of these things. They would all be on the next plane, rushing to her rescue, because they would assume that she had suffered some kind of head injury if she was extolling the virtues of being a domestic servant.

And she did not need rescuing. She never had.

This is all very mysterious, Auggie pointed out in the text chain later that night. Irinka, have you moved to Venice forever? Since when do you keep secrets from us?

I always keep secrets from you, Irinka replied. This you know.

I thought the entire point of Irinka was that she's endlessly and needlessly secretive, Lynna agreed.

Secrets, Maude chimed in, are like walled gardens.

Irinka stared at that text, baffled. And also flooded with the usual surge of affection she felt for Maude and her gardens.

Yes, she texted back. Exactly that.

And she wasn't particularly surprised when her door opened once again, on the other side of midnight.

"Some people knock and wait to be invited in," she pointed out.

"Some people lock their door," Zago replied.

This time he simply crossed to the bed and climbed into it. And she turned to him without any further words and slowly, carefully, *recklessly* they pulled each other into pieces.

And this went on, one week into the next.

Until one night, as they lay there tangled into their usual knot, panting into the crooks of each other's necks, he shifted so he could look down at her.

"I think I've had enough of this," he said.

"That's a crying shame," Irinka murmured. She moved her hips sinuously and smiled when his eyes went blank, because she could feel him harden inside of her. "I'll miss this."

"That is not at all what I mean," Zago replied in that dark way that thrilled her, because she could feel it in her bones.

He stood then, pulled on the trousers he'd worn here only to toss them off upon arrival, and then picked her up. He did not bother to cover her. And Irinka couldn't decide if she was startled, horrified, or wildly entertained when he simply walked out of her room and carried her through the house.

The palazzo was quiet all around them, but those famous paintings on the walls seemed to look askance at her, no doubt as taken aback as she was.

Zago carried her in no great hurry through the grand palace until he reached his own suite and then installed her in his bed.

Where she hadn't been since that summer, but that didn't bear thinking about just then.

"But *il padrone*," Irinka said, smirking at him, "I am but a servant girl."

"I wish you were," he growled at her. "I wish you were anything that simple."

He then demonstrated his feelings on the topic by tying her to the bedposts, because there, in his bedchamber, no one would hear her when she screamed out her pleasure.

So she did.

In the morning she woke to find the light streaming in, which meant that it was late. She sat up in a rush, then froze.

Because Zago was there, lounging in the sitting area near the great fireplace. There was no fire at this time of year, and she thought that was a pity, because even during the stifling-hot summer she'd spent here she'd wished for one.

Though she supposed they'd made their own.

He did not look up from the newspaper that he was reading with a skeptical look on his face. "How nice of you to join us this morning."

"You have made me unpardonably late for my duties," she said. "The staff will be in an uproar."

"They are far too well trained for that," Zago said. He took his time setting the paper aside. And then gazed at her. "I'm sorry to tell you that your tenure as a housemaid has come to an end, Irinka."

He was so beautiful that he made her throat hurt. She could feel a lump forming there, and an ache in her ribs, because something about this man made her feel blurry all over.

As if, given half a chance, she would throw herself into him and disappear.

Three years ago the prospect had terrified her.

She wasn't sure why it was that this time around she could see something almost tempting about such a freefall.

"So it's the dungeons for me, then?" And she really did try to keep her voice light.

"I cannot deny that I've enjoyed these weeks," Zago said, in that deliberate way he had. Yet his amber eyes had that gleam. And she could feel something prickle all over her skin, some kind of warning. "But then, this has always been the problem, has it not? Three years ago I assumed that the only way to contain this was to formalize it. You disagreed."

She actually laughed at that, because it was so unexpected. Like a sucker punch. "How funny." Irinka did not think it was funny at all, but still she kept laughing. "That is not how I remember it."

He had always been so good at this, she thought now. He could sit there as if someone was painting his portrait, a picture of dark masculine serenity, because that was what most people saw.

When all she could see was that simmering fury right there beneath the surface.

"What would you call it?" he asked, in a tone that suggested he was attempting to be reasonable. For her sake. As a gift.

It set her teeth on edge, but then, it was likely meant to.

"I don't see any point in talking about this," she said quietly, instead of succumbing to the lure of indignance. But he only looked at her, one arrogant brow raised high. And she had no doubt that he would keep her here, naked in his bed, until she had the conversation he thought they ought to have. That being the case, she decided there was no point in arguing. Better to fight with a weapon she had, she'd always thought. "If that's your recollection, there's no point arguing about it. Call it whatever you like."

That amber gaze of his was searing, then. "I am sorry that it is still such a burden to you to have a simple conversation. Three years have passed from the night you ran off without a backward glance. How silly of me to imagine that some maturity might have occurred in the meantime."

He intended that to be a blow, she could see that. And it was. She felt her temper surge in response, but she tamped it down. "If you think I am a silly little fool of a girl, the way you did back then, what purpose is there in having this conversation?" When he only glared back at her, she smiled wide, though it made her lips hurt.

"I've never denied the chemistry between us. I was as overwhelmed by it as you were. But surely you understand that it was toxic."

"What I recall is that you told me you loved me, Irinka," he said, in that intense, low voice of his. "And that it was a lie."

The unfairness of that swept through her like some kind of dark tide.

It was a wonder that she stayed where she was, sitting up in his bed—the very same bed where she had lost her virginity to this man and experimented with sensuality and sex, love, and longing for the whole of that breathless, airless summer. He had taught her so much pleasure, so much joy, so much despair. She had felt something like *skinless* in his presence, so attuned to his every move, his every whisper, his every thought.

It was right here in this bed where she had learned that despite all of her mother's teachings over the years, she was actually fully capable of the deepest, wildest emotions.

It was also here, in this bed, where she had come to understand that if she did not leave this place and this man, she would *combust*. And there would be nothing left of her but ash.

And everything she'd ever been taught about the ways foolish women lost themselves in powerful men would have been for naught.

Even if she'd toyed with the idea, back then, that somehow she might be able to handle involving her heart the way Roksana had sternly counseled her never, ever to do. Not ever.

She could remember the exquisite grief of that summer vividly, knowing that she had only so much time before she would lose herself to the black hole of this passion that she knew even then could only eat them both alive.

Because that was what a passion like that did. Irinka was the result of such a passion herself, no matter what vile things the Duke liked to claim in the aftermath. She had known better.

But oh, how she had loved him. As well as she could, for as long as she could.

"You know perfectly well that it was no lie," she said now, and it was a grueling sort of effort not to give in to the urge to shout at him. He wanted that, she knew. Because it proved that what he said about her was true and it *wasn't.* "What you won't accept is that there was no way to control this. No matter how hard you tried. Making me into some perfect Venetian housewife couldn't have changed that."

"Baldisseras are not housewives," he retorted with a silken fury. "But even if they were, I fail to see the issue. I thought you took great pleasure in these roles you play."

"I might enjoy playing a role, it's true." And this time, the way her temper rose was different. It wasn't a combustible fire, or any kind of explosion. It was a slow kind of simmering thing. She didn't think it would eat her alive—she thought it might scald her if she didn't let it out. "What about you, Zago? No matter what act *I* put on, I always know the difference between the stage and me. Can you say the same?"

He stood then, though he did not move any closer. Not yet. "I don't know what you mean."

"Don't you?" She let her head tip to one side, but she didn't look away from him. "You hide away here in this half-ruined palace in a sinking city, telling yourself that what you're doing is building out your family's legacy. You can never measure up to the things your father claimed were required of the heir to all this because he made them impossible on purpose. Impossible duties. Unacceptable responsibilities. The weight of all that history and a moral code he did not live up to himself. And yet you can never make up for what your mother—"

"If I were you," Zago said, very, very quietly, "I would not speak about my mother."

"Why not?" Irinka asked him. Or dared him. "Isn't she the real reason this house is so haunted? Isn't she the reason that your father all but abandoned his own children? Why he decided that he could lose himself in your family's illustrious past, making up wilder and wilder stories as to why it was that he would need to live forever and—"

"I warned you."

Zago was moving then, crossing the room swiftly until he was there at the bedside. And so Irinka moved too, meeting him. Going up on her knees so that they were face-to-face.

So that he would see that this time she had no intention of backing down.

"You were the one who thought it sounded like a fine idea to tear into our past this morning," she pointed out. "Or is it only my past that you think needs interrogation?"

"Your past is complicated, is it not?" His voice was like ice, his eyes like chips of obsidian. "It is no wonder you walk around with a chip on your shoulder. You have been forced to carry the shame of your parents' affair, forced to answer their sins, all your life."

"I spent almost no time at all thinking about my parents' affair," Irinka said with a laugh that was not forced, exactly—but was also not precisely *organic*. "My mother has had a great many affairs, as it happens. I spent time considering precisely none of them."

"I don't believe you."

"That's all right," she replied, and her voice was something like soft now. Something like it, anyway. "Shame requires secrets. When a secret shame is in every paper, there's actually a ceiling on it. There is no further shame once that ceiling has been met." Irinka took a breath, and said the rest of it. "I'm not sure the same thing can be said about guilt. Especially the misplaced guilt of a son who thought he should have saved everyone in this family, but couldn't."

Including your sister, she wanted to say, but didn't quite dare.

She could see from the look on his face that he wanted to put his hands on her. There was a part of her that wanted that, too. Because maybe he'd forgotten this, in their years apart from each other. It wasn't that they hadn't talked the last time, it was that they hadn't had their discussions in *words* back then.

It had all been heat and disaster, wildfires and regrets.

Maybe it made it easier to mischaracterize people.

But he did not touch her then, despite the temper and heat in his dark amber gaze. And she couldn't tell if she wanted to celebrate him for that or mourn it.

"My mother was not like yours," he told her after a moment, all that old pain in his voice. And Irinka found herself holding her breath, wondering if he was actually going to talk about something she had only ever read about in anodyne news articles and taut little paragraphs of snide speculation. "She was a fragile, emotional creature. She was raised for sunlight and ballrooms, laughter and parties. And my father may have wished to grant her those things at some point, but he was a man burdened by his obsessions."

"I hesitate to point out that such a burden runs in your family," she said. "And in your case, involves kidnap."

She would not have dared to say something like that to him three years ago.

His eyes blazed. "I've talked to every servant who was in this house back then," he told her. "I have made it clear that it was only their honesty I was looking for, to gain some kind of perspective on events that occurred before my birth. So that I could better understand what happened later."

"You don't have to dig this up," she said then, because it hurt, and that was the part that she'd forgotten. That when this man hurt, she did, too. It was so unfair. And it made everything else that much harder.

"Venice is a city of graves," Zago told her darkly. "We float upon our ancestors and sink, in time, to meet them. The veil between these things is cracked, eroded, washed away. And my mother was not made to live in the in-between." His jaw worked. "Over time, she grew sadder, and I do not think there was any cure for it. But I also think that neither she nor my father thought to look for one."

There was no part of Irinka that wanted to have this conversation any longer. But she couldn't seem to stop herself from merely…kneeling there. Sitting back on her heels, studying his face, trying to understand him at last.

She couldn't pretend that wasn't what she was doing.

"And this is never something I would say to my sister," Zago told her, gruffly, "but it is a certainty that our mother did not recover after giving birth to her. She was already frail and a shadow of herself, and then…"

He trailed off and shook his head, his shoulders stiff as if even this was a responsibility he carried.

"Zago." Irinka said his name deliberately. She interlaced her fingers before her and held his gaze as best she could. "I didn't bring her up because I was trying to hurt you."

"Why not?" he threw back at her. "I should have expected it."

That felt like a low blow, so low it took her breath away. "Because I'm so terrible?"

"Because I did it first."

And that emboldened her, somehow. "I only meant that the way you look at what happened between us before doesn't take into account that, perhaps, neither one of us is well-equipped to handle that much emotion. That much…"

But she had never known what to call this. How to quantify it.

"Is that why you went out and became who you became?" Zago asked, quieter now. But that fire in his gaze still burned. "Did you really believe—*do* you really believe—that spending your life breaking up relationships for these cowardly men who cannot do it themselves was preferable to marrying me?"

She had not expected him to *say* it. Sometimes she thought she had imagined that part, there at the bitter end.

Sometimes it was easier to think she must have.

"Zago—"

His gaze gave her no quarter, then. "Or is it that you thought that marrying into this family was a death sentence?"

And she must have known that he would go there. Wasn't that where this conversation had always been heading? Wasn't this why they'd avoided it in the past?

Because Zago kept going. "Just as it was for my mother when she took her own life."

CHAPTER SIX

HE COULDN'T BELIEVE that he had actually asked that question. When he'd promised himself, time and again, that he would not. That it didn't matter.

That *why* was a fool's game and he had never been much for games. He'd never had the time to indulge himself in such frivolous pastimes.

And in any case, she hadn't married him. She had left him.

Those were the only facts that mattered.

But Irinka looked…winded. She sank back a little farther on her heels, as if she'd deflated, there before his eyes.

"That had nothing to do with it," she said after a moment. "I wouldn't say I was aware of all the ghosts here that summer. There was only you. And this. I'm not sure I thought about anything else until afterward."

"I find that hard to believe."

Meaning, he did not believe it at all. There were so many scandals and tragedies in Venice. Every ruined palazzo was a treasure trove of loss and pain, family secrets and shame. Sometimes he thought he'd like to make a map of the sorrows here that marked this city through the ages.

But he had only ever been intimately acquainted with *this* family and *this* palace.

And the woman who had run from him as if he was the ghost here, all along.

"Zago. You and I..." Irinka shook her head, her blue eyes clouded, then. "It wasn't healthy. Nothing that happened between us was *healthy*. It was overwhelming. It blotted out the sun. It was unsustainable and I don't understand why you don't see that."

"Anything is sustainable if you *try to* sustain it," he said, darkly.

She blew out a breath that sounded far too much like a sob. And he hated seeing anything but brightness in her gaze. "Imagine if you considered the possibility that everything I do or say is not designed to hurt you, Zago. What then?"

And he opened his mouth to immediately refute that, like some kind of knee-jerk reaction that wasn't his to countermand—

But he stopped himself.

A memory teased at the edges of his thoughts, then seemed to bloom into being. Some deathly-dull meal with his parents, long ago. He had only been a boy, though he had considered himself a man, and he had viewed these forced family moments as a torture designed deliberately to plague him.

As was his custom, he had tuned his parents out completely, since they were given to their tedious discussions of the things he was certain *he* would never lower himself to care about, like politics and the weather and the opera.

But something in their tones caught at him and he'd

lifted his head from his daydreams, focusing on the two of them for a change. There had been a shift.

His mother had sighed. His father had been frowning.

If it was something that could be fixed, I know you would fix it, his mother had said. *Like you do every other broken thing in this house.*

Zago had looked away again, assuming they were talking about the usual repairs or floods. It wasn't until many, many years later that the memory had come back to him and he'd thought to wonder if it had been a very different sort of conversation after all.

And then he'd had to wonder if his father's obsession with the family's history was his way of coping with what couldn't be cured in the present.

Even after his mother had died, his father had hidden himself away in the libraries, chasing down arcane little bits of fact and fable and painstakingly piecing it all together, as if a finely researched mosaic of the Baldissera past would redeem what had happened to him.

To all of them.

Was what he was doing here—to Irinka—really all that different?

She had offered him hope, that summer. That he could do this differently. That he could navigate this life better than his parents had done if she was with him. That they could find their way, together.

Then she had taken that hope with her when she'd gone.

And so he had hunted her down. He had—happily—arranged for her to be bodily removed from London and brought here. He had insisted that it was all about Nicolosa and yet, behold—here was Irinka, naked in his bed.

Was he any less obsessed than his father, in the end?

Or any less sad than his mother?

That settled on him like the weight of a new palazzo, with all its history and legend, bills and renovations.

And Zago had always considered himself the most rational of men. He hadn't had any other choice, had he? Growing up in a house where his mother was so fragile, so often ill, and forever victim to the voices in her head, and his father retreated further and further into the past while leaving it to Zago to take charge of things.

Which he had.

How could he have done that if he was not all that was reasonable and rational?

But he was staring down at Irinka now. This woman who, little as he wished to admit it, had been haunting him for years now.

This woman who he had imagined was a terrible party princess and an entitled brat. He'd been certain he could bring her here, put pressure on her, and expect her to crumble.

Instead, she had taken on her so-called Cinderella role with good humor and a surprising work ethic.

He could admit, now, that she'd shocked him.

And then there was what had happened between them since.

Zago couldn't pretend that he hadn't entertained the thought of what might happen between them if they were ever together again. But he hadn't truly believed that would happen. He had imagined that he would confront her here. Perhaps rake over the past. That he would find some grim satisfaction in that, or better still, find himself indifferent.

And instead, there was this.

There was Irinka in his bed again and the taste of her in his mouth. There was Irinka, kneeling there before him with her blue eyes wide, her hair a mess, and a distraught look on her face.

Not the expression of the shallow, selfish girl he'd imagined she was these past three years—and certainly this past month.

But then, did he really believe that she was the woman he'd decided she was in her absence? The woman he'd pretended she was, because that made it easy to dismiss what had happened between them, or cast himself the victim, or otherwise excuse himself from what had happened that summer?

When, as she had just said, it had been all-consuming between them, but it had not been *healthy*.

Zago wasn't sure he knew what *healthy* was.

Thinking these things made him feel a bit too much as if he was standing on shaky foundations. The same way her question had done.

What if you considered the possibility that everything I do or say is not designed to hurt you, Zago?

Maybe he was afraid that if he admitted any of that, if he allowed that question to alter him in any way, it would be worse.

But Zago had not lived a life that had ever allowed him to worry over much about the things that made him afraid. Whether he was afraid or not of something had very little to do with his actions.

He'd learned that here, too.

"Are you going to answer me?" she asked, and he realized he'd been standing there too long, all these things racing through his head.

So he blew out a breath and told himself that might clear his mind. He moved closer to her and really took in how she reacted. She didn't move. She didn't brace and she didn't flinch, which was, perhaps, a low bar.

Her eyes widened even more, however, and he wondered how he'd never noticed that she really seemed not to know that nothing on this earth could compel him to hurt her.

Not with his hands, anyway.

He climbed onto the bed next to her, then shifted them both around until they were lying on their sides, looking at each other.

Though he noticed that she was holding her breath.

"All right, then," Zago said, trying this out. This new *consideration* she'd suggested. "You are not trying to hurt me. What happens now?"

Irinka looked startled. She blinked, and then, slowly, a smile began to take over her face. A benediction Zago had not realized he needed.

"I…don't know what happens now. I don't think I imagined it was possible that you would listen to me."

He reached over and pushed a hank of her black hair back, then tucked it behind her ear. "Am I really so overbearing?"

"Intense," she said. Still smiling. "Always so very intense."

"And you think that this intensity is inhibiting me in some way?"

She laughed, and then changed her expression, frowning thunderously. Then she made her voice deep when she spoke. "Of course not. Because here in this palazzo that has been in the Baldissera family from time immemorial, intensity alone keeps the stones from sinking beneath the waterline."

It took Zago a long, stunned moment to understand that she was mocking him. Teasing him, he amended. He didn't like it—

But in the next moment, when she smiled at him again, he decided that it was not so bad. It was not terrible to be the reason she smiled like that.

So he moved forward, and she did too, and it was so different to kiss like this. The sun beaming in. laughter between them, and none of that dark, driving need and desperation that colored every memory of every moment he'd ever had with her.

He felt like it was some kind of gift, that laughter. This moment. This kiss.

So he took his time moving his way down her body, spreading that heat. Losing himself in that fire.

Until he could settle himself between her legs, lick his way into her core, and set them to gleaming bright like the sun.

He was too conscious of the way they'd shifted. The magic of it, dancing within him, and he wanted to give that back to her. He dedicated himself to casting that spell.

Zago pressed incantations into her most tender places, encouraging her with the sounds he made low in his throat as he lifted her up toward the pinnacle, then backed away. Once. Again.

"I will kill you," she managed to cry out, her back arched and her arms over her head. "If you don't kill me first."

"No need to fling yourself into the abyss so quickly, Irinka," he murmured, smiling as he traced her soft heat with his fingers. "Martyrdom is so messy."

Then he bent his head to her once more.

And only when she was sobbing with pleasure did he crawl his way back up her body. He memorized her as he went, etching her into his bones.

Tattooing her every response, her every scent and taste, deep into his skin.

Exploring this light they made together with her, while he could.

She pushed him onto his back and he let her, sprawling out on the bed while she took a turn at making spells, letting her hair brush over him as she slid her way over his chest, his abdomen, then lower still to take the length of him deep into her mouth.

And he let her play with him, for a time. It was exquisite. It was too much.

It was Irinka. The agony and the longing and the glory. All her.

But he did not intend to end this in her mouth. Not this time.

When he could take no more, Zago pulled her back and laughed at the half crestfallen, half outraged look on her face.

"I wanted to—" she began, hotly.

"You can bear the tragedy, I promise," he told her.

And then he crawled over her and thrust deep within her, smiling as she broke into pieces. He held her as she shook and sobbed, and then, as she came back to him, he began to move.

Slow and steady, until she broke apart again. Then faster the next time.

Until she was moaning his name and he was something like feral, incapable of anything like control until he lost himself, too.

Only with her, he thought as he spun out into eternity, holding her tight. *Only Irinka.*

For a long while afterward, they lay there together, holding on to each other while their breath stayed wild.

Later, they sat together on the balcony and looked out at the *vaporettos* and *gondolas* going by on Grand Canal. He called down for food and Irinka seemed entertained to greet the friends she'd made among his staff when they served her.

"Bit of an upgrade," she murmured to them as the meal was laid out. "I rather think it's because of my excellent scrubbing of that front step."

And when the staff were unable to muffle their laughter, something that would have been unthinkable in any other circumstance, Zago reminded himself that it was not necessary for him to be *quite so* intense all the time, and allowed it.

He found it a particular pleasure to break bread with this woman. To talk of things that were not so emotional, or so personal. To share an anecdote or two, and not look for land mines in every sentence.

It reminded him of all those conversations he'd thought were boring when he was a child. Were they simply a bit of plaster over the cracks, smoothing out the bones of the place, a way to keep things humming along like this—all sunshine and a smile?

That felt like another revelation.

And so he was unprepared for it when Irinka turned to him at the end of the meal, the afternoon sun bathing her in a golden glow, and smiled ruefully. "You know I can't stay here," she said.

Zago was unprepared, and his first reaction was the searing shock of betrayal.

But there was something wise and knowing in those blue eyes of hers, as if she could see his reaction all over him. As if she was waiting for him to backtrack and start hurling accusations at her again, as if he hadn't learned a thing today.

He would obviously rather tear off his own head.

"This is gorgeous. Venice is like a dream and I'll even admit I didn't mind the hard labor." She smiled at that, inviting him to find the housework she'd called *hard labor* as amusing as she clearly did. "But I do have a life in London. I have commitments."

"That tasteless job of yours," he said, before he could think better of it.

"You and I will have to disagree about what it is I do," Irinka said, but not as if she was taking offense. "And I cannot compromise a client's privacy, of course, but I can tell you that there are no repeat clients on our roster who I would recommend as a love interest for anyone. Much less your sister."

There were a thousand things Zago wanted to say to that. He said none of them.

She nodded, though. As if he'd said enough. "I have been here for weeks now. Surely there can be no more reckoning required."

He wanted to tell her to apologize to Nicolosa, but he remembered something she had said at the start. When she'd pointed out that he wasn't off pounding down Felipe De Osma's door, demanding apologies from *him*.

And the truth that was sitting on him strangely today, despite how rational he believed himself to be, was that the moment he'd seen Irinka's name he had thought of nothing else. Nothing and no one. "I will certainly point out to my sister that a man who would hire someone like you was never the man she thought he was in the first place."

"And never will be," Irinka said in soft agreement.

Then she sat there before him, an odd sort of look on her beautiful face, and it took him a moment to realize that she was waiting.

She was waiting for him to decide what it was that he would do now. She was giving him that space and he didn't know what to make of it.

Or, something in him whispered, *you do know.*

He thought of his poor, lost mother, who had never been able to get past her own broken heart and the twisting paths in her brain. He thought of his father, who had lost himself completely in his fantasy over what the past might have been, if only he could prove it.

He thought of his sister, who could not let go of a man she never should have dated in the first place.

And here he was, once again trying to hold on tight to someone who didn't want to stay.

Did it really matter why?

He already knew that if he dragged her back here, they would end up the same place. The way they had this time. And he liked this place more than he should, but it was no different from that summer they'd shared.

Fleeting. Temporary.

Because he wanted things she either did not wish to give, or couldn't.

Maybe what he was having trouble with here was nothing more or less than the oldest story there was. A person, no matter their strength and power, will, or determination, could not make another do anything they did not wish to do.

Not really.

And did Zago truly want something he had to force?

He already knew the answer. Which was, he was certain, the reason he had never asked himself that question before.

And so, even though it made him feel as if he was cracking wide open and shattering in half, burning down like the front part of this palazzo once had and with less hope that there could be any kind of reconstruction, Zago Baldissera did the one thing he had never done in all his days.

He surrendered.

"Very well, then," he made himself say, perhaps more gravely than necessary, but it was all he was capable of when her smile was too knowing and the sun seemed to taunt him. "When will you leave?"

CHAPTER SEVEN

NEXT TO DREAMY, breathtaking Venice, London was a grim, gray sprawl of concrete and exhaust.

It was well into May now, and the weather was often pretty, but it still felt gloomy to Irinka. She walked to the Tube in the morning, paying no attention to the hints of spring flowers in boxes and gardens along the way. And it was often a bright, happy sort of evening on her walk home, but to her it might as well have been storming down pellets of rain on her head.

Maybe it was fairer to say she couldn't tell the difference.

There were clients to soothe in the wake of so many canceled appoints, each of them with a vast male ego that required she cater to them as if they were the only man alive—the sort of thing that Irinka normally did on autopilot. But she'd left that particular skill behind in the Grand Canal, it seemed.

Because try as she might, she couldn't seem to find the will to return those calls. She couldn't even listen to the usual outraged messages, because the sort of men she worked for were always ruffled and stroppy until they felt appropriately catered to, and she simply didn't have it in her to *murmur encouragingly* and make *as-*

senting noises until they decided they'd shouted long enough.

This was not a problem she'd ever had before.

It was almost as if she'd come back home as someone else.

One night Irinka walked back from Notting Hill Gate. She walked and walked, and only noticed that she'd sailed past her own front door when she found herself tramping about in North Kensington. The part of North Kensington that only dreamed it was Ladbroke Grove. When she finally noticed that she was taking herself on an impromptu walking tour, it was the better part of a half-hour's walk back to her own front door.

"So you took a holiday in Venice," Auggie said at a Work Wives lunch one day, purportedly so they could gather and discuss work, but mostly to celebrate the fact they were all back in London at the same time. A rare occurrence these days. "And yet you look like you need a holiday to recover from your holiday."

"Doesn't everyone?" Irinka asked dryly.

"Perhaps not quite so much of a holiday, then," Auggie murmured.

But Irinka ignored her. She tried to focus on the others, because she didn't need reminding that these sorts of nights were rare. Back at university, there had been nothing but time. Long nights piled into common rooms or loafing about in each other's rooms in halls. Dreaming up glorious futures at the local, dancing madly in the discos for each other's entertainment more than anything else. They'd plotted, planned, dreamed, and they'd done it together.

Irinka knew she wasn't the only one who viewed these friendships as something more like sisters, taking the place of many of their rather less congenial family relationships.

Or maybe that was just her.

And in any case, it would only get more rare to have the four of them together now.

Because her friends were happy. They were in love, and it was the kind of love that made each of them *better*. She could see it in the way they all…inhabited their own skin differently than they had before. Maude was talking about landscape architecture with a smile on her face. Lynna held forth on her strong opinion that pies should be savory, not sweet, but she was laughing as if she'd finally decided it was okay to be a little silly, if she liked.

It was Auggie who kept watching Irinka's face, as if she was that close to giving herself away. And the mad part was that Irinka couldn't tell. All her friends were more authentically themselves than ever, loved up and gleaming, and she felt as if she'd had to put on a costume to play the role of herself today.

Like all her bones had been rearranged in Venice and she still didn't know how they worked.

Auggie tuned back into the conversation, which had something to do with Lynna's disdain for the pub's lofty menu and Maude's stinging critique of the herbaceous border and shrubs, which Auggie claimed meant they might need to ascend to a wine bar next time.

"Maybe we are no longer the sort of women who pile into a pub on a Friday and get the pints in," Auggie said.

"Let's not get ahead of ourselves," Maude said with a laugh.

And Irinka decided that the strange emptiness she was feeling was actually freedom.

Not everybody got to revisit a defining, disfiguring love affair that had altered her life once already. The real madness was imagining that she might come out of it unscathed, just because it had been less of a bitter, acrimonious ending this time.

Not everyone got to go back to the scene of the crime that had broken her heart and repair it.

Because she was absolutely repaired, she assured herself. Stitched up and made new.

She smiled when everyone looked her way and leaned in, dropping her voice. "Guess what scandalous, outrageous gossip I heard only yesterday about a selection of minor nobles we may or may not have met at university."

Irinka decided that the only thing that was required of her was to enjoy this lovely late evening in an outdoor pub garden that regrettably did not meet Maude's standards, gathered around the picnic table until well after dark.

And sitting there spinning stories for her friends felt right—like she was finally fitting back into her body, and her life.

"Why do you seem sad?" Auggie asked later, as she and Irinka broke away from the other two and headed toward a different Tube stop.

"I don't know what you mean."

Auggie laughed and bumped Irinka's shoulder with hers. "You forget, I was there when you came back from

Venice that summer after university. You look like that again, pale and wobbly."

"I'm not the least bit wobbly." Irinka made herself smile. "I'm not even wearing treacherous heels."

"Repeatedly saying that you're not a thing when I can see with my own eyes that you are doesn't change it," Auggie observed.

Irinka stopped walking and faced her friend, waiting for a rumbling double-decker coach to go by. "I appreciate that you're looking out for me," she said quietly. "Really. But I'm fine. You don't need to save me from anything. Not even myself."

Auggie gazed back at her, but a bit too shrewdly for Irinka's taste. "You do know," she said, almost carefully, "that the great mystery of Irinka Scott-Day might be why you get attention wherever you go, but it isn't why *we* love you, right?"

Irinka thought she would have preferred if Auggie had taken out a dagger and stabbed her straight through the heart. It hurt to smile, but she made herself do it.

"It's been a lovely night," she said. She gave her friend a hug, and she meant it, but then she turned and strode off, leaving Auggie standing there.

No doubt burning holes into her back with her glare, but that was better than carrying on with that conversation.

Irinka was grateful when she made it back to Notting Hill, and did not wander off in a daze this time. She made her way through the throngs crowding in along the Portobello Road, reveling in the mild weather and the hints of the summer ahead.

She wanted to find that kind of hopefulness. She wanted to tilt her head back and spin around, or do whatever it was *actually* free and unfettered people did in these circumstances.

But instead, she walked to her door and looked around—a bit longingly—to see if there were any black SUVs lingering at the curb, dispatched on strict orders to redo her kidnap. There were none. Only the usual drunks singing in the streets and the sound of traffic in the distance.

Feeling let down all over again, Irinka let herself inside.

She'd loved this little house on sight. It was one of the smallest terraced houses in this stretch of the road and like many of the others, had been falling apart until the 1980s or so, and was now valued at an extraordinary price. Buying it had felt the way she thought freedom should, because it was the first place that was entirely her own. Not one of her mother's flats or house shares, and happily purchased with her father's court-mandated settlement to make her love it even more.

Irinka thought that keeping the double-barreled surname that forever linked her to him, shaming him every time she signed her name or was mentioned in a news item, had been a lovely punishment for the Duke. But she also enjoyed living off his begrudging support, too.

A better person would be humiliated to take forced charity, the Duke had said to her once.

You mean, like the rest of your children? Irinka had replied. *Thanks, Dad.*

And over the years, she'd taken great delight in making the little house her own. She loved that it was small, suitable for only one person if that person truly wished to be comfortable. Or possibly a couple, if that couple got along well. There was room for guests, but only the sort who did not intend to stay too long.

Because Irinka had made every room hers.

She bought art from the stalls in the Portobello Market. She liked to haunt the galleries in Notting Hill, finding things she liked from emerging artists. Whenever she traveled, she liked to pick something up wherever she landed, so that the house was an eclectic mix of all the things that made her happy.

But tonight she stood just inside her door, breathing in *her space* the way she liked to do, and it hit her that it was all just...*things*.

She didn't know why she'd never noticed that before. She had a lot of stuff, but it was just that. *Stuff.* No different from all the statuary scattered about the palazzo in Venice.

But Irinka was absolutely not thinking about Zago.

Back in her kitchen, she set about toasting some bread, slathering it with butter and a bit of Marmite. Then she took her plate and a cup of tea up through the house to the tiny little rooftop deck that was half the reason she'd bought the house.

She sat outside in her favorite chair, crunching on her toast and waiting for a sense of peace to take her over, but it didn't come.

Instead, she could see Zago's dark amber gaze on the day she'd left. She'd promised herself that she would walk away from him without looking back, and she'd made it down that long, stone path. She'd worn the clothes she'd come in, though without her mobile stuck in her boot this time. And with every step, she'd assured herself that she was doing the right thing.

The *only* thing.

She'd climbed into the water taxi that he'd called for her, and that was when she'd looked back.

Like she wanted to give Orpheus a run for his money, she'd turned and looked.

Zago had been standing on that balcony again, his hands braced on the rail, his face expressionless.

But she'd felt the burn of his gaze like a torch.

It still woke her at night.

And even now, she felt heavy. Out of sorts, which she could admit was just another form of *wobbly*.

Maybe the real truth was that she'd expected Zago to fight her when she'd told him she wanted to go.

Up on the roof of her little house, Irinka blew out a breath at that.

But at least that was better than a sob.

That same sob that was lodged there behind her ribs like a bruise that never healed.

Irinka decided that she'd had enough of sitting out there as the night grew colder and London clanged all around her. She finished her tea and then she went back inside. It was odd to walk around her little house now, suddenly overly sensitive to all her *things*, so she tried to shower it off. And the city with it.

Then, still strangely wound up and in no mood to sleep when she knew exactly what would greet her once she crossed over into dreams, she called her mother.

"What is it?" Roksana demanded, not bothering with a greeting. Irinka wasn't sure she'd even heard a ring. "What has happened?"

"Hello, *momochka*," Irinka said ruefully, already rolling her eyes, because of course she should have expected this reaction. Roksana was always primed for disaster. "Nothing's happened. I just…wanted to hear your voice."

There was a pause. Irinka could imagine her mother rising from her bed in her current flat, a modern eyesore of edges and angles and low-slung cubes masquerading as furniture, all courtesy of her latest lover. This one was much younger than her and liked it when Roksana treated him as if he was a naughty puppy.

"At this hour, even I do not wish to hear my voice," Roksana said after a moment.

This was sentimental for her mother, Irinka knew. It was practically a good cry and a long hug, when most of Irinka's childhood had been arranged around various ways to toughen her up.

Irinka already regretted the impulse. "I'm sorry. I don't know what came over me. I wouldn't want to disturb your beauty sleep."

Back when she'd been young, messing with Roksana's rest had been akin to starting a war. But while her mother still prized her sleep, she was no longer quite so militant.

"Is this a call to merely…catch up?" Her mother sounded baffled. "Have you been at the vodka? Remember what I have always told you. Vodka spoils everything—"

"But the glass," Irinka finished for her. She sighed, frowning up at her ceiling. "You do know that some daughters call their mothers as a regular thing, don't you. They actually like to talk to each other on the phone. They're more like friends, really."

"I did not raise you to have friends." Roksana's voice was cool and untroubled. Irinka could hear her moving around her sterile flat with its commanding views, and wondered if that was happiness. Maybe she'd been getting it wrong all this time. "I raised you to survive under any circumstances, as I have done."

"But are you happy?" she dared to ask.

Roksana went quiet. So quiet that Irinka lifted her mobile away from her ear to make certain the call had not dropped.

"Are you at risk of bodily harm?" her mother asked after a long pause. "Do you need rescuing? Otherwise there should be no such calls."

"I don't know whether to take that as a vote for or against happiness."

Roksana sighed. "If you chase two hares you will end up with neither," she said. Her way of saying that a person couldn't have their cake and eat it, too. "Sleep, Irinka."

But after her mother rang off, Irinka did not sleep. She found herself thinking a little too much instead, as if her ceiling had transformed itself into a cinema where she could watch what had happened between her and Zago like a film.

She had asked Zago to look at things between them differently, and he had.

Why did she keep coming back to the conclusion that she should have done the same?

Irinka couldn't answer that. But as she lay there she

accepted that leaving him was, in many ways, worse this time. Three years ago she had been so torn apart, so shredded into pieces, that she'd had no choice but to throw herself into absolutely anything that would take her mind off of Venice. That palazzo.

Zago himself.

She was certain that had contributed hugely to her zeal in setting up His Girl Friday with her friends and how she'd managed to round up clients relatively quickly.

But this time around, the thought of storming into anything—much less her client list—made her feel… sordid.

"This too shall pass," she told herself, and to lull herself to sleep, she decided she would watch nothing but frivolous things until she drifted off to sleep.

A few weeks more of that and she thought she might explode.

"Are you still in the doldrums?" Auggie asked when they ran into each other at the office one day.

A run-in that Irinka suspected Auggie must have planned, because Irinka had gone out of her way to choose a time when no one else was meant to be there.

"I've never met a doldrum in my life," Irinka told her as cheerfully as possible. "I exude happiness, Auggie. Is that not clear?"

"What's his name?" Auggie asked quietly.

And Irinka felt strung out on some kind of precipice, then. She hadn't spoken about Zago, ever. Not to anyone.

Because if she did, wouldn't that make it real?

And once it was real, how was she meant to survive

it? She hadn't had an answer for that three years ago. She didn't have an answer now.

But it was clear that *not* speaking about him hadn't exactly been helpful thus far.

And maybe her friend had meant it when she'd said that it wasn't Irinka's mysterious side that she loved. That all her friends loved.

She didn't have to believe that to *wish* it was true. And maybe she was weak after all, soft in all the ways she'd been taught not to be, because she went with it.

"His name is Zago Baldissera," she heard herself say, almost as if someone else had possessed her body to spit out that name.

Auggie blinked. Then she started typing into her mobile and, a moment later, swiveled the screen around so that Irinka was staring directly at a picture of Zago himself.

Zago crossing Saint Mark's Square in Venice, the basilica rising up behind him. He looked like a dream. A dream she often had, and in far greater detail than this photo.

She sighed. "That's him."

And then sat there feeling as if her skin was trying to crawl off her bones as Auggie started reading out facts about Zago.

"Ancient Venetian family. Extraordinary family fortune. A palazzo, no less." She set her phone down on the desk between them. "Back then, too?"

Irinka didn't pretend to misunderstand her. "Back then, too."

"That was your summer of travel." Auggie frowned

as if she was trying to think back those three years. "I don't even remember the names of those girls you were meant to travel with, off on some sort of Grand Tour."

Irinka did, and named them. "We all went to the opera in Venice. That's where I met him. When they moved on toward Croatia, I…stayed."

She and Auggie sat with that a moment, all the unsaid things that could be packed into that word. Into *staying*.

"And you went back last month. All these years later." Auggie frowned. "Why now? What changed?"

Irinka smiled. "That was more of an invitation that couldn't be refused. What I told you about the brother of a woman who I was hired to brush off is true. It was his sister. I didn't recognize her, but then, I really never have paid much attention to the women in those scenarios."

"The women in those scenarios weren't paying us," Auggie said, pragmatically.

"Funnily enough that was my argument, too."

And then Irinka found herself sitting there telling Auggie the entire story of Zago and her, even including her weeks of drudgery.

"You *cleaned his house*?" Auggie asked, her eyes round.

"I am nothing if not committed to a role," Irinka said loftily. "And I rather fancied myself a Cinderella, if I'm honest."

"And now you're here." Her friend crossed her arms and eyed her with something that looked a little too much like pity. "Irinka. You cleaned the man's house out of some form of malicious compliance because you knew that would get under his skin. You're sad when you leave him. Last time you built up an entire career arranged around reliving your breakup. Now you can't even bear to do it."

"That…is not how I would put it."

"Is it untrue?" When Irinka couldn't claim that it was, Auggie nodded. "Then what are you doing in London?"

And that was how, the very next day, Irinka booked herself on a flight and went back to Venice.

Of her own volition, this time.

Once she landed, she found herself a water taxi and had it deliver her straight onto the dock of the palazzo. She marched up the stone path she'd scrubbed on her hands and knees and presented herself at the grand door, smiling at Roderigo when he opened it.

"*La signorina* has returned," he said, not unkindly. But not in a particularly welcoming manner, either. "But without an invitation, I fear."

Irinka, who did not consider herself particularly impulsive, had actually not considered this part of her impromptu visit. And she should have.

"Will he see me?" she asked.

Because it didn't occur to her until then that he might not.

So she stood at the bottom of the steps, staring back out at the canal and the boats. She soaked in the impossible splendor of this magical place, this floating city that seemed more dream than reality. She paid attention to the curious way that sound carried, dancing where it shouldn't and finding ways to sink in so unexpectedly.

And when she thought she heard a faint noise behind her, she turned and he was there.

Zago.

Somehow even more beautiful than when she'd left.

He gazed at her for a long moment, and everything was that amber, that fire. Then he looked past her, out at the water, and it shocked her how much that felt like grief.

After a moment he came down the steps and stood there—near her but not touching her.

Irinka wondered what a picture this made for the tourists passing on the *vaporettos*, the two of them standing there so awkwardly at the front of an ancient palazzo surrounded by June gardens and polished stone.

It almost made her feel as if she was a part of the sweep of history that sang its way up out of the stones in this place. As if this was all another way of claiming that what burned between them still was destiny.

Almost.

Because wasn't *destiny* just another word for surrendering to the things that refused to allow you to control them?

"You don't seem happy to see me," she said when she began to worry that she was, in fact, going to turn to stone where she stood.

"Should I be?"

And when Zago turned to look at her then, his amber eyes were blazing hot and that brooding intensity of his seemed to wrap itself around her as surely as if he'd put his hands on her body.

But he didn't.

There was something almost like sadness on his face, she thought then. Or maybe it was resignation. Whatever it was, it made something in the center of her chest go hollow, then seem to become its own, terrible drum.

"Have you come to stay?" Zago asked her, his voice that silken threat. "For good?"

She balked at that, she couldn't help it, and he saw it. Irinka watched his eyes track the movement, then shutter.

"For good?" she repeated.

And out there in all that golden light, he reached over and fit his hand to her cheek as he had before. As he had many times before.

It made that hollow drum inside her seem to stretch tight, then shiver into something else. Something she couldn't name.

"Letting you go gives me no pleasure," he told her in that dark, low voice. "And I want to welcome you in. But Irinka, there will be no more playing games. When you come back, *if* you come back, there will be no more half-measures. It's all or nothing. Are you ready for that?"

He waited, but everything inside of her seemed to seize, then shudder. Hard.

And she couldn't seem to make her own mouth open.

She couldn't seem to do anything but stare.

"That's what I thought." His thumb stroked her cheek-bone.

Once, then again.

And then she stood there, stricken straight through, while Zago climbed the stairs and then closed that grand door behind him.

Leaving her there on the stones with a hollowness where her heart should have been and no earthly idea what she should do next.

CHAPTER EIGHT

ZAGO REGRETTED THE decision to turn Irinka away immediately.

He closed the door with great finality but then stood there on the other side of it, cursing himself. Cursing the weakness that still allowed her to haunt him like this, whether she turned up at the palazzo or stayed in London.

Because one place she always was, night and day, was in his head.

But he did not turn around, throw open the door again, and welcome her in, because he'd meant what he'd said to her.

That night he barely slept, certain that he had made the greatest mistake of his life—but then, that was every night. He had to believe that sooner or later, he would get used to it.

Sooner or later, he would stop worrying about how a man could live a whole life without his own heart.

Yet by dawn it was clear to him that the only thing he needed to learn to live with was his surpassing weakness. Because he knew as he watched the sun bloom into being, caressing the ruined old buildings and illuminating the water outside, that if she came back again this day, he would not have the fortitude to deny her entry once again.

But Irinka didn't come.

"And there is your answer," he told himself darkly that following night, as he lay awake in that bed that he might as well go ahead and burn, now. Because it was little more than an altar to his memories of her.

It might as well have been a mausoleum.

When he drifted off to sleep, he kept thinking that he caught her scent—like she was just out of reach on the same mattress—and he would spring awake to find her and touch her, but he was always alone.

And there came a point where he could no longer bear being a ghost inside his own home, like all the rest who were trapped in the old walls. Yet it was as if the ancient, floating city itself—murmuring and sighing all around him—was trying its level best to make him feel as haunted as possible.

Venice was ever a city of echoes. Ghosts were noisy here, and the dead were never truly buried. It was the easiest thing in the world to turn down the wrong, narrow lane and find a part of the city he didn't know.

It is like falling in love with a woman, his father had told him on one of their rare walks through the old city on a pretty evening, when Zago had still been young and both of his parents had still been here and he had not understood, yet, how drastically things could change. *She is ever-changing. She is always herself, always a mystery, unknowable and eternal. This city must be the love of your life and to love her, you must lose her and find her, again and again, a thousand times a day.*

Zago hoped he never grew too old or too bitter to enjoy the simple things in life, like following an echo wherever it led and then wandering the streets of Venice until he found his way back home.

He threw himself into the routines of his daily life as a lifelong resident and the scion of an ancient family, who had spent many years deeply involved in the local community. It was already summer and the cruise liners came in daily, hunkering over the city and discharging their hordes into the Piazza San Marco. Like most Venetians, he supported tourism insofar as it kept the city alive, yet grew weary of the summer hordes.

Still, he walked to have his morning espresso in cafés that were not in guidebooks. It was important to meet with friends and neighbors, have a coffee, and ground himself in the world of the living again. To speak again of art and literature and local politics.

To remind himself that there was more to his life than a woman who had left him.

Twice.

But the ghosts would not leave him alone.

It was a few days after Irinka had turned up at his door—and had been turned away with a great strength of will he was still surprised he'd had in him—when he caught, out of the corner of his eye, the figure of a woman.

Zago lost track of the story his friend was telling him in an animated fashion, leaning against the side of a high-top table. He looked again, and then shook his head, not certain why he had reacted so strongly to a mere glimpse of this woman. A closer examination only baffled him more.

It was not Irinka. It was a different woman entirely, blonder, huskier. Older.

And yet the sighting left him almost winded.

He even dreamed about it that night, the blonde woman changing into Irinka as he watched, then melting off into the bright sun outside...

"You sound strange," his sister told him when he made his daily call to her the following day. She laughed. "Stranger than usual, I mean."

"I beg your pardon," he protested, but mildly, because he hadn't heard her laugh in some while. "That is no way to speak to your revered and beloved older brother."

"Sometimes, Zago, I think you are a ghost yourself," Nicolosa told him, and though she laughed again then, it did not make him quite as happy as before.

Because how could he tell her that he was haunted entirely by his own hand?

A few days later, Zago left the crowded tourist areas behind, making his way through the snarl of lanes and bridges that led into the part of Venice that was largely without signs. A person either knew their way here, or they did not.

This was one reason that the farther he walked, the fewer people were about.

It was late into the evening, the lamps aglow and the sky still flirting with the last of its blue. He was heading into one of the neighborhoods only locals tended to know about and one of his favorite *osterias* to meet up with friends, enjoying the particular joy of Venice in the evening, The canals and the hints of music and laughter, dancing down the alleys.

Zago was halfway over a small bridge when the sound of a footstep behind him echoed strangely. He glanced back in time to see the side of a woman's head as she retreated back into the shadows of the alley he'd just come through. And he knew immediately it wasn't Irinka.

This woman had short hair and was dressed like an American tourist, in torn jeans and dirty sneakers, and she was swallowed up by the darkness before he could look at her straight on.

There was no reason that he should think twice about it.

But that night, sitting in a loud, happy group of friends he'd had since childhood, Zago found himself thinking about that American again and again. For one thing, tourists did not usually make it that far away from the bright piazza and famous bridges, the *gelaterias* and mask shops. And certainly not alone.

And for another, she had to have been following him, or he would have passed her on the bridge. There was no other way to get to that particular alley.

Zago couldn't shake the odd notion that she had retreated back into the mouth of that alley when he'd turned to look at her.

And later that night, he found himself pacing in his bedchamber, wondering if he was losing it. If these odd sightings of strange women were a sign that his weakness was more mental than emotional. If he was destined to tear out his own hair and become one more ghost story the enterprising storytellers of this city would use to titillate the visitors on their nightly spooky tours.

But apart from finding himself fixated on strangers, he felt relentlessly the same. His work was the same. He tended to the accounts, he supervised the endless and ongoing maintenance of the palazzo, and he made certain that the financial portion of the family legacy was self-sustaining and would outlive them all. He allowed himself more access to *la bella vita*, as all Italians should.

His only trouble was that he kept thinking he saw Irinka everywhere.

Once more near an ancient church, its small square thick with guided tours and ill-behaved children, though she turned out to be a hugely pregnant woman. And again, standing on a bridge as his boat passed beneath it, half her face obscured with a camera—though something about her jawline lingered.

"If you'll forgive my saying so, *il padrone*," Roderigo intoned one afternoon, "you have seemed rather on edge of late."

"I feel on edge," Zago agreed, closing his laptop and standing. He accepted the espresso that the older man set before him with a nod. "Tell me, Roderigo. Are you worried that I'm losing my grasp on reality?"

His *maggiordomo* slid a look his way, his face almost too blank. "I am now," he said.

"I cannot be the only man who sees ghosts in Venice," Zago said, perhaps more to himself. "Though I know that we will all become ghosts ourselves, if the water has its way."

"I prefer to do without a haunting, if at all possible," Roderigo said, sounding only slightly reproving—but that was a comfort. Even now, when he spoke of Zago's mother, it was with that same gentle kindness that he remembered from back then. If Roderigo had been at all concerned about Zago, he would not be *reproving* at all.

The older man picked up the small cup and saucer after Zago tossed back the espresso. "This is already a city of too many masks, is it not? A ghost seems like overkill."

Zago didn't think much more about that conversation. The days grew warmer, the city more crowded, but also more musical and less haunted than it seemed in the darker months, where melancholy seemed to float along the canals like memories and barges.

He thought he caught the sound of Irinka's laughter on the breeze one fine morning, but when he turned, reluctantly, there was no one nearby—save an old woman and the birds she was feeding on the other side of the narrow waterway.

A few nights later, he made his way through the city at dusk, picking his way through the crowds waiting outside overpriced restaurants and eying glass beads through shop windows. He was heading for an art gallery not far from the Piazza San Marco and decided that tonight he was determined to be on guard against the tricks his memory intended to play on him.

No ghosts, he told himself sternly.

When he got there, the gallery was loud and full. Zago knew many of the guests, as well as the patron and the artist herself.

He took his time with the exhibit, lingering on each work to really take it in, and then it happened. As he moved from one grand canvas to the next, he thought he saw a particular smile flash just beyond the nearest pillar.

So much for his *no ghosts* rule.

Zago was tired of himself. He kept his eyes trained on the canvas before him, a lavish painting of one of Venice's masked balls.

And he thought about what Roderigo had said a few days ago. That theirs was a city of masks. That these masks allowed intimates to move amongst each other, unseen. Every family in Venice had stories about masks and balls and the particular delights of being anonymous in this place where they were all known too well.

Every Venetian child was raised on these stories.

And then, perhaps inevitably, he thought about Irinka. But this time he found himself considering that job of hers. The tasks she performed for those clients of hers.

And the fact that she billed herself as a master of disguise.

Those disguises were how she was never recognized. They were how she could pretend to be the girlfriend or wife or long-term mistress of any man at all, and was always believed.

She can dress up as anything or anyone, one of her happy repeat clients had told Zago with great admiration. *I reckon she could pass you on the street and you'd never know her.*

His pulse was pounding through him.

Irinka.

It had been Irinka all along.

Zago turned, slowly and with all apparent ease, but he did not look toward the pillar where he had last seen her. She would not be so foolish. He would have caught her already if she was that kind of foolish.

He ambled through the gallery, smiling and nodding at all the familiar faces. He had a drink, told a story, laughed with his acquaintances.

But all the while he was scanning the room. Not for the black hair and blue eyes he knew so well, but for other tells that she could not hide so easily. Her height, or someone hunched over to pretend she was shorter— he thought again about the old woman and the birds the other morning—and that was how he found her.

Once he knew what he was looking for, it was easy.

She was hiding by standing out tonight in a blazing red wig in loose, tumbling curls. And he thought from this distance that her eyes were green, suggesting that contacts were involved, and the kind of heavy cosmetics he had never seen on *his* Irinka.

But it went further than that. He was not a poetic man and yet Zago felt that he could easily write a book of sonnets concerning her particular lithe, lean form. The woman with the red hair, by contrast, was voluptuous. Padding, he assumed.

None of that mattered. He knew it was her.

He could make out those cheekbones he liked to trace with his fingers. He could see the mouth he had kissed too many times to count.

And then there was her smile. He would know it any-where.

He knew it now.

Zago pretended not to notice her at all. Instead he tracked her movements through the gallery, waiting for an opening. For the right moment.

It came later, after the artist thanked everyone for coming and there were toasts and applause, and the voluptuous redhead who was no ghost after all slipped out the side door, clearly thinking that no one was watching her.

He followed, tracing her into the shadows as she moved from the art gallery, and then wound her way down one crowded, narrow little alleyway into another, before she burst out into the Piazza San Marco itself where the famous clock tower stood watch and the Basilica gleamed in the dark.

It was a mild and pretty summer night. The restaurants were full, orchestras dueled, performers wandered, and the crowds were replete with pasta and gelato and the sea air. Irinka slowed as she wound her way into the thick of it and let the packs of tourists carry her along.

Zago was glad of it. It allowed him to track her all the better. And as he did, he could see that any tension in her body eased away as she let the hordes of people direct her this way and that, no doubt imagining she was in the clear.

Because she always had been before.

She navigated her way across the square toward the Basilica, then ducked around it, back into alleys and byways that led her along a canal off the piazza. Zago knew immediately that she was heading for one of the hotels on the other side.

So he lengthened his stride and caught up to her right there on the crest of the bridge that arched up over the canal. By day there would be a steady stream of people here, moving from one neighborhood to another. But tonight it was only them, a gondolier singing lustily into the night, and the simple satisfaction of the way his hand closed over her wrist at last and tugged her around to face him.

"Can I help you?" she asked boldly as she looked up at him, complete with an Irish accent.

"I told you not to come back unless you planned to stay," he reminded her, filled with that pulse that hammered at him and the silken menace that was taking him over. "And instead you have taken it as a personal project to turn yourself into a hundred different women, then haunt me in every corner of my life." She looked as if she was about to argue that, so he tugged her closer, or maybe he simply leaned down into that face that was all hers and not hers at once. "Did it not occur to you that I might worry that the ghosts I kept seeing were an indication that the family madness had reached me, too?"

He saw her eyes change at that, even though they were the wrong color. "I did not think about that," she admitted. She blew out a breath. Then, more quietly, she said, "I'm sorry. That wasn't my intention."

"You will have to explain to me what your intentions were, I think." The gondolier moved around the corner, heading deeper into the stillness and night. They were alone, now, in this pocket of quiet, as if the city floated only for them. "Was this a punishment in kind? You thought you would haunt me for the great sin of turning you away? When you have already left me twice?"

If he had imagined he would confront her with calm rationality, well. That was as unavailable to him as the gondolier, now only a faint melody in the distance.

"I don't know," Irinka said, and she hardly sounded like herself. Her voice seemed too high-pitched, as if something had changed inside her. As if she wasn't quite the woman that he remembered, and he wanted to take some kind of joy in that.

But he didn't believe it.

Because these were still games and he was tired of playing them.

"Irinka." And her name still tasted like a song on his lips. "I told you exactly how you can come back to me. It is simple enough. But it cannot happen in costume and deceit, clambering about in alleyways pretending to be someone else."

She did not look anything like herself and yet his chest hurt when she looked away, off toward the Bridge of Sighs in the distance, not quite visible from here.

"You say you want everything," she said, then. Softly. "But that's not true. You want total capitulation. You want me to come crawling to you."

"I cannot imagine you crawling." He turned her wrist over in his grip, tracing the delicate skin on the inside, where her pulse beat like his. "Then again, I did not imagine that you would take to the streets of Venice in costume, your very own Carnival."

She looked down at the way he was holding her wrist, and he thought he felt her tremble.

"I don't understand," she said quietly, and it was becoming something like an out-of-body experience to hear her voice coming out of the wrong woman. As if she was presenting him with the essential issue between them with her disguise—the Irinka he longed for and the woman she pretended she was. He could touch them both, but only one of them was real.

What Zago did not know was *which one* that was.

Irinka lifted her head to look at him, then, her distractingly green eyes solemn. "You say one thing, and I think you believe it, but the truth is that you don't want *everything*. No one ever does. So where does it leave me if it turns out that I am a whole lot more than you bargained for?"

He moved closer and lifted her hand as if to put it to her face, but dropped it again. "I can't look at you while you're dressed like someone else. It's disturbing."

She made a frustrated kind of sound at that. Then she flipped her wrist so she could tug him along with her as she continued across the bridge, and he let her do it.

Because despite what he'd told her, he didn't know what he wanted. He was outraged, obviously. But there was also a part of him that couldn't help but like the fact that she hadn't left Venice. That she had stayed all this time, and had stayed close.

Irinka led him off the bridge and then directly into one of the hotels that waited there on the other side, built on the canal. She swept inside, waved at the dazzled man at the desk, and brought him up a narrow set of stairs to a hotel room with casement windows that opened up over the bridge below.

Once the door was closed behind them, she pulled off the wig and tossed it onto a table, where he could see many other bits and pieces of disguises. Torn jeans. Blond hair. She shot him a look and then strode off into what he assumed was a bathroom.

And when she came out again, she was herself.

His Irinka.

And that was both worse and better, all at once.

"Tell me what you want," he demanded. She looked haunted, and something like furious, and he didn't know what to do with that. He didn't know what to do with any of this. "If you wish to haunt me, tell me why. Because otherwise it feels like torture, Irinka."

"I thought it would be entertaining," she said and she smiled, somewhat self-deprecatingly. "More fool me."

He moved toward her then, something wild inside of him that was clawing at the inside of his chest. He backed her up until they moved straight out onto a tiny balcony overlooking the canal, the lights of San Marco in the distance.

But there was only the real Venice here, secrets and sighs, and he could not help but indulge himself.

He knew better, but he pulled her into his arms and then swept her back so he could kiss her. Again and again, as if to assure himself that he hadn't made this up. That he hadn't been driving himself mad.

That she really had been here in Venice the whole time.

He kissed her and he kissed her and when he thought he might lose control, he set her back on her feet. She gazed at him, her properly blue eyes blurry, and she looked dazed and soft.

And Zago had never wanted anything more than to pick her up in his arms, carry her inside to lay her on that bed inside, and lose himself in her.

But he knew too well that losing himself like that was losing her for good.

So he did not pick her up again. And he kept his hands on her shoulders until she could stand without swaying.

Then he waited until she looked at him. He held her gaze, and didn't recognize his own voice when he spoke. "If you want to come back, come back. Don't pretend."

Her lips parted, and she looked at him as if he'd said something terrible.

Or painful.

"But…" She shook her head, then pressed her lips together. There was a suspicious sheen in her eyes. "But what if pretending is the only thing I know how to do?"

CHAPTER NINE

ONCE AGAIN, IRINKA felt skinless.

Exposed and naked, though she had clothes on.

Not that silly dress with all the padding built in that had made her look like some kind of silver screen goddess. But an old T-shirt and a pair of lounging pants that she'd thrown on in something like a panic, half-convinced that by the time she came out of the bathroom—no longer in any sort of disguise—he would have left.

She wasn't sure she would blame him if he had done so.

Instead, he had kissed her on the balcony. It should have been swooningly romantic, wildly hot and beautiful, and it had been.

Everything with Zago was all of those things.

But somehow, Irinka wanted to cry. She wanted to dissolve into that sobbing thing that still camped out there in her chest, threatening to spill over at any moment.

She almost wished that it would.

Zago stared down at her, his gorgeous face carved into something stern—but the light in his amber gaze felt like hope. She told herself it was, because it had to be.

Though the truth was, she didn't have the slightest

idea what it was she ought to hope for here. All the possibilities seemed designed to take her breath away, and not necessarily in a good way...

"It is very easy to stop pretending," Zago told her with that *certainty* of his that made her bones feel like melting. Like it was an imposition for them to hold her upright. "You simply...stop."

Irinka actually laughed at that, and the sound of her own laughter reminded her that they were still standing out on the balcony. And more, that Venice was an echo chamber at the best of times, but especially at night. Stiffly, waiting for her bones to betray her, she moved inside.

And felt out of sorts all the while, as if she thought her body might mount its own revolution at any moment. She sat, gingerly, on the end of her hotel bed, not entirely certain that her own limbs would obey her.

Then she found herself gazing up at Zago as he stood in the windowed doorway to the balcony and studied her where she sat, his expression unreadable.

"I don't know that I've ever seen you so uncomfortable," he said after the moments seemed to expand into separate eternities. "Is it that much of a trial to simply be yourself?"

"You seem to have no trouble with it." It felt like much-needed action, to throw it back on him and see how he fielded a question that made her whole body ache. "How do you go about it?"

His lips curved, but it didn't look like a happy sort of smile. "By now you must realize that I was born with a destiny, a set of immovable expectations, and very clear directions on how to achieve all of the above." Then, as if he was quoting someone, "Baldisseras are not merely born, but carefully and deliberately bred."

"I never thought your childhood sounded quite so structured." But Irinka considered that a moment. Had he actually talked to her at any length about his childhood? Or had she made assumptions based on what had happened to his parents later—and then filled it in with what she imagined it must have been like to live in the same place for an entire life? "Then again, it is not as if you speak about it that much."

"There are two versions of my childhood and the older I get, the more I realize that both are equally true. And equally false." Zago shook his head, that same bittersweet curve to his lips. "In one, it was a magical time. I explored the palazzo, and this city of myth and memory, as I chose. What is not to like about such a life?" He tipped his head slightly to one side, as if that was a trick question. "And in another, I was tutored from a very young age to think more of a ruined old building on its rickety foundations than any of the people I encountered. To place it above all else, and do whatever was necessary to restore it or revive it, as needed. And in the midst of all of that, of course, there were the usual expectations of a man in my station. The kind of education it was expected I would procure, to be a credit to my name. The kind of people I am expected to know and maintain relationships with throughout my life, because we are all rotting away here together."

His amber gaze seemed to blaze straight through her.

"I have never gotten the impression that your childhood was bucolic and sweet in any regard."

And maybe she was going to have to get used to the fact that she felt winded in his presence.

"I knew I was a bastard before I knew what it meant," Irinka told him quietly, and without realizing she'd intended to say such a thing. It was as if it welled up from that same space inside of her where that un-sobbed ache still *hurt*. "I used to tell my mother's friends what I was at parties as it always got a big reaction. In some circles, it still does."

Zago's expression shifted in a way that made everything inside her list a bit to the side, like she really was melting in on herself. He moved into the room and crossed to the bed, and Irinka thought for a brief, dizzyingly sweet moment that he was simply going to pull her into his arms and kiss her senseless again. Or bear her back down onto the bed and make all of this simply swirl away into all the bright colors they made together, the way he always did.

The way she desperately wished he would.

Instead, he came and stood before her for a moment, then squatted down so he was almost at her eye level. She had to look down at him, just slightly.

"You are not pretending now," he pointed out in that measured way that she wanted to rail against, even as it felt like some kind of caress. "How does it feel?"

"It feels silly that we both have our clothes on," she replied.

She expected to see that heat in his gaze. Was banking on it, in fact.

And so there was nothing in her that was prepared for the way that sad smile took over the whole of his beautiful face, making her worry that once that ache inside of her let go, there would be nothing left of her. Not one shred or scrap or shattered little piece. That it would all swirl away into the mess of those tears she was afraid to cry.

Her heart was pounding so hard that she was shocked she couldn't hear it echo back at her from across the canal. "Whatever you might think of the costumes and all the rest, you know as well as I do that at least *that* has always been real between you and me, Zago. You know that it is."

He didn't dispute that, but it was no comfort. "You have been hiding since the day I met you," he said, very distinctly.

She felt something in her shaking, like her body was trying to tear itself apart from the inside. "I met you at an opera. I was in the stalls like everyone else. You were the one in the box, hiding."

"I met you at the café in the interval," he corrected her. "And if I had to guess, I would say it was your first time at an Italian opera, that you didn't understand a word, but you happily assumed the role of an opera patron anyway. And the thing is, Irinka, you're very, very good at it."

"And what…you think I was pretending that whole summer?" Her throat was on fire. Irinka was tempted to imagine that she was coming down with some terrible fever, but she suspected she only wished that she was.

Because, unfortunately, she was not feverish at all.

She was frozen solid, incapable of movement, and yet hanging on his every word even while she wished that he would stop.

"I think that at first, you were overwhelmed," he told her, and there was something inevitable about this. As if she had known that he would say these things and had avoided any circumstance in which he might. "And then, as best as you could, I think you were pretending that you could really do it. That you could stay with me. Marry me. Live with me ever after, even though it all happened so quickly. So unexpectedly."

Her lips felt chapped. Her throat was aflame. "It was a love affair. Affairs end."

"How would you know?" And that dark amber gaze of his was like fire. "You have only had the one, spread out over the course of all these years. And last I checked, *tesoro mio*, you couldn't let go of it yourself. You settled in, changed your appearance, and held on tight. So what do we call a thing that does not end?"

She moved then, as if to reach out for him—

But he caught her wrist and held it there, between them.

"No," he said, and that he sounded almost *kind* did not help. It made that feverish thing all over her seem to burn all the brighter. "I meant what I told you on the steps of the palazzo. It is all or nothing."

"Yet you accuse *me* of playing games," she managed to say, while everything in her seemed to be going haywire. She couldn't *breathe*. Her heart actually hurt where it beat inside of her. And she simultaneously wanted to melt into the grip he had on her wrist and tear it away from him, because if he wouldn't give her what she wanted—

But it was too tempting to get angry when it wouldn't solve anything, only delay it. And she doubted it would help her, anyway.

"I have had a lot of time to think about you," he told her, with that same disarming, disquieting intensity. "That summer. The three years after. The month I spent fuming over my sister's disappointment. And all the time since I brought you back here, up to and including the little haunting you have treated me to these past weeks. When I take myself out of the equation, it all seems obvious." There was something like laughter in his eyes, when she had never felt less like laughing in all her days. "I know you like to think of yourself as deeply mysterious, Irinka. But in the end, you're not."

She tried to swallow past the fire in her throat. "I suppose I can comfort myself with the knowledge that you can apparently read me like a book, yet keep reading."

"I think your childhood was not kind to you," he said in that darkly quiet way, as if she hadn't spoken at all. "I don't think there were any different versions of it to confuse the issue or pretty it up. Your mother, for all her beauty and success, is a harsh woman. Famously so. Your father was prepared to put you and the rest of his family through hell to keep from owning up to the reality of the fact that you were his. How could these things not take a toll?"

This time she did pull her wrist away from him, and then held it in her lap as if it was burned. "I've always wanted therapy. I thought it would be so soothing, so lovely and sweet, to sit about on comfortable couches and talk about my troubles. Another notion disabused."

He did not rise from where he squatted before her, and he did not move that intense gaze of his from her face. "I think you learned how to be whoever you have to be, Irinka. I think you can change the versions of yourself at will and as needed, and you do. That summer, I think you felt deeply vulnerable for the first time in your life and you hated it, so you decided to make a profession out of it. Because no one could accuse you of playing games when it was your job, could they?"

Irinka stood up then, in a blind rush. She moved away from the bed, jerkily, skirting his body and putting space between them until she found herself standing there near the table where she'd arranged all the different disguises that she'd used while wandering around after him. And she couldn't tell if she felt foolish, indignant, terrified, or all of the above.

And still her heart kept up that calamitous beating. And still, her whole body felt singed to a crisp, inside and out.

"You talk a lot about playing games," she managed to say, and even managed to keep her own voice even and low. As if this wasn't wrecking her the way it was. "But I seem to recall that you're the one who had me picked up off of the street in London, transported across Europe, then dropped down into a choice between sexual favors or domestic labor."

"Perhaps I was trying to speak to you in a language you understand."

She looked back at him over her shoulder. "I don't think you were."

He stood then, too, and they faced each other with the floor between them, but still not nearly enough air. "You're right. That's the thing, Irinka. No one is entirely in control of themselves or entirely aware of the reasons they do things, not every hour of every day. But, to be clear, I never thought you would take either one of those options. I suspected that you would not be too scared—"

"By a kidnapping? That's quite an expectation."

"—which is why I sent an entirely female crew to collect you. To help assuage any doubt."

"You are too kind, Zago. As always."

Irinka wanted to rage at him. To throw things. To turn this all around and use it like a weapon but she didn't have the appetite for it. She kept feeling that everything was lost already, and possibly always had been, and the harder she tried to hold on to it the further away it got.

It was a lot like panic, now that she thought about it.

"What I thought," he said, in that steady way that only seemed to poke at that panic, and make it worse, "was that it would force an honest conversation with you that I felt was three years overdue."

"I've always been honest with you," she blurted out, because that felt like an attack.

But he didn't reply. Instead, he looked past her to the table piled high with all the various disguises she'd worn.

Irinka felt herself flush, and worse, felt a wave of something too much like shame wash through her, staining her. Inside and out.

"I'll tell you once more," Zago said with that quiet finality. "All or nothing, Irinka. And this time, I do not want to see versions of you out of the corner of my eye every time I turn around."

"You seem very certain of my response," she said, and her heart was going so fast and so hard that she was terrified that at any moment it would slam straight into that trapped sob, and then she would be in pieces.

At which point, she thought she might simply collapse, because she couldn't see past it. She couldn't see anything behind that pulsing ache in the center of her chest.

And all he did was raise a dark brow, so there was nothing to see but searing amber and calm query.

"Am I incorrect?" And there was a darker current in his voice, then. "I'm delighted to hear it. You wish to gather up your life in London, set it aside, and move here for good? You wish to live with me in the palazzo, marry me and have my babies, and lie beside me every night as long as we both live? What a glorious day. Shall we mark it as our anniversary, do you think?"

She put out her hands, hardly understanding what she was doing. "Stop," she whispered. "Please, Zago. *Stop.* I have to think."

"No," he corrected her, and though there was a dark fury in him, his voice was quiet. "You do not have to think. You would *prefer* to think, because that is what you do. You think up barriers, you think up long absences, you think up disguises and subterfuge. You don't need to *think* a thing, Irinka. You just hope that if you do, you can get your brain to tell your heart that it's a liar."

She felt a great trembling come from deep inside of her. It felt cataclysmic, as if her bones were trying to separate from themselves, and at any moment she might simply—

"If you're so bloody *certain* about everything, I don't understand why you don't just say so," she threw at him. "I don't understand why you didn't say so from the start."

"Because you can't handle it," he bit out at her, that dark fury more obvious now, and that did not feel like the victory she'd expected. "I was foolish enough to think that we both understood what was happening that first time and that even when you left Venice that summer, you would be back. I was wrong. And you're right that the way I brought you back into my orbit was its own kind of game. But now I am forced to think that if I hadn't done it, it would never have happened. I would never have seen you again."

Her breath *hurt*. "I would be glad of that."

That, too, did not have the effect she expected. All Zago did was shake his head.

A great deal as if he despaired of her, and that made her feel bruised all over.

"Irinka." Her name sounded like a curse. "You maddening, impossible woman. *You are the love of my life*."

And he did not wait for her to absorb that. He seemed to know it was a blow, or maybe he didn't care, because he laughed in that way he did when he didn't find anything funny at all.

"Do you think that pleases me?" he demanded. "Do you think that three years ago, when you were moments out of university, heedless and reckless, I was looking for this kind of mess? Do you think you were what I had in mind as the next Baldissera wife? The mother of the heirs to my family legacy, who must shepherd it long into the future? But there you were. Standing there in La Fenice and it was over the moment our eyes met."

Irinka remembered that moment with perfect clarity, as if it had only just happened. She had been transported and though she hadn't been fluent in Italian then—and was only slightly further along now—that hadn't been required to fall in love with it. The opera was timeless, universal. She had been floating on air when she and her friends spilled out in the interval to join the crowd at the café on the third floor.

She couldn't remember what she'd ordered or if she'd ever gotten it, but she remembered turning, her head wild with the music as if she was half-drunk on it, and there he was.

It had been like falling off of a great height, and perhaps the real truth was, she was still falling.

"I'll admit that there was an instant connection—" she began.

"It was love at first sight, and you know it," he threw at her, and it wasn't that he was loud, it was that she could feel the intent behind each word, as if he was hammering each one directly into her heart. "You have always known. You know it now, little as you wish to admit it."

Irinka felt torn asunder. The cataclysm inside of her was ongoing and she could not understand how it was possible that she might survive this moment. There was so much tearing, so much cracking and shattering, that she expected her body to simply implode into ash at any moment.

Yet somehow she was still standing. She couldn't make sense of it.

"I don't understand why we can't go on as we are," she managed to say. "It doesn't require all of these wild declarations, surely. There's no need for them. We don't have to *declare* anything, we can just—"

"Tesoro mio," he said, and that endearment—again—stopped her cold. He came toward her and his gaze was intent, a dark amber blaze. His mouth was a grim line. "Until you believe that you deserve more, you will never, ever have it. And until then, Irinka, you will also never have me."

He was close then and she thought that when he leaned in it was going to be one of those terrible, glorious kisses—

But instead he traced the line of her cheekbone, that gaze of his stamping into her, leaving impressions behind that she wasn't certain she would ever get out.

And in the next moment, he was gone.

Irinka heard the door to her hotel room close. Or she thought she did, somewhere over the clamor of her heart.

And inside, still, everything was shifting, changing, *hurting*.

Without conscious thought, she rushed to her balcony and gripped the rail as she looked down at the canal below.

In a few moments, Zago appeared below and she watched the fine lines of his gorgeous form as he strode up and over the bridge.

She ordered him, silently, to turn around to look up at her. She begged him to look back, but he didn't.

He didn't even pause.

Zago swept over the bridge and then disappeared into the dark embrace of the Venetian alleyway on the other side, as if he had never been here at all.

And it struck her hard, like a blow to the back of her head. All deadly force and no quarter given.

Irinka staggered back, his words like a litany inside her head, competing with the rattle and thump of her heart against her ribs.

She looked around at the hotel room. At Venice out her window and the pile of disguises that she had taken so much pride in, because so highly did she rate her ability to disappear.

It was love at first sight, he had said. *And you know it.*

And it felt like an accusation. It felt like a punishment.

That terrible sob in her chest began to grow, that ache sharpening so much she almost thought it might kill her, and maybe she wished it would—

But then it burst.

And for the first time in as long as she could remember, since she was a very little girl and in all honesty she couldn't remember it even then, Irinka sank down onto the floor, buried her head in her hands, and cried.

CHAPTER TEN

THIS TIME, WHEN Irinka went back to England, she did not wallow.

She did not waft about London, trying to match the Big Smoke in all its gray sprawl.

And that was handy, because it was a lovely summer. Bright and clear—and that meant there was no pretending that she wasn't, in fact, the great cloud currently storming her way all over the British Isles.

She spent her first night home in her little house in Notting Hill, but everything seemed different to her now. Had she collected all of these things because she truly liked them? Or because she'd liked thinking up a different persona to go with each purchase?

Because she could remember each and every one of them as if they were friends, not parts she'd played. At the same time, she could remember how it felt to play each character, how soothing it was to slip into a different skin, and see the world out of different eyes.

Just as she could remember all the time she'd always liked to spend here, alone, reacquainting herself with those characters. As if she was always auditioning to see which one might fit the new moment she was in.

Irinka had always viewed it as her secret weapon, this ability to become someone else when it suited her.

But now she found herself wondering if what she'd actually been doing her whole life was trying on characters, waiting to see if one fit. Changing roles with every new person to lessen the possibility that anyone might get fed up with her and discard her.

No wonder her own skin felt so strange.

She didn't call her friends. She did check her voice mail and wasn't entirely surprised to find a series of increasingly unhinged messages from her clients. Though she would have preferred to ignore work entirely, she decided that the last thing she needed was these men in her life any longer.

So she called each and every one of them and noted that they were all confounded when she did not lapse off into character—the flirtier, sweeter, more amenable character she usually played for them—while talking to them.

"I don't know what you expect me to do," said one man, who'd had Irinka staging scenes to break up with a girlfriend for him for the past two and a half years. On a strict seasonal schedule.

"The way I see it, you have two options, Craig," she told him calmly. "You could stop dating women that you don't like, thereby skirting the necessity to get rid of them every three months. Or—and this might come as a shock—you could also break up each one of them yourself. Like a man."

And perhaps there was something wrong with her that she found herself smiling at his outraged, sputtering response.

But she held that closely, like a personal security blanket, as she went and got on the train. And then sat back, staring out the window as the train slowly heaved itself out of London proper, and on into the countryside.

It only took a bit more than a quarter of an hour before she found herself in the old market town and decided—it being such a lovely day, summery and blue but not too warm—to walk out along the hedgerows into the rambling, wildly green land that made up this part of the countryside.

She had always wanted to walk here.

And so she did, enjoying the feel of the sun on her face and the way her body responded to the motion. Her feet on the ground, her arms pumping.

No characters, just her.

Irinka turned in at an old stile, climbing up and over it, and then followed a path that rambled along until it turned into a bit of a lane. She wandered past a selection of lakes, one complete with its own dramatic folly, before walking up a drive rich in ancient oaks whose branches created a dense green canopy overhead.

And when she got to the top, an imposing stately house sat there. The way it had been sitting there, proud behind its gates and deep in the heart of all this beautiful land, for centuries now.

There were flags flying at the top of the house, because, just like royalty, the Duke always wished the common folk to know when he was in residence. Not so that they would think to call upon him, but so that they would know better than to trouble him at all.

Irinka had no such qualms. She marched herself right

up the formidable front steps and rang the actual bell that graced the epically grand front door.

Then smiled at the dour-faced butler who answered. Eventually.

Really, she was becoming an old hand at presenting herself at the doors of historic old houses and demanding entrance.

"His Grace is not accepting visitors," the butler told her, with scandalized affront, to make it clear that it was not the done thing to simply *appear* at the door of a house like this. As if she was a tinker selling her grubby wares.

She only smiled wider. "Luckily enough, I am not a visitor. I am His Grace's disgraced and illegitimate daughter."

The butler was unmoved and, in any case, she suspected he knew exactly who she was. It was his job to know such things.

So Irinka shrugged. "If he does not wish to see me, I will simply call the first tabloid that comes to mind and see if they can provide a more sympathetic ear."

And as she'd known it would, that got her ushered right in. The butler stalked off into the bowels of the house and Irinka followed. When she'd been younger, as much as she'd disliked her father, she'd found herself wondering what it might have been like to grow up in a place like this. So crushed beneath the weight of its own self-importance that even the ceilings seemed to hang lower than they should.

But now she thought of Venice. She remembered the airy rooms of the palazzo, always opened to the world of water and wishes that was just outside. And now as she walked through the Duke's ancestral home, all she could wonder was how many ghosts lingered in these hallways—and how lucky she was that she'd never spent enough time here to see them.

Because the mean old ghost she saw when she came here was always the same one.

And, tragically, he was still alive and what passed for well. Or so she assumed, because surely someone would have told her if he wasn't. And she knew perfectly well she would be swept back up in the news coverage once he died.

Something else to look forward to, she told herself tartly as she walked down the hushed corridor decorated with medieval suits of armor on podiums every few feet and ancient banners from old wars proudly displayed.

The butler led her to the same room that she was always led to when she came here. Or was brought here, the way she had been long ago. He opened the door, looked at her as if she was a deep, personal insult to him and this house, and then waved her inside.

Where the Duke, her father despite how arduously he wished to deny it, stood in front of his vast and important desk, vibrating with rage.

At least she assumed it was rage. It wasn't as if she'd ever seen a different expression aimed in her direction, and every time she saw him, she was forced to reflect that it wasn't the best look on a man so red of face. And with a belly that made her think that perhaps he was too committed to his puddings, and likely plagued by gout.

She considered it a sign of great personal growth that she wasn't even *tempted* to say such things to him.

"Hello, Dad," she said instead, and yes, she was fully aware that he would probably have preferred to discuss his ailments than listen to her call him *Dad*.

Irinka had planned this all out on the way back from Venice. After she'd picked herself up off the floor sometime much later that same night. And then had soaked herself in her bath for so long that she thought she'd never unpickle herself. Once she'd dried off, she'd collapsed into bed and had passed out into an exhausted, dreamless sleep.

In the morning, she'd begun plotting out her next move.

But this time, she had no intention of playing her usual games. She winced at the word. This time, she had particular questions she wanted to ask, that was all. And she intended to get answers.

Even from the Duke.

Yet before she could launch into the things she wanted to ask, her father took the opportunity to speak instead. Jowls trembling to indicate that he was appalled by her, as usual.

"I knew you would come crawling back," he spat at her. "I suppose you've blown through all the money I already gave you, haven't you? I told you then that I won't be footing the bill for your lavish, irresponsible lifestyle. I've paid, and I won't pay more."

Irinka stood there, gazing at him. Looking at him the way she would any person she might encounter on the street and not coloring the experience with the clips she'd seen of him and her mother when they'd been dating. Not weighting it down with the fact he'd fathered her.

What she saw was an old, sad, unhealthy man who

thought his wealth would save him from everything that irked him, even death. Maybe especially death.

"I'm very well," she said quietly, after a moment. "Thank you so much for asking."

"You have spent your life skating about on my good name," he frothed at her, his brows practically tangled together, his frown was so deep. "Embarrassing my family with your shamelessness."

"Oh, no, Your Grace," Irinka replied in the same quiet tone. "I'm afraid they do that all by themselves."

And it was tempting to remind him that his heir was a gambler, his spare was an addict, and his daughter was on her third divorce, but she was certain he knew that. Just as she was certain that somehow, he would find a way to blame her for it.

"I won't give you a single sodding pound," the old man told her, his voice trembling. "If you ran through your settlement, that's on you. I can only hope that you and your mother *finally* descend into the sewer from whence you came."

And Irinka couldn't decide if what she felt as she stood there before him was temper or sadness. It was a kind of grief, that she was sure of, but she couldn't quite put her finger on what kind.

Because she didn't want a relationship with this man. She had only meant to ask him why he'd thought it was necessary to be so cruel to an innocent girl who had nothing at all to do with what had happened between him and Roksana. She had wondered if now, all these years later, there might at the very least be a frank discussion.

But instead there was this. The same as always.

It wasn't that she was surprised. This was the man she'd met when she was a girl. This was the man who had revealed himself in all of those tabloids, and in court, as small and mean. Over and over again.

Maybe she had been hoping that in the fullness of time, there could be something other than vitriol between them.

"Do you have nothing to say for yourself?" he demanded. "After all the fine schools I paid for?"

"I had quite a lot to say, actually," Irinka replied, thinking that she would have been better off having this conversation with one of the empty suits of armor outside. She would have gotten more back. "But now I don't really see the point of it. I don't want your money."

He scoffed. "A likely tale."

"I think you are confusing me for every other person in your life," Irinka said gently. "I'm sure you will be delighted to know that I not only have *not* run through the funds you provided me so generously when ordered to by the court, but have significantly expanded my portfolio since then. No thanks to you."

His face began to mottle, so she smiled. "I would rather sleep rough than take anything else from you, ever. I wanted only to ask you a question, daughter to father. But I suppose you've answered it, haven't you?"

"You can see yourself out," the Duke snarled at her. "And don't come back."

Irinka shook her head. "I don't think you have to worry about that."

And it was the strangest thing, but as she walked away, out of the gloomy halls of his old house and into all that waiting sunshine, she felt as if a set of weights she hadn't known were strapped to her came loose. She could almost imagine they were floating off like rogue balloons, and no doubt getting trapped in the eaves.

But it didn't matter where they went. They weren't hers any longer.

She took that long walk back into town, and took her time with it. Then she sat and waited for the train, understanding that this time, she really wouldn't be returning.

This time, she really was done with everything involving that man.

Except, of course, his good name.

Irinka laughed about that all the way back into London.

And once there, she didn't head toward her little house again. Instead she made her way over to her mother's current flat in a desperately chic and outrageously expensive block of them on the Thames. She announced herself in the lobby and then took the dark, metallic elevator up high. She was not surprised to find her mother waiting for her when the elevator opened directly into that sleek, dramatic living room, the low-slung mid-century modern pieces disappearing against the view of London from every vast window.

In the midst of all that, Roksana looked like a goddess.

Perhaps that was the point.

"Now we are dropping by?" her mother demanded. "Without even a call?"

She was as brusque as ever, but Irinka noticed that she came closer as she spoke. Her gaze moved all over her daughter's body, as if she was looking for signs of damage.

"I have some questions for you," Irinka said, when it

looked as if Roksana was slightly mollified not to find any blood or obvious bruising. "I think I've been waiting to ask them all my life."

"Beware a question whose answer must be excavated to be known," Roksana intoned. "I would sooner take my chances with wolves."

Another question Irinka wanted to ask her mother, but not now, was why wolves featured so significantly in her conversation when as far as Irinka knew, her mother had never encountered one. Nor the woods she often claimed was their home.

But that wasn't why she was here. "Do you love me, *momochka*?"

Roksana flinched, as if Irinka had taken a swing and punched her straight in the face.

"What is this question?" She sounded cross, but Irinka had seen that flinch with her own eyes. "Have you taken ill?"

"I know you won't answer me," Irinka said. "But I wanted to ask anyway."

She looked at her mother and, as always, it was like looking into her future. The same black hair. The same blue eyes. Irinka had always thought her mother was more beautiful because of the way her face was sculpted into near otherworldliness, though she knew some people considered that a kind of hardness.

They had the same build. At different points, they'd shared the same clothes. People had often said they looked like sisters, and Irinka had never found that insulting. How could she? Roksana was still considered one of the most beautiful women on the planet.

Besides, her mother had only been eighteen when she'd had Irinka. She had already been famous for years. And Irinka had read many articles that claimed that a fame like Roksana's meant she wasn't any sort of typical teenager. That she'd had been *wise beyond her years*, which was the thing that men always said to excuse the fact that *they* were apparently too immature for theirs.

Roksana had been told by everyone who mattered that her career would be over if she had her baby, much less kept it. Irinka knew that she had always taken great pleasure in proving them wrong.

"Of course I love you," her mother said, belting the words out as if she thought that if they lingered on her tongue, they might bite her. "Can this be in any doubt?"

"What about all of your lovers over the years?" Irinka asked. "Did you love them, too?"

She had made a pact with herself long ago only to remember the ones she liked. Mats, the Viking, who had made them all laugh so much. Olivier, the great reader, who still sent Irinka book recommendations from time to time. Byron, whose sweetness had seemed like a miracle to her in the midst of a rather bruising few years there.

Roksana looked at her for a long moment and then she turned, making her way across the vast living space. She paced across the room like it was a runway and managed to look the part despite wearing the most casual of clothes, and then settled herself dramatically in the chair she preferred, likely because it resembled a throne.

She picked up the drink that she'd left there. There was a time when Irinka might have investigated to see if it was vodka or not, but that didn't matter now. Her mother could do as she liked. She had earned that.

Surely they all had.

"I think you must tell me why you are asking me these things," Roksana said, in a neutral tone. That was her mother at her most suspicious.

"These aren't questions meant to trap you." Irinka trailed after her mother, and sat down on one of the low couches. "I honestly want to know. The thing is, I don't..." It was so hard to say out loud, even to Roksana, who made a habit out of not reacting to anything. It had always made her a safe space, really. "I don't know how to love anybody. I think I've been pretending."

"Don't be silly," her mother said at once. "You have those friends of yours." She swirled her drink around in its tumbler. "I have always been impressed that you were able to do this, Irinka. Have these friendships and maintain them. This is not something that was available to me."

"Was it not available to you or did you not know how to do it?" Irinka asked.

Roksana looked out toward that endless view over London for a moment, though Irinka didn't think she was examining Big Ben in the distance. She took her time looking back again.

"I was terrified to bring a daughter into this world," she said, in a voice very different from the one she normally used, so brusque and harsh. Roksana sounded... hushed. Irinka would have thought her *uncertain*, but that was not a state she could imagine her mother inhabiting. Not even for her. "I already knew what it was like to be a girl and I could not recommend the experience. I learned many things too young. And I did not want you to have to figure out how to survive those things as you went along, so I did my best to make you tough. If you started tough, you would not have to learn tough-ness the hard way, by surviving." She did not smile. She looked at Irinka, her gaze stark and direct. Blue to blue. "I did what I thought was necessary to keep you safe."

What she did not say, because everyone else who had seen them always said it for her, was that she had understood that Irinka was beautiful. Just as she had been. And she'd understood that their kind of beauty was as much a burden as it was a boon.

Roksana had made sure she'd comprehended that young.

Your face is so lovely that the rest of you must be sharp, like a knife, she had told Irinka when she was very young. So it would sink in early and stay.

And Irinka really did love her mother, despite the things she'd done, and hurdles she'd made her daughter jump over, time and again. She really did love this woman who she knew, with every fiber of her being, would have died for her a hundred times over.

Sometimes she thought that's what Roksana's court case against the Duke had been about. She'd had her own money. She hadn't needed his.

But she didn't like the way he'd felt he could talk about her daughter.

Roksana might not have been a tender parent. She was not cuddly. Irinka had heard her say, more than once, that she was not tactile and that had extended to her child.

But her love was fierce and dangerous. Her love was like a weapon, and Irinka had always known that it was hers whenever she might need it.

So she did not tell Roksana that some of the ways she'd made her daughter tough had broken her where it counted.

Because maybe that was her own fault, in the end. There was a certain point that everyone had to take responsibility for their own lives, wasn't there?

It was love at first sight, Zago had told her, and his voice still rumbled around inside her. Like thunder.

Irinka went over and hugged her mother. And then held on, even though she knew Roksana hated it. Because even though she did hate it, and stiffened at first, Roksana eventually relaxed. With a sigh.

And patted Irinka on the back. Again and again, until she let go.

"There," Roksana said, looking somewhat wild-eyed, as if she had passed a treacherous test of some kind. "All is well, yes?"

"I love you, *momochka*," Irinka murmured.

Then she kissed her on the cheek, and left.

She thought a lot about her friends that evening when she was tucked up in her house with a takeaway. And the fact that a woman like Roksana, who trusted no one and was proud of that, had noticed that Irinka's friendships were real. And good.

A glance at the text chain showed that her friends had

moved on to a rousing conversation about the potentially dueling weddings they were all planning.

Irinka joined in, presenting them with hastily assembled mood boards designed to make each one of them scream in horrified laughter, and found herself laughing too, sitting cross-legged on the cozy sofa in her living room as she sent them all a barrage of images.

Each one more outrageous than the last.

When she looked around and saw all the characters she'd played up there on her walls, she realized that she'd forgotten to include her friends in all of this *reckoning* she was doing.

These women who had loved her no matter what state she was in, or what character she was playing. These women who had supported her, and laughed with her, and were never afraid to tease her or call her on her nonsense.

These friends who allowed her space and always welcomed her back as if she'd never been away.

These friends who asked for nothing but her, however she showed up. In whatever role she was playing that day.

How could she say that she didn't know love, when *of course* she did?

How could she think that she didn't have the slightest idea how to have a relationship, when she'd been having four rather deep and consuming ones all this time? Individual relationships with each one of her friends, and then the group relationship they all had together?

Why did she think that love only mattered when it involved a man?

She had to sit with that one some while.

And eventually, it led her around to her job. And how she'd researched all the details in each case, but had never spent any time figuring out who the woman was in each instance whose heart she was pummeling with her antics.

It wasn't that she thought she was *more* responsible for the way those men had handled their relationships than they were.

But she also had to wonder why it was she'd never given a second thought to any of those women.

Except one. And only because her brother had insisted she think about her actions.

And that was how she got the bright idea to go find Nicolosa Baldissera and apologize to her.

Not only because she was Zago's little sister, but because she was representative of all the women that Irinka had believed she was saving. When, maybe, she was more like Roksana than she wanted to admit—and her version of saving a person was harsher than she wanted to admit.

Maybe she'd learned that cruelty was kindness a long time ago and had never had occasion to question it until now.

"But now," she told herself as she left her house that evening, "you are questioning *everything*."

It had been easy enough to find the younger girl. Because it was easy enough—if a person had a particular set of skills and access to certain databases—to locate the properties owned by her brother, look them all up, and then determine which one she thought would appeal to a younger university student.

Then it was nothing at all to turn up at the lobby of Nicolosa's building, pretend to be one of her friends, and have the very nice security man—who probably should have been less forthcoming, and likely needed someone to tell him that, though it wouldn't be her— tell her in a chatty sort of way that Miss Baldissera had popped out for dinner.

"Over the road at the brasserie," he confided. "If I heard it correctly."

Irinka smiled. "I'm sure you did."

She walked back outside and decided that she felt different as she made her way down to the zebra crossing, then over the road. It was a pretty night and the light was lingering. The air was cool, and even though she thought that ought to have felt gray straight through after all the revelations she'd had since Venice, she didn't.

Maybe she couldn't.

There was a freedom in confronting both of her parents, choosing what to take and what to leave. There was a freedom in acknowledging that she didn't know how to love, and hadn't, for years now. Not the way she wanted to.

Not the way Zago did.

She had to think that there would be a freedom in this, too. In acknowledging the role she had played in another person's life. No matter what her intentions might have been, she had contributed to someone else's pain, and she wanted to acknowledge it.

And she didn't think about what her reception would

be or what it might accomplish. She knew she needed to do this and she wasn't thinking about the future. She wasn't tallying up these revelations, like she thought a certain amount of one thing or another would help her find her way back to a man with dark amber eyes in a flooded city.

The future would do what it would.

That, too, felt like a freedom.

Irinka walked into the brasserie, not surprised to find it high-end and crowded. She smiled at the maître d' as she walked past him. She looked around, certain that she would be able to recognize Nicolosa based on the pictures she'd seen online.

Maybe she was a little bit embarrassed that she couldn't remember her from that night in Felipe De Osma's flat.

But she saw Zago instead.

And she froze.

He was seated at a table with a pretty young girl, and she knew immediately that it was his sister. Something she probably would have guessed even if they didn't look so much alike, and she hadn't just been examining Nicolosa's pictures online.

But there was that moment first.

That split second when the pit of her stomach opened and it was like concrete dropped straight through, making her feel sick and dizzy at once.

And she understood in that moment how little she'd really grasped about the service she'd been performing.

Irinka stood there, watching Zago and his sister talk.

She saw him smile engagingly, and tease an answering smile back.

And it was like a key into a lock.

The bolt was thrown, and now she understood at last.

It was a wonder that it had taken her this long. But, by the same token, if events hadn't happened in the precise sequence they had, she knew she never would have gotten here at all. She would likely have been in a new costume, haunting this very restaurant.

"May I help you, madam?" asked the maître d' from beside her.

And when Irinka turned, she made sure to keep her back to the table until she was sure she was out of sight, smiling at the man as she went.

"I was looking for someone," she told him. "But I think… I think I must have gotten it wrong."

Deeply and surpassingly wrong, she told herself when she pushed her way outside.

She took a deep breath when she hit the street, filling up her lungs and then letting out again. Then she walked all the way back across Central London to her sweet little house on the Portobello Road, and cried again the moment she shut the door behind her.

This time, for the opposite reason.

Not because of what she'd lost.

Not because of what hurt, what was broken, what she was hiding.

But because, at last, she knew exactly who she was.

And better still, what that meant.

CHAPTER ELEVEN

ZAGO THOUGHT HE'D handled his trip to London well.

He had caught up with a few old friends, as was his usual habit. He had taken care of the usual business concerns, and had subjected himself to the usual, tedious meetings.

Notably, he did not *accidentally* find himself wandering about Notting Hill, dressed as a stranger. Though he could not claim that the notion had not occurred to him, just to see what it was like. Just to inhabit her skin a while, and get a better sense of the woman who—it turned out—haunted him with great effect even when she was only in his mind.

When he had satisfied himself that Nicolosa was well and recovering from her heartbreak, even intended to go back to university in the fall, he took himself home again.

And every time he left Venice, returning to this magical city where his ancestors had lived for some thousand years, it always reminded him exactly who he was.

Because it wasn't simply that it was heart-stoppingly beautiful to arrive in the evening and take a boat into Venice at night, though it was. It wasn't only that all the regal houses along the Grand Canal were lit up and lovely, with the lamplight spilling over the water and music echoing as if it was welling up directly from all the cracks in the weathered old buildings. It was more than that. It was more than pretty views and old bloodlines.

This was *recognition*, he thought. This was the love that he been raised on, for good or ill. The sense of place and belonging that felt as if it was a part of his bones and his very biology, and Zago did not intend to settle for anything less than that in his private life.

He would not.

And it wasn't that he second-guessed himself, he thought as the boat pulled up to his dock. Though he had certainly been tempted to, especially in London. It was more that he was bolstering up the decision he'd already made.

It also wasn't that he thought any love could exist without its challenges. That seemed impossible as long as humans were involved. But at the base of it all, he was certain it should feel like *this*.

Instant recognition. That feeling of homecoming. The knowledge that no matter where he went in this whole wide world, all these beautiful places filled with adventures and temptations aplenty, that he might love them in his way but he would always long to be *here*.

That there could be nothing on this earth that would ever suit him better than this city. And this ruined old house that he had loved since before he could walk.

For better or worse, Zago had only ever had one home.

He walked slowly up the long stone path, looking up at the palazzo that stretched high into the night, gleaming with the same soft, thick light. And he was halfway to the impressive front door when he lowered his gaze and saw a figure sitting there on the wide stone steps.

He recognized her instantly.

In truth, he would recognize her anywhere. He had looked for her in London, in costume and out. He had puzzled over passing strangers, looking for the telltale line of her cheek, or the arch of her brow. Even the way she drew in a sharp breath. He had looked in all those crowds, forensically examined everyone who came into his field of vision, and he hadn't found her.

Yet somehow, it was no surprise at all to find her here. Waiting.

He kept walking. He did not alter his pace. And Zago stopped there at the bottom step, his eyes on her.

Irinka, back again.

He was aware of the staff who moved around them, but mostly because Irinka smiled at them and nodded her head in greeting. Only when they were alone again, save the passing boats in the canal, did she look at him once more.

Zago let his gaze move over her. It was warm here, much warmer than it had been in London, but she had dressed for the humidity. Her black hair curled all around the way it had that first summer, even though she piled it on top of her head. She wore an easy sort of dress that looked as if it was fastened by two bows at her shoulders, then left to do what it would. He wondered if he would always notice everything. That her manicure was repaired and back to its former glory. That her toenails matched, the color of champagne. That she wore sandals that wrapped around her ankles.

And that she looked as if she had gotten sun somewhere. There was a hint of that sort of flush on her skin, right there across the crest of her nose where some people were given to freckle.

It was just the two of them, out here in the soft light of a warm Venice night.

He could hear opera echoing down the Grand Canal, though he could not take that as a sign of anything except the fact that this was Italy. Opera was a part of who they were. It had nothing at all to do with how blue her eyes were.

Or the fact that it was once again time to test his resolve.

"I saw you in London," Irinka said. But before he could respond, she lifted a hand. "I wasn't skulking around in costume, which I'm sure is your first thought. I can't blame you. But I was actually seeking out your sister, entirely as myself. I planned to apologize to her, but then I saw the two of you having dinner together and didn't feel I should intrude."

Zago didn't know what to say to that. How had he felt her so many different times, in so many different places, but not then? How had she been so close and him none the wiser?

It felt like a fundamental breakdown on the part of the universe.

"But I realized something as I was standing there," Irinka told him. "First, that an apology would be for me, not for her. I saw her smiling and it seemed cruel to go over there and bring the whole thing up again. It could possibly have made it worse. And right when you'd clearly made some headway." She took a breath. "And then I had asked myself why it was that I wanted to apologize to her, specifically, and not all the women who'd been broken up with in this particular way. By me."

Zago thought he could have jumped in there and answered, but he didn't. Surely he had said enough.

Irinka was frowning down at her hands.

"I've been on something of a journey, actually," she said after a moment. "I kept looking for the wounds."

She looked up and searched his face, and it took everything he had to stay as he was. Not precisely impassive, but not engaging, necessarily.

I am simply here to listen, he cautioned himself.

Irinka looked down again. "I kept thinking that if I could just find the thing that was broken in me, then everything would make sense."

He had never wanted to go to her more. But he couldn't let himself. It was almost like he wasn't *able* to move. He felt like some kind of statute, as if he had finally turned to stone and become one more part of this palazzo that would one day sink into the mud.

"I went to see the Duke." That moved in him like a physical blow, but he still didn't speak. "I talked to my mother. I thought about my lovely friends and the way we've always been with each other and *for* each other." Her chest moved as if she couldn't quite get a breath in. "Then I finally realized that I kept failing to ask myself the critical question."

Zago shifted his weight, then thrust his hands in his pockets. Because it was that or put them on her.

As much as he longed to do that, he could not. He could not allow himself to intervene in this. Whatever this was.

And he didn't dare hope.

"Finally," Irinka said quietly. "*Finally* it occurred to me to ask why it mattered what anyone told me or thought of me or called me. Because it shouldn't, unless I agreed." She smiled then, and he thought his heart might have shattered if it hadn't been broken into pieces already. "And I realized, at last, that this was what you've been trying to tell me. I don't think I deserve *any* of this. My father's name. His begrudging blood money. My gorgeous, marvelous friends. Even the clients I was able to round up to help out the agency. And you." That smile again. "I am certain that I don't deserve you, Zago."

It caused him physical pain not to say her name. Or to reach out and touch her, at last.

But all he could do was stand there and listen. And wait to see where she went.

Irinka's smile faded. "All this time, I kept thinking that if I really let you close, if I truly let you in, you'd see that there's nothing there. My friends still think I'm mysterious. Because I am. Because fundamentally, deep inside, I've never thought that it made sense that I was the subject of all that speculation when I was little. But I was center of so much drama and I thought that meant I had to be *worthy* of it, so I made sure no one could ever find out that I'm not. That I'm just me."

She took a breath, then blew it out a bit raggedly, and

he saw what looked like a gleam of moisture in her blue gaze. "I don't know how to love anyone the right way, Zago. But I want to try. And maybe there isn't a right way. Maybe there's just you and me and this thing that I've been fighting against since I first saw you at that theater." Her breath caught. "I know it doesn't make sense, that I could enjoy being naked with you so much and yet I'm terrified of being too vulnerable. But I know that once I do this, once I *really* do this, it will be like a death. There will never be this version of me again. She will be gone forever and despite everything, I have grown rather fond of her."

For a long moment, they were both quiet. There were so many things he wanted to say. Arguments he wanted to mount and facts he was dying to point out to her, but all of it was to sway her to his side.

And he'd meant what he'd told her, more than once.

He didn't want what he had to force. Or beg for.

He wanted her love freely given. He wanted her to meet him here.

"But death is only terrifying if life is," she said quietly. "Look at this marvel of a city, propped up on little more than hopes and dreams and wooden posts. A thousand years or more of stories, ghosts, secrets, memories. Floating on. Because maybe death is just the beginning."

She stood then, and Zago had to look up, but that was no hardship when it was Irinka he was looking at. She came down one step. Another.

"Zago," she said, with a kind of solemnity that made his throat ache, "I fell in love with you so fast that it terrified me."

And something must have changed on his face, because she smiled and he saw a tear form in the corner of her eye. Then trail down her cheek.

"That first summer was so overwhelming. Maybe I died then the first time, but over and over again. I told myself it was just physical. I was sure that it was toxic. Because everything I'd always been told was that sex should be light and fluffy, a happy little pastime. I wasn't prepared for *you*, Zago. For all this intensity. For not only what you did to me, but what you demanded in turn. How fully and completely you wanted me to be present, with you, right here." She shook her head. "I couldn't do it."

Irinka came down another step. "It's more true than I would like to admit that I went back to London and found new and interesting ways to reenact our breakup with all those men, my clients. I got to throw crockery. I got to flip tables. I got to rant and scream and carry on." Her gaze was wide and shadowed. "But you and I know that our real breakup was so quiet. You looking at me with all that disappointment and me sneaking out under cover of darkness, so I wouldn't have to say goodbye. So anticlimactic. So cowardly."

She came down the final step and then she stood before him, her head tipped back and her eyes on his.

He had never seen that expression on her face before. Then again, he wasn't sure that he was breathing.

"As soon as they told me that they were taking me to Venice, I knew it was you," she confessed. "And I told myself that there were practical reasons not to cause a scene, but I didn't even try. I got on that plane and I let them bring me straight here, straight to you, because I wanted that plausible deniability. If you were a kidnapper, that made me the victim. And if I did the thing that you asked and made myself a servant, that made you look like the bad guy." Her lips curved. "And Zago, I desperately wanted you to be the bad guy."

She looked as if she was going to reach out to him, but she didn't, and it felt like a new, bright grief.

"And when I left you that time, I was convinced it was so civilized. So adult, at last. I told myself all the way home that it made up for the first time. I was drawing a line underneath it, under *us*, at last." Irinka laughed at that. "But then when I got back to England, I was a disaster. Everything was gray, inside and out. So I thought that I would come back and convince you to try again, but you were having none of it. You were saying all the things that I was afraid to even look at directly. It was terrible."

She shook her head again, but there was a different light in her eyes, now. "And I think I underestimated how hard it must have been for you to turn me away, but you did it. So of course I did what I always do. I hid. But I did it in plain sight. I followed you around, like a mad woman. And you caught me anyway. And then… you kissed me like a fairy tale and walked away without looking back." Her breath sounded ragged. "You told me that I needed to believe that I could deserve you."

This time she did reach out, and she fitted her palms to his torso, carefully. As if she was checking to see if he was real. Not stone at all, but a living, breathing man who hadn't died each time she left.

A man who had been waiting a long, long time for her.

For this.

"And I don't know what it really means to truly deserve anything," Irinka told him. "But I want to be the woman you imagine that I could be. I want to see myself in the mirror the way I can see myself in your eyes. I want to love you, as much as I can and for as long as I can, and with everything I have inside of me, until it feels like the love *you* deserve. I want to figure out how you have always been so certain, and give that back to you like the gift it is."

Tears were running down her face now, and she did nothing to hide them. She went up on her toes and tipped her face back, and he could see everything.

No games. Nothing held back.

And, if he wasn't mistaken, forever in her eyes.

"Zago," she said, this woman who had stopped his heart from the first, "I want it all. I want to marry you. I want to rattle around in this palazzo and keep it floating. I want to have your babies. Maybe a lot of them. And I want to love them all in ways that they will recognize, so they'll know, their whole lives, that no matter what else happens…they are loved. And I want to love you the same way, but more. I want to give you everything. I never want to make you wonder, ever again, that this is anything but meant to be. You, me, and no more masks." She considered for a moment, then smiled. "Except, perhaps, at Carnival."

Finally, then, Zago moved. He pulled her deeper into his arms and then his hands found her face, cradling her head in his palms while he rubbed his thumbs beneath her eyes to pick up all that moisture.

And once again, there were so many things *right there* on his lips. Vows he would make. Promises he intended to keep. Declarations and opera and all that poetry he only seemed to have inside him where she was concerned.

But what he said was simple. "What took you so long?"

And his beautiful, magical Irinka threaded her arms around his neck. She went up higher on her tiptoes and pressed her body to his, and it wasn't that he didn't feel that instant chemistry, that wildfire implosion. He knew she did, too.

But he understood when she pushed into him that what she wanted was simply to feel the way they fit together. That sweet, impossible perfection that had haunted them both all these years.

Because that was how he felt, too.

She smiled at him, ear to ear and her blue eyes sparkling. "Don't worry, my love," she said, her voice husky with all of the time they'd wasted, and all of the ground they'd covered. "I plan to make up for it with a lifetime or two. If you'll have me."

"Tesoro mio," he said, as he swept her up in his arms and held her there, like a fairy tale that would end the right way, this time. "I have only been waiting for you to say the word. Our forever starts now."

And then he showed her.

CHAPTER TWELVE

IT BECAME A year or two of marriages and babies.

Each one of Irinka's friends went before her, and for a time it seemed that all four of them were moving from one blessed event to the next. There was ample opportunity not only for them to congratulate each other and enjoy each other's company, but for their formidable billionaire men to form a most unlikely friendship of their own.

Given that each and every one of them was so...intense. Each in his own way.

At one wedding or another, they all stood together in the corner and Irinka pointed out the fact that the four men were doing the same thing on the other side of the dance floor. Huddled together like a pack of wolves, each one of whom clearly considered himself the alpha—which was likely why they got along.

"It's almost as if they've become their own set of work wives," she said.

Lynna grinned. "I can't wait to tell Athan that he has *three* work husbands."

Maude smiled serenely, holding her baby to her shoulder. "Dominic might consider it something like déjà vu."

Auggie laughed. "I informed Matias that they have no

choice but to become the best of friends. But I do like the fact that they do seem to *actually* enjoy each other."

After all, they all knew by now that trying to order around men like theirs made herding cats seem like a walk in the park.

Good job they were all particularly good at that sort of thing.

His Girl Friday changed, which was perhaps inevitable. Irinka no longer performed her previous services, but that didn't mean she didn't have other skills. She did, after all, have inroads into some of the highest levels of society. They all did now, but she was the one who was most likely to sail in, armed with a smile, and drum up business.

So that was what she did.

"I've decided that I'm going to put *rainmaker* on my business cards," she told Zago one night in London. They had decided to keep her little house on the Portobello Road. She had taken a great deal of delight in showing him around, presenting him with all the different pieces that she'd collected, and watching him study each one as if it was a window into her soul.

Maybe she hadn't appreciated the view because she'd been on the wrong side of it.

"Rainmaker?" Zago asked lazily, stroking her hair as they sat together on her rooftop. "Because something like *client acquisition specialist* is too boring?"

"I'm happy to be anything, my love," she told him. "Except boring."

This she had proved already, deciding that it wasn't

only Carnival where she could experiment with her love of costumes, but their bedroom.

He had yet to complain.

She put off introducing Zago to Roksana for as long as she could. When she finally made everyone sit down around a dinner table in her cozy house, where she could contain any damage, she was surprised to find that her mother was apparently capable of being charming when she wished.

"I had no idea you could have an entire conversation with a man without mentioning death or dismemberment," she muttered at her mother when she walked her out later. "Where has this charmer been hiding?"

"You do not think that I have had so many lovers because I cannot *charm* them, do you?" her mother replied, arching a smug sort of brow. "Silly girl."

As for their own shining, happy forever, Irinka and Zago took their time.

Nicolosa finished with university and got her first, appropriate boyfriend, who doted on her and treated her like a princess she was.

Neither Zago nor Irinka thought it wise or necessary to tell her the identity of that woman who had happily removed her from Felipe De Osma's clutches.

And while all of Irinka's friends were settling down to marriage and motherhood, she and Zago made up for lost time. He showed her the boundlessness of true love. She showed him the parts of her she had never showed anyone else, ever.

Together, they experimented with the very outer limits of vulnerability, and love, and everything in between.

When she had the urge to run away, she learned how to run to him, instead.

And when his ghosts became too much for him, she reminded him what it was like to be alive.

Irinka thought that she would have been perfectly happy to go on like this for some time. A forever or two, in fact.

So it was not until she was six months' pregnant with their first child, and quite obviously so, that Zago took her out to the balcony that looked out over the Grand Canal at another summer sunset. And as the most golden, glorious light poured over her, and him, he went down on one knee.

He looked up at her, and said, "*Tesoro mio, amore della mia vita*, I am afraid it is time."

"Already?" Irinka smiled down at him. She reached her hand down so she could hold his beloved jaw and move her thumb over his cheekbone, because it turned out she could delight in that, too. That imprinting. That muscle memory. "I was thinking we could live in glorious sin for at least the first three children."

"I would live with you in sin in a thousand lifetimes," he told her, and leaned forward to kiss her rounded belly. "But in this one, I am a Baldissera, and there are legacies to consider. And so I must beg of you, my heart and my soul and my life, to make an honest man out of me after all."

"Well," Irinka said with a sigh. "When you put it that way, how could I refuse?"

And her heart was catapulting around in her chest, but there was a lot more room in there than there had used to be. She did not hold on to age-old sobs for a lifetime, not anymore. She laughed more. She cried more.

Sometimes she shouted out her feelings without thinking them through.

Sometimes her brain got in the way of her heart, but they had found delightful ways to untangle them.

And no matter what happened, every time she reached over, Zago's hand was there to hold hers.

They were there to hold each other.

So she watched as he pulled out a ring that she had seen in the austere portraits in this grand old house. A huge diamond that she did not have to ask to know had belonged to a great many women who had lived right here, in this ancient place, surrounded not only by history but also by the history they would make.

"Will you marry me, my beloved?" Zago asked. "At last?"

"I will," she told him, and it was the easiest vow she'd ever made. "I love you so much, it almost seems as if being your wife will be too much joy to handle." She leaned down and kissed him. "But somehow I think I will rise to the occasion."

And she did.

Thus, one day not far from then, Irinka Scott-Day gave up the name she'd kept her whole life out of spite, and took up a far better one for love, instead.

And then kept it, and cherished it—and the husband and children that came with it—all the days of her life.

* * * * *

MILLS & BOON®

Coming next month

RUSH TO THE ALTAR
Abby Green

As if being prompted by a rogue devil inside herself, she blurted out, 'I couldn't help overhearing your conversation with your solicitor earlier.'

Corti's mouth tipped up on one side, and that tiny sign of humour added about another 1,000 percent to his appeal. For a second Lili felt dizzy.

'What was it you heard exactly?' He folded his arms now, but that only drew attention to the corded muscles of his forearms.

Lili swallowed. 'About how you have to marry and have an heir if you want to keep this villa.'

'And this is interesting enough for you to bring it up...why?'

The night breeze skated over Lili's bare skin, making it prickle into goose bumps. She was very aware that she was wearing just a swimsuit and a tiny towelling robe, her wet hair streaming down her back. The sense of daring fizzled away. She was being ridiculous.

She shook her head. 'It was nothing. I shouldn't have mentioned it.'

'But you did.'

There was a charge between them now. Something that felt almost tangible. 'Yes, I did.'

Continue reading

RUSH TO THE ALTAR
Abby Green

Available next month
millsandboon.co.uk

COMING SOON!

We really hope you enjoyed reading this book.
If you're looking for more romance
be sure to head to the shops when
new books are available on

Thursday 22nd May

To see which titles are coming soon, please visit
millsandboon.co.uk/nextmonth

MILLS & BOON

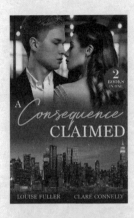
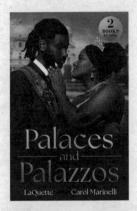
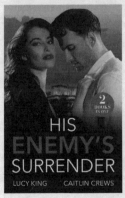
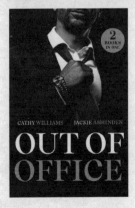

afterglow BOOKS

Afterglow Books is a trend-led, trope-filled list of books with diverse, authentic and relatable characters, a wide array of voices and representations, plus real world trials and tribulations. Featuring all the tropes you could possibly want (think small-town settings, fake relationships, grumpy vs sunshine, enemies to lovers) and all with a generous dose of spice in every story.

♪ @millsandboonuk
⊙ @millsandboonuk
afterglowbooks.co.uk
#AfterglowBooks

For all the latest book news, exclusive content and giveaways scan the QR code below to sign up to the Afterglow newsletter:

SCAN ME

LET'S TALK

Romance

For exclusive extracts, competitions and special offers, find us online:

f MillsandBoon

X @MillsandBoon

⊙ @MillsandBoonUK

♪ @MillsandBoonUK

Get in touch on 01413 063 232

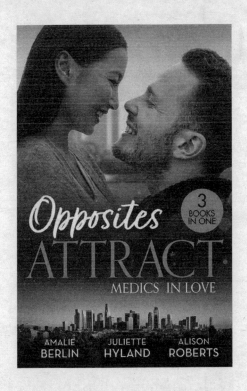